MW00459607

# FLASHBACK

# ALSO BY IRIS & ROY JOHANSEN (IN ORDER OF PUBLICATION)

**KENDRA MICHAELS SERIES**
(written with Roy Johansen)
"With Open Eyes" (short story)
*Close Your Eyes*
*Sight Unseen*
*The Naked Eye*
*Night Watch*
*Look Behind You*
*Double Blind*
*Hindsight*
*Blink of an Eye*
*Killer View*★
*More Than Meets the Eye*
*★Starring Jessie Mercado*

**EVE DUNCAN SERIES**
(Iris Johansen)
*The Face of Deception*
*The Killing Game*★
*The Search*
*Body of Lies*
*Blind Alley*★
*Countdown*★
*Stalemate*
*Quicksand*
*Blood Game*★
*Eight Days to Live*★
*Chasing the Night*
*Eve*
*Quinn*
*Bonnie*
*Sleep No More*
*Taking Eve*+
*Hunting Eve*+
*Silencing Eve*★+
*Shadow Play*+
*Hide Away*+
*Night and Day*
*Mind Game*★
*Shattered Mirror*
*Dark Tribute*
*Smokescreen*
*The Persuasion*★
*The Bullet*
*A Face to Die For*★★
*Captive*★
*The Survivor*★★
★Starring Jane MacGuire
+Featuring Margaret Douglas
★★Featuring Riley Smith

**CATHERINE LING SERIES**
(Iris Johansen)
*Chasing the Night*
*What Doesn't Kill You*
*Live to See Tomorrow*
*Your Next Breath*

**JOE BAILEY SERIES**
(Roy Johansen)
*Beyond Belief*
*Deadly Visions*

**IRIS JOHANSEN STANDALONES**
*The Ugly Duckling*
*Long After Midnight*
*And Then You Die*
*Final Target*
*No One to Trust*
*Dead Aim*
*Fatal Tide*
*Firestorm*
*On the Run*
*Killer Dreams*
*Pandora's Daughter*
*Silent Thunder* (Iris & Roy Johansen)
*Dark Summer*
*Deadlock*
*Storm Cycle* (Iris & Roy Johansen)
*Shadow Zone* (Iris & Roy Johansen)
*The Perfect Witness*
*No Easy Target* (featuring Margaret Douglas)
*Vendetta*
*Chaos*
*High Stakes*

**ROY JOHANSEN STANDALONE**
*The Answer Man*

# FLASHBACK

IRIS JOHANSEN

ROY JOHANSEN

*New York Boston*

This book is a work of fiction. Names, characters, places, and incidents are the product of the authors' imagination or are used fictitiously. Any resemblance to actual events, locales, or persons, living or dead, is coincidental.



Grand Central Publishing
Hachette Book Group
1290 Avenue of the Americas, New York, NY 10104
grandcentralpublishing.com
@grandcentralpub

First Edition: June 2024

Grand Central Publishing is a division of Hachette Book Group, Inc. The Grand Central Publishing name and logo is a registered trademark of Hachette Book Group, Inc.

The publisher is not responsible for websites (or their content) that are not owned by the publisher.

The Hachette Speakers Bureau provides a wide range of authors for speaking events. To find out more, go to hachettespeakersbureau.com or email HachetteSpeakers@hbgusa.com.

Grand Central Publishing books may be purchased in bulk for business, educational, or promotional use. For information, please contact your local bookseller or the Hachette Book Group Special Markets Department at special.markets@hbgusa.com.

Print book interior design by Marie Mundaca

Library of Congress Cataloging-in-Publication Data
Names: Johansen, Iris, author. | Johansen, Roy, author.
Title: Flashback / Iris Johansen, Roy Johansen.
Description: First edition. | New York : Grand Central Publishing, 2024. | Series: Kendra Michaels series ; book 11
Identifiers: LCCN 2023054970 | ISBN 9781538726266 (hardcover) | ISBN 9781538726280 (ebook)
Subjects: LCGFT: Thrillers (Fiction) | Novels.
Classification: LCC PS3560.O275 F63 2024 | DDC 813/.54—dc23/eng/20231213
LC record available at https://lccn.loc.gov/2023054970

ISBNs: 978-1-5387-2626-6 (hardcover), 978-1-5387-6650-7 (large print trade), 978-1-5387-2628-0 (ebook)

Printed in the United States of America

LSC-C

Printing 1, 2024

# FLASHBACK

# PROLOGUE

Is my mommy dead?"

San Diego police detective Paula Chase looked at the two little girls in her rearview mirror. The question had come from eleven-year-old Chloe Morgan, who was in the backseat with her nine-year-old sister, Sloane.

Paula exchanged glances with her partner, Detective Todd Williams, who was in the passenger seat. They were in her car riding to a popular walking trail in Tecolote National Park.

"No, honey," she said gently. "We haven't seen anything to make us think that happened to your mother. What makes you ask that?"

Chloe shrugged. "That's what Aria Watkins said in school today. She said our mommy was dead and no one wanted to tell us the truth. I got in a fight with her after she said that. That's why I was in detention when you picked us up."

Paula sighed. As if these poor girls hadn't been through enough. Their mother had disappeared four days before, while exercising in her wheelchair on this park nature trail. Her Toyota Sienna van was found on an adjacent gravel parking lot, but so far there had been no trace of Alyssa Morgan.

Until an hour ago.

Maybe.

Williams turned to face the girls. "Don't listen to Aria Watkins or anyone else about your mother. They don't know sh—" He stopped himself before completing the expletive. Paula smiled. Williams was obviously as angry as she was.

He took another moment to compose himself. "Just know we have a lot of people working on this. We're doing everything we can to bring your mom home, okay?"

Sloane looked around at the wooded park. "Why are we here? This is where Mommy likes to ride."

"We know. We need you to look at something for us."

This appeared to unsettle both girls. Paula had been afraid it might. "What is it?" Chloe asked.

Paula hesitated a long moment before answering. "It's a wheelchair."

Both girls gasped. Sloane began to cry.

"We don't know if it's your mom's," Paula added quickly. "It looks like it might be from the photos we have, but we can't tell for sure. That's what we need you for."

While this information only caused Sloane to crumble further, Chloe's face tightened into a determined expression. It was a strength Paula had observed in her first interviews with the girls. "Where is it?" Chloe asked.

"Up ahead. Some hikers found it in the middle of the trail."

Chloe shook her head. "But we looked there. We looked everywhere around here."

"We know. We looked, too. Our department has

combed this trail from one end to the other. I guarantee you, that wheelchair was not there before today."

"But why would it be here now?" Chloe said.

Williams shrugged. "I don't know. Somebody might be playing a sick prank. Pictures of your mom in her wheelchair have been all over the news these past few days. That's why we need you to look at it for us. Okay?"

Chloe grasped her sister's hand tightly and nodded. "Yes."

They parked in the same gravel lot where the woman's van had been found, then trudged up the path that had consumed so much of their attention in the past few days. Soon they were greeted by the sight of several uniformed officers, a pair of forensics specialists, and several yards of yellow police tape.

One of the officers stepped aside to reveal an ultralight manual wheelchair.

The girls froze for a long moment, transfixed by the sight.

Paula turned toward them. "What do you think? Have you seen it before?"

Chloe and Sloane didn't answer. They stepped forward as a hush fell over the group. The investigators backed away, clearing a path to the chair. Chloe and Sloane approached and knelt beside it, still mesmerized. Sloane reached out, but Paula gently pulled back her arm. "Please don't touch it, honey. It's evidence."

Sloane looked up. "It's my mom's chair."

"Are you sure?"

Chloe pointed to tiny lightning bolt decals on the left and right footrests. "Mom loves Harry Potter. She put these here herself. And these blue scratches on the handles came from our front railing at home. This chair is hers."

Paula flinched and then nodded. "Okay." She spoke to her partner. "Let's make sure our teams go over this whole trail again, Williams. Maybe somebody saw this chair being moved out here today. If so, there's a chance—"

Everyone was suddenly looking behind her. She turned to see a grim-faced uniformed officer climbing through a clump of brush and back onto the trail. "Detectives…You should take the girls away now."

"No! Why?" Chloe screamed as she jumped to her feet. "Why do we have to leave her? I have to find my mom!"

Detective Williams put his hand gently on Chloe's shoulder. "Let's get back to the car and let these people do their work."

Chloe broke free and bolted toward the brush. "Mom!"

The uniformed officers rushed toward the girl and tried to block her path, but Chloe bent over and dove into the brush. Williams grabbed her ankles at the last second and pulled her back. She was still screaming and crying as he carried her back toward her sister.

Paula looked at the faces of the officers coming back from the other side of the hill. Grimmer than grim. Shit.

She pushed through the brush and looked down the ridge.

There, hanging from an oak tree, was the body of Alyssa Morgan. Her hands and feet were bound by the same green-and-white nautical rope used to wrap around her neck and the highest tree branch.

Paula turned away. In her years on the force, she'd seen more than her fair share of monsters. But with this poor woman's little girls now sobbing less than a hundred yards away, she was sickened in a way most of the others couldn't touch.

She sat on a large rock at the ridge's edge. And rocked herself back and forth. "Jesus," she whispered. "Dear Lord Jesus."

# CHAPTER 1

FIFTEEN YEARS LATER

Kendra Michaels looked at the sea of faces in front of her. She was in the general-purpose room at the Pacific Villas Senior Living Community, where she'd set up her synth keyboard in front of a dozen residents afflicted with profound dementia. She'd greeted each of them as they were brought in, but the audience members were not even remotely responsive to her or, as far as she could tell, any outside stimuli.

"You want to hear some music?" She smiled at the group.

No reaction.

She smiled again. "I'll take that as a yes." She began playing Frankie Valli and the Four Seasons' "December, 1963" on her keyboard. Aside from rhythmic swaying from a few staff members, there was still zero reaction from the crowd.

Kendra wasn't surprised. She was a music therapist with a successful practice in San Diego, and she'd seen the same response—or lack thereof—literally thousands of times. Much of her academic research focused on the ability of music to reach and help certain patients form connections with the outside world. She'd had greater success with younger subjects, particularly autistic children, but she had recently begun a promising study involving elderly patients in advanced stages of dementia. Unfortunately, none of the seniors in front of her were exhibiting any positive signs of—

Wait.

In the second row, a woman in a floral sweater began to bob her head in time with the music.

*Don't get too excited,* Kendra told herself. The woman might just be drifting off to sleep.

No. She was listening.

And feeling it.

The woman's eyes opened wider.

And was that...a smile?

Kendra smiled back and raised the keyboard's volume. Staff members smiled and gestured toward the woman, obviously surprised and pleased at her engagement.

But her attention faded after a couple of minutes, and despite Kendra's best efforts to re-engage with her, the woman never responded to the twenty minutes of music that followed.

Kendra concluded her mini-concert, and the staff began the process of moving the residents away from the area.

Bill Dillingham stepped toward her. He was in his late eighties, and he looked elegant with his stylish slacks, well-coiffed hair, and neatly trimmed silver mustache. "Tough crowd."

She hugged him. "Good to see you, Bill. Just so you know, I wasn't here to entertain them."

He chuckled. "That was painfully obvious."

"You know why I'm here. And I appreciate your helping arrange it."

"It was my pleasure, Kendra. You seemed to be reaching Sophie for a minute there."

"The woman in the floral-print sweater? You know her?"

"No, I can't say I do. As you can imagine, our dementia residents keep pretty much to themselves. They live in a different building from the rest of us. But an orderly told me that he hasn't seen her so responsive to anything since she's been here."

Kendra unplugged her keyboard and wrapped the power cord around a spindle. "That's nice to hear. I'd like to do some follow-ups with her. I'll speak with her family about it."

"I'm sure they'll be glad to hear from you."

"Hard to say. If a patient is here in that wing, the family has probably already given up hope that they can improve. With good reason, most likely. But even if I can't help them, they can help add to the body of research that my colleagues and I can use to help others. That may not be good enough reason for them. I spend a lot of my time with this, believe me."

"I believe you."

Kendra smiled as Bill greeted several others as they walked past. He was obviously one of the institution's most popular residents, which didn't surprise her a bit. He was a gregarious, charming man who liked to tell stories from his colorful career as a sketch artist with the San Diego Police Department. But he was also a wonderful listener, a major reason he'd been so good at his job.

She slid her keyboard into its long vinyl sleeve. "How about I take you to lunch, Bill? I know a good restaurant near here."

"Sounds fun. But there's something I need to talk to you about first."

"Sure."

"You're not gonna like it."

She put down her keyboard and turned toward him. "Well, that sounds ominous."

"It isn't. Not really. I just know how you feel about investigative work."

"Oh, no."

"Sorry, kid. You have a gift, so you shouldn't be surprised when people ask you to use it."

"A gift? Sometimes it feels more like a curse."

"You don't mean that."

"Don't I?"

He nodded. "I know you better than that, my dear. Think of all the people you've helped. And I'm not talking about the police departments and the FBI. I'm talking about the lives you've saved."

A voice came from behind Kendra. "He's right, isn't he?"

She turned to see a woman in her mid-sixties stepping toward her. She extended her hand to Kendra. "Detective Paula Chase, San Diego PD, retired. It's a pleasure to meet you, Kendra."

Kendra shook hands with her and turned back to Bill. "You didn't tell me I was walking into an ambush here."

"Detective Chase is an old friend of mine," Bill said. "There's something I thought maybe you could help her with."

Paula smiled at Kendra. "And even if you can't, I knew I'd enjoy meeting someone I've heard so much about."

"From Bill?"

"From Bill, from my other former colleagues, from everyone. How could I not? It's an impressive story. You were blind for the first twenty years of your life, and after you gained your sight thanks to a surgical procedure, you still had all those other senses you'd improved during your years as a sightless person."

"You do know my story," Kendra said. "But I honestly don't think my senses are better than anyone else's. Like all blind people, I just learned to pay attention to what my senses of hearing, smell, touch, and taste told me about the world. It's not something I'd ever forget how to do just because I'm fortunate enough to see now."

Paula nodded. "But from what I understand, you're now also extremely observant about things you see."

"I guess that's because sight is such a wonderful gift to me. I don't take anything I see for granted, so I'm constantly absorbing and processing whatever passes in front of me." Kendra shrugged. "Again, I think it's a natural response."

"Interesting," Paula said. "I suppose all this is what makes you such an amazing investigator. I know the FBI has tried to get you to join their ranks, and I'm sure the SDPD would love to have you on their payroll."

Kendra laughed. "Depends on who you talk to. A few people there would be happy never to see me again."

"Only the insecure ones," Bill said. "There's a reason why Kendra is brought in to consult on the tough cases. Which is why I wanted you two to speak."

Kendra turned back toward Paula. "But you said you were retired. Are you a private investigator now?"

Paula rolled her eyes. "Lord, no. When I say I'm retired, I'm most definitely retired."

"So what's this about?"

Paula took a deep breath before launching into it. "You probably would have been a teenager at the time...But have you heard of the Bayside Strangler?"

Kendra thought for a moment. "Sounds familiar, but I honestly don't have any real memory of that."

"You're not alone. It was fifteen years ago, and most people have forgotten about it. The Bayside Strangler was a serial killer who murdered five women in a four-month period, all just south of downtown San Diego. Not all of them were near the bay, but the name stuck."

"The case was unsolved?"

"Yes, unfortunately. It was my case, and I eventually led the task force."

"Ah. Needless to say, you've never forgotten."

The years of pain were suddenly etched on Paula's face. "No, never. Not for a single day."

"I can imagine."

"Anyway, the FBI had just started to get involved when the murders stopped. The profilers thought the killer might have moved, gone to prison for something else, or died himself. It's rare that a serial killer can just stop and lead a normal life for the rest of his days. We continued to investigate, of course, but the case just went cold. The task force was disbanded, and we moved on to other things."

Kendra could see that it still pained Paula to talk about the case. "Most investigators I've known have at least one unsolved case that haunts them years later."

"It's true. This was definitely one of mine. But the thing that has really stayed with me all these years is the daughters of the second victim, Alyssa Morgan. I was with them when their mother's body was found. Alyssa was a single parent, and she'd done a wonderful job with those girls. They were nine and eleven when their mother was taken from them. They were smart and beautiful. Their aunt raised them as her own, but sometime during their high school years, they started asking more and more questions about what happened to their mother. I got calls from them almost weekly, and I tried explaining to them there was no place for us to go in the case. Eventually I realized they were investigating the case themselves. It consumed them, especially the older girl, Chloe. They each graduated from college, but over the years, a lot of their free time has been spent working on the case. It got worse in the past month or two. They were obsessed. According to their aunt, they were convinced they were onto something, but they wouldn't say what. Then, a week ago yesterday, both girls disappeared."

Kendra raised her eyebrows. "By disappeared, you mean..."

"It's as if someone snapped their fingers and made them vanish. Their cars, purses, wallets, and phones were at their homes. There's absolutely no sign of anything wrong at either of their places. They're just gone."

Kendra stepped closer to her. "The police have talked to family members and friends?"

"Of course. They didn't talk about going on a trip or doing anything out of the usual. They both had jobs and co-workers who were expecting to see them. Their financials were untouched, no credit card or banking activity whatsoever."

"That's not encouraging."

"No, it isn't. And I guess I'm feeling some responsibility. All those years I told those women there was nothing that can be done, that all the leads had been exhausted...They felt they had no choice but to take matters into their own hands, and now they've gone missing."

Bill put his hand on Paula's arm. "You did what you could. You can't blame yourself." He turned back to Kendra. "I told Paula I'd make an introduction and let her tell you her story. No obligation, of course. But it's a story I thought you should hear."

Kendra nodded. "I'm flattered that you think I can help, but the police have far more resources for a case like this. I wouldn't even know where to begin."

Paula turned around and pointed to three stacked shipping cartons, all secured to a dolly with bungee cords. "Well, you could start with those. It's over ten years' worth of photographs, newspaper clippings, interview transcripts, and everything else Chloe and Sloane Morgan have gathered as they investigated their mother's murder."

Kendra walked around the stacked cartons. "Shouldn't the police have this?"

"Their aunt tried to give it to the detectives investigating her nieces' disappearance, but they weren't interested. The police aren't convinced that Chloe and Sloane were closer to finding the killer than any of the official investigations have been."

"What do you think?"

"I don't know. But those women have been relentless in uncovering everything they could about the Bayside Strangler cases. There are things here I never knew."

Kendra unfastened one of the bungee cords and lifted the lid on the top box. The items were neatly labeled and organized, with dates and supporting information handwritten on the file folders.

"Their aunt gave you these?"

"Yes. Chloe kept them in her home office. I spent last weekend going through every single page and photo, believe it or not."

"I can't even imagine. What did you find out?"

"A lot of possibilities and several dead ends. But nothing that obviously points the way to what may have happened to them, I'm afraid."

"What do you think?" Bill said to Kendra.

Kendra lowered the lid and refastened the bungee cord. As much as Bill was trying not to pressure her, he clearly wanted her to look into the case. He'd cheerfully helped on several of her investigations; what kind of friend would she be if she didn't return the favor the one time he asked something in return?

Paula smiled. "I know it's a lot to ask. And frankly, I have no idea if Chloe and Sloane's disappearance has anything to do with those fifteen-year-old murders that they were investigating. They've already been through a lot in their lives, and I'm concerned for them. I wouldn't be here otherwise."

"I know. Chloe and Sloane are lucky to have you in their corner."

"I'd love to have you there, too. But whether you think you can help or not, I was wondering if you could do something for me."

"What?"

"Tell me about myself."

"I'm sure Bill told you everything about me you would ever want to know."

"No. I want you to tell me about myself."

"I'm not sure I understand. We just met."

"That's never stopped you before, from what I gather. If what I've heard about you is true, you can tell a lot about a person or place from just one glance. I'd love to see it for myself."

Kendra looked over to Bill. He was raising his eyebrows in excitement. As much as she tired of performing her parlor tricks, she didn't want to disappoint him.

She turned back to Paula. "It's really not that big of a deal."

"That's not what I hear."

Kendra shrugged. "You're a dog lover. It wasn't that long ago that you had one large dog, one small. Sad to say, you've recently lost your big dog. I'm sorry. I know you give your pets a lot of love and attention, and I'm sure it still must be hard for you."

Paula looked as if she'd had the wind knocked out of her. "How in the hell…?"

"You have allergies, but you're more susceptible to mold than pollen. And there's a good chance you're a diabetic. If you haven't been diagnosed or gone under a doctor's care for it, it might be a good idea to get checked out."

"Pre-diabetic," she said, sounding dazed. "I'm trying hard not to go all the way there." Paula looked at Bill, who was thoroughly enjoying the show. She turned back toward Kendra.

"Good. You're taking care of yourself. I guess your visit to Massage Envy this morning is part of that."

Paula smiled. "Deep tissue. I go every other week. Sometimes more if I'm feeling extravagant."

"Nice. I've gone there for facials a couple times."

Paula shook her head. "Wow. Anything else?"

"Well, speaking of extravagant, you've stayed in a Waldorf Astoria Hotel recently. Maybe in New York?"

"Park City. I went on a ski trip with some college friends."

"Fantastic. I've never been there. I hear it's nice."

Paula held her head in her hands. "This is unbelievable."

"Not at all. I just learned to pay attention at a time of my life when I had to."

Paula crossed her arms in front of her. "How could you possibly know I recently stayed at a Waldorf Astoria?"

"Your hair. You brought home some hotel shampoos and you happened to use one today. I'm smelling their house brand, Salvatore Ferragamo. The Waldorf Astoria version is the only one that smells this way."

"I never would have guessed."

"Then you wouldn't have guessed that Massage Envy uses Obagi Professional-C Serum. It's available other places, but almost every time I've smelled it, the wearer has just been there for a massage."

"Huh. Allergies? I don't have itchy eyes or anything that shows."

"No, you usually see that in the springtime with grass and ragweed pollen. This time of year, when we get almost all our rain, it's more about mold and getting a post-nasal drip. I thought I could hear a slight rattle in your breathing a couple of times."

"A slight rattle? I could've had a cold."

"You could have if I hadn't seen a distinctive outline in your front right pant pocket. It looks like a wide squashed tube with a straight bottom. That happens to be the exact shape and size of the most popular allergy medication in the country. It's Flonase, right?"

Paula reached into her pocket and pulled out the green-and-white bottle. "Yes, it is. I didn't want to meet you with snot running down my face."

"I think we both can be grateful for that."

Paula pocketed the container. "But I'm not carrying diabetes medicine."

"No. That brings us back to smell."

Paula's eyes widened. "You can smell a diabetic?"

"You have a slight fruity smell on your breath."

Paula covered her mouth with her hand. "Oh, God."

"It's not a bad odor. Seriously. It's sweet smelling, a product of diabetic ketoacidosis. That odor is an early sign of diabetes. It's good you caught it so early, before it's taken hold."

She put her hand down. "Good to know. But I think I'll start carrying travel-size mouthwash, just in case." She looked down at her clothes and shoes. "Still, there's no way in hell you could know about my dogs. Bill didn't even know about them. There's nothing on me that could tell you that."

"Sure there is."

"What?"

"Look at the backs of your hands."

Paula raised her hands.

"Like a lot of dog owners, most of the sun you get each day comes when you walk them. You obviously use retractable leashes with handles you slip your fingers through. I say 'obviously' because those handles have left untanned stripes across the backs of your fingers. You see those on a lot of dog walkers, especially if they don't wear sunscreen on their hands. The stripe on your right hand is larger than the one on your left, clearly because that leash handle was a bigger size for a bigger dog."

"You're right." Paula suddenly sounded sad. "I always held Bruno with my right hand. But how did you know he—?"

"That right-hand stripe isn't as distinct as the other. It's now red. There's a sunburn there now because you've recently been walking your other dog, but no longer carrying a leash in your right hand."

"Yes." She managed a smile. "You're absolutely right. Bruno died just last month. He was a good boy."

"I'm sorry."

"Well, this just shows that the stories about you are true. Will you consider helping me find Chloe and Sloane?"

Kendra thought for a moment. Bill was now trying his damndest to look like he didn't care either way, but she knew better. "I'm not sure what help I can be, but of course I'll look into it."

Paula smiled. "Thank you, Dr. Michaels. That's all I can ask. Where would you like to begin?"

"You said it yourself." Kendra motioned toward the stacked boxes. "With those. I'll see where they take me and get back to you."

---

"Sir, can I help you?"

Rod Wallace was standing on the far side of the parking lot, watching Kendra Michaels load the three file boxes into her Toyota 4Runner. He'd considered snapping her neck and seizing them when a muscular man in a red Pacific Villas polo shirt approached from seemingly nowhere. He was obviously an employee.

"Can I help you?" the employee repeated.

"Uh, yeah." Wallace glanced around. "I'm thinking of bringing my dad here. He's not crazy about the idea of moving to a retirement community, but this place looks...nice."

"It is. But you'll need to go to the welcome desk and get a visitor's badge. Did you make an appointment, sir?"

"No. Is that really necessary?"

"I'm afraid so. But if you'd like to follow me, I can take you to someone who can set up a time for a tour. Maybe your dad can come with you."

Wallace looked out of the corner of his eye and saw that Kendra Michaels had climbed into her car and started it. Dammit. Now he wanted to snap this employee's thick neck.

Patience.

He couldn't risk tipping his hand now. He had come too far.

"Thanks," he told the man. "But I'd better check my schedule. I'll call this afternoon. Thanks."

Wallace turned and walked away.

Patience.

He'd been following that retired detective, but when she handed off that stack of files, he now had *two* people to be concerned about. Dammit. Either of those women could now be a danger to him.

He would have his turn with the Michaels woman yet.

All things came to people who were willing to wait…

## CHAPTER 2

Stop!" Kendra shouted across her condo living room.

Olivia Moore froze in the main doorway. "Jeez, Kendra. You sure know how to make a girl feel welcome." She pocketed her key. "Should I just go?"

"Of course not. But you're about to run smack-dab into a four-foot tower of file boxes. Three steps to your left will give you a clear path in."

"Thanks."

Kendra stood to greet her friend and downstairs neighbor. As children, she and Olivia had attended a school for the blind, and their friendship had only deepened in the years since Kendra gained her sight. Olivia had never shown the tiniest bit of jealousy at Kendra's good fortune, though she still hoped she would one day reclaim the sight that had been taken from her in a childhood car accident.

Olivia hugged her. "You need to stop bringing your work home, Kendra. We talked about this."

"It's not work. It's a favor."

"A favor that involves...a murder?"

She shrugged. "Maybe even a bunch of murders."

"Ooh, I gotta hear about this." Olivia pushed back her long black hair as she walked over and plopped down onto the couch. She was stunningly beautiful with her olive complexion and high cheekbones, made even more attractive by her stubborn refusal to believe she was good looking at all.

"Don't get so excited," Kendra murmured. "It's a tragic story."

"It always is. Got any wine?"

Kendra smiled. "Of course." She walked to the kitchen counter and poured them each a glass of Malbec. "Do you have any memory of a killer called the Bayside Strangler?"

"No. Was he around here?"

"Yes, but it was a long time ago. We were in school then, at Woodward. I really don't remember any of the details, but he was never caught."

Olivia grasped the wineglass that Kendra put in her hand. "That's what this is about? No one's asked you to work a cold case before."

"Well, that's only part of the story. The only reason I'm considering it is that two women's lives may be in danger. If they're even still alive." Kendra filled her in on the facts of the case as related to her that morning. As she spoke, she felt the same sense of dread she'd heard in Detective Chase's voice.

Olivia sat in silence for a long moment after Kendra finished. "You have to try to help them. You know that, right?"

"It's getting more clear by the minute."

"Good."

"But this is different from anything I've done before.

You said it yourself. I don't do cold cases. Whatever skills I have, they may not apply to a fifteen-year-old investigation that went absolutely nowhere."

"Which is why you could be perfect for it. They might be able to use a fresh pair of eyes." She raised her wineglass. "So to speak."

"You know...Right before I came home, I looked online and saw the news story about the Morgan sisters' disappearance last week. There was a picture of the two of them, and you could almost see the sadness in their faces. Their mother was taken from them when they were children, and they've also lost so much of their lives trying to get justice for her. And now it may have cost them their own lives."

"Do you think they were really close to finding out who this Bayside Strangler was?"

"Nobody knows. That tower of files over there is everything Chloe and Sloane Morgan gathered over the years as they investigated the Bayside Strangler case. Detective Chase went through it, and she didn't see anything that convinced her. I'll look and see if there's anything I can follow up on."

Olivia made a face. "Are we talking hundreds of sheets of paper over there?"

"Maybe thousands. That's what you almost collided with. It's stacked about four feet high."

"That's horribly inefficient."

"Well, when the Morgan sisters turn up, you can tell them that."

"No, I mean...for you to sort through."

"You got a better idea?"

"Scan it all. A good PDF software program could index all the text and make it searchable. If you see something interesting, you can cross-index and bring up every instance that appears in any of the other documents."

Kendra smiled. Naturally, Olivia would have a high-tech solution right off the top of her head. She ran a popular web destination called *Outasite* that was geared toward the vision-impaired. Packed with reviews, profiles, and other articles mostly written by Olivia herself, the internationally acclaimed site earned her an income well into the six figures. "Good idea," Kendra said, "but I don't have time for a scanning project."

"You don't need the time. I have an intern."

"What?"

"I have an intern who's desperate for something to do. He's taking a semester off from USC to intern for me. I wanted a blind student, but she got a better offer from a Wall Street firm at the last minute. So I got Zack. He's studying online marketing, which I already have covered pretty well."

"I'd hate to impose."

"He's an intern. These kids sweep floors, pick up dry cleaning, and walk dogs for course credit. At least he'll be doing something that'll give him some useful skills in the real world."

Kendra thought about it for a moment. "Okay, fine. It makes sense to put all that information into some kind of searchable order."

"Definitely. And it'll be a relief for me to not have to come up with stuff for him to do. I've been a one-woman show for so long that it's a real effort for me."

"I've been telling you to get an assistant. You're practically running a media empire alone out of your condo.

Maybe this will show you how to delegate some of the work you've taken on."

"We'll see." Olivia took a long sip of her wine. "Maybe you could use an assistant yourself. You've been crazy busy even when you're not moonlighting as a crimefighter."

"Don't remind me. I've been playing catch-up from those three weeks I spent in Spain."

"I still think you should have stayed longer."

Kendra smiled. She couldn't remember the last time she'd felt so relaxed and happy. Maybe too happy. Spending three weeks in a Marbella beach house with an exciting, beautiful man who adored her. How could it not be paradise? "Lynch wanted me to stay another two weeks, but I have clients back here. On our last day, he bought the beach house we were renting so we could go back whenever we wanted."

"Wow. You left that part out when you told me about the trip."

"It made me a little uncomfortable. The trip was supposed to merely be a two-week vacation. All of a sudden it seemed to be something else."

"The guy bought you a multimillion-dollar beach house. That's the kind of discomfort I could live with."

"He didn't buy it for me."

"Did he give you your own set of keys?"

"Yes, but—"

"Aha. He did buy it for you. He obviously wants you to go back there with him as much as you can."

"Well, it's been almost a month, and I haven't seen him since."

"Which foreign capital has Lynch been toppling, or saving, now?"

"I lose track. In our last phone conversation, he said he was in Geneva, but I swear I could hear gunfire in the background."

"Of course. Those Swiss love their assault rifles."

Kendra laughed. Adam Lynch was a former FBI agent who had spent the last several years as a freelance agent who brokered sensitive deals all over the world. He'd helped negotiate prisoner releases, peace accords, and whatever else needed to be done in the pressure-cooker situations that were his specialty. He was often out of the country for weeks at a time, and Kendra admitted she appreciated the emotional distance it allowed her to keep from him. Lynch could be overpowering, and she was never certain how deeply she wanted to lose herself and her independence when she was with him. During those weeks in Spain she'd felt as if she'd been on an emotional roller coaster. Kendra leaned back on her couch. "Okay, I have to admit, he can be fascinating and I find myself missing the guy."

"Good," Olivia said. "And you know, it wouldn't be the end of the world if you told him that?"

"Heaven forbid. He thinks quite enough of himself. Everyone treats Lynch like a combination 007, Sam Spade, and one of the Marvel superheroes. It's difficult enough to keep a reasonable distance."

"I believe you'd manage to do it. Though it might be more interesting just to dive in and enjoy."

"Which you would probably never do."

"Just a thought..."

---

*Assholes.*

*A couple of total and complete assholes.*

Paula Chase turned off the I-5 freeway and took the road that led to her suburban home in San Marcos. She'd been spitting expletives during the entire drive from the downtown San Diego Police Headquarters, where she'd been trying to convince two arrogant young detectives that they needed to give more attention to the Morgan sisters missing persons case. They'd insinuated that Chloe and Sloane might have left on an impromptu road trip to Mexico or Las Vegas.

Right, Paula thought. And both women just happened to forget their cars, keys, phones, and credit cards.

She'd worked with lazy assholes during her twenty-five years with the department, but it seemed there were more of them now. The two detectives, Breen and Danforth, looked at her as if she was some kind of hysterical relic. She wasn't sure if it was sexism, ageism, or both.

Guys like that made her happy to be retired.

At least Kendra Michaels seemed to take the case seriously, though it still wasn't clear that she could be persuaded to join the investigation. According to her friends in the department, Kendra turned down far more cases than she accepted.

In any case, it was worth a shot.

Paula pulled into her driveway as the last tinges of sunlight disappeared behind the row of palm trees at the end of the nearby cul-de-sac. She opened her garage door with the visor-mounted remote, parked her Honda CR-V inside, then closed the door behind her.

She stepped inside her house and froze.

The place was a wreck. Someone had ransacked the

place, pulling out every drawer, clearing every cabinet, even emptying the refrigerator and freezer. She glanced at the wall where her alarm panel should have been. It was gone.

What in the holy hell?

There was rustling from the next room. Oh, shit. Her intruder was still in the house.

If anyone else was in her position, she knew what she'd tell them.

Get the hell out of there.

But she wasn't just anyone else. She had a gun, and she knew how to use it.

Paula crept toward her bedroom, on the opposite side of the house from where she could still hear her visitor opening desk drawers and emptying the contents of her office closet. What the hell was he looking for?

She peered through her bedroom doorway. Jesus. This room was in even worse shape than the rest of the house. Her mattress had been sliced open, and the padding was on the floor with every book and every object from the tall shelves. She scrambled toward her bed and felt underneath for her holstered automatic.

"It's not there anymore."

The man's voice came from behind her.

Dammit.

She looked at her television cracked and lying on its side and saw the reflection of the man standing in her bedroom doorway. He was dressed totally in black and wore a ski mask.

He was also holding her gun.

"Stand up."

She stood and slowly turned around. "What do you want?"

"I think you know the answer to that." He spoke in a low rasp. She wasn't sure if he was speaking that way to disguise his voice, or if that's the way he usually talked.

"I really don't. But before you destroy any more of my house, how about you just ask me? Is it money? If that's it, you're out of luck. I'm living on Social Security and my pension."

He raised the gun and aimed it at her head. "Fine. Maybe I should just do this."

He squeezed the trigger.

Click!

It didn't fire. He tried again.

Click!

She punched him in the face and elbowed his head until he dropped to the ground. She pounced on top of him.

"That gun jams all the time. Been meaning to take it in to the shop. Good thing I haven't, huh?"

Even through the ski mask, she could see his cheekbones rising in a wicked smile. A second later, she felt an icy coldness slicing into her right side. She gasped for air as her lung collapsed.

The intruder pushed her off him and pushed his knife into her again.

This time it went into her heart.

# CHAPTER 3

"Kendra, what in the hell have you gotten yourself into now?"

Kendra turned over in her bed and looked at the clock: 3:15 A.M. She was only barely aware of the phone in her hand. But she knew she recognized the voice. "Lynch?"

"Sorry for the insanely early call."

"You should be sorry. Where in the world are you right now? Are you still sticking with the Switzerland story?"

"I'd rather not say. I'll tell you about it later."

She smiled. Pure Adam Lynch. Someday he'd tell her about his mission in some exotic locale. "Okay, so maybe you can tell me why you're calling me at three in the morning."

There was a short silence. "Then I don't suppose you've heard."

"Heard what?"

He was silent for a long moment before replying. "You recently met with a retired San Diego police detective. You're helping her with a cold case."

If she hadn't known him so well she might have thought that he had someone spying on her, but she knew Lynch had close contacts with the police and FBI. Still, this was invasive even for him.

"You're incredible. I haven't even known her for twenty-four hours. Her name is Paula Chase, and for your information, I still haven't decided if I'm helping her or not. I'm not sure if I could be of value."

"I'm afraid that may not be an issue, Kendra...She's dead."

"What?" Kendra sat up in bed.

"I'm sorry. I'm sure you'll soon hear it from the police or maybe the news, but I wanted you to learn about it from me first. You tend to become involved."

"Of course I do," she said numbly. Kendra was still having trouble comprehending what she had just been told. "I suppose you even know what happened?"

"Justice thought I might be interested since you were involved." He added roughly, "Of course I was interested. Why the hell didn't you tell me that you were dealing with this kind of shit? You didn't even mention it."

"It wasn't any of your business. Besides, all you had to do was access another of your contacts about Paula. I'm sure no one would chance upsetting you by keeping you in the dark about anything concerning me. How did she die?"

"She was murdered in her home. A neighbor called it in last night. The first officers on the scene thought she might have interrupted a burglary, but it turns out she was just at the downtown station yesterday, trying to get some help on a missing persons case that may be related to an old investigation of hers. She told the detectives that she'd gone to you for help. I guess she thought that might light a fire under them."

"I can't believe it."

"My source in the SDPD was a bit incredulous, too. But since it concerned you, he knew I'd be interested. He didn't give me many details, but her murder did accomplish one thing: The police are now taking that case much more seriously."

"Good."

"So there's really no need for you to get involved."

"I don't know how you can say that. Or was that a command?"

"No. Be for real. I know you better than to try that. You don't respond well to commands, from me or anyone else. It was just an observation. That missing persons case is now a priority, and I'm sure they'll be searching to see if there's any connection to the old cold case. It's all being covered."

"Maybe."

Lynch clicked his tongue. "You're going to do it anyway, aren't you?"

"You do know me, Lynch. I don't see that I have all that much choice."

"Of course you do."

"Paula Chase didn't have to get involved. She's been retired for years, but she put herself on the line for those two young women. Which is more than anyone else was doing. She may have died for them."

"I suppose you're right."

"Which means I have to do what I can."

He sighed. "Of course you do. Where will you start?"

Kendra threw the covers off and swung her feet over the bed. "Her house. Now."

"Will you keep me informed?"

"Why should I bother? You're a busy man. But I'm certain that you'll be able to check your usual sources."

"Kendra."

"Sorry. I'm a little irritated. And I liked Paula. But I might be inclined to forgive and forget if you pull some strings that help me find out who the devil killed her."

"Did it occur to you that I was feeling helpless and wanted to touch base with you occasionally?" he asked quietly.

"No," she said. "You never feel helpless. You rule the world."

"Have it your way." She could almost imagine him shrugging. "I'll see if I can run a little of it your way if I get the chance. Take care of yourself, Kendra."

"Always."

"That's the problem I've been having. 'Always' is a word that's not in your vocabulary on a regular basis. You're too damn independent. Perhaps we'll both have to make a few adjustments."

---

Less than half an hour later, Kendra was driving through Paula Chase's pleasant San Marcos neighborhood where, she was sure, local television stations would soon be interviewing shocked residents about the horrible crime that had shattered their peaceful hamlet. It was still a good hour before sunrise, making it easy to spot the work lights and police flashers from almost a mile away.

Kendra parked her car, climbed out, and ducked underneath the yellow-and-black police tape stretched across the driveway.

"Kendra?"

She stopped and turned around. FBI agent Roland Metcalf was just a few steps behind her, slightly favoring his left leg. "What are you doing here? Somebody must have really begged you to be a part of this."

"Somebody did." Her lips tightened. "The victim."

"The victim?" Metcalf pushed back his mop of thick brown hair. He was a handsome young agent, about thirty, who had recently spent several weeks in the hospital recovering from a killer's booby-trap explosion. He'd been far enough away that he avoided the worst of the blast, and Kendra was happy that his recovery seemed to be going so well.

"Yes, the victim. Paula Chase herself. I just met her yesterday. But why are you here, Metcalf? This doesn't seem like the FBI's beat."

"Normally, it wouldn't be. But she'd been pushing us to follow up on an old serial killer case that our office had been helping investigate back in the day." His eyes widened and he gave a low whistle. "She got you to help her, didn't she?"

"It wasn't definite. I hadn't decided yet."

"Neither had we. But when this call came in, Griffin sent me to represent the Bureau in case there might actually be some connection to that Bayside Strangler case."

Metcalf flashed his badge at the officer guarding the scene, and he and Kendra stepped inside the one-story house. Kendra stopped. The place was a shambles, with every drawer, every cabinet, even the stove and refrigerator opened and contents spilled onto the floors.

"Wow," Metcalf said. "I take it Detective Chase didn't usually live like this."

"I doubt it." Kendra scanned the scene, trying to get some sense of what the intruder might have been looking for.

She'd seen several murder scenes where the killer ransacked the place to give the appearance of an interrupted burglary, but this wasn't one of those. It was clear the searcher had been on a mission, and didn't leave until every nook and cranny had been explored.

A photographer and four forensics techs were working the scene, and a red-haired detective with a wrinkled shirt and blue sport coat emerged from a back doorway. Kendra had seen Detective Ronald Breen a few times before, and he still wore a short strip of facial hair above his upper lip that creepily resembled a Hitler mustache.

Breen reacted in surprise at seeing them. "Huh. No one told me the FBI was taking over the case. Fine. Give me a sec to pull my guys out."

"Just the guys?" Kendra said. "Two of the techs and the photographer are women."

Breen pulled a thin-lipped smile. "No sexism implied, Dr. Michaels. So nice to see you again."

His voice was dripping with sarcasm. Although several cops had resented her involvement over the years, Breen was often one of the most hostile.

"The Bureau isn't taking over anything," Metcalf said. "This is San Diego PD's show all the way."

"So you're just here for an evening's entertainment?"

"Trust me, I'd rather be in my nice warm bed. Paula Chase was in our offices in the past few days about a missing persons investigation and how it might relate to an old cold case."

"She's been beating down our door, too. As a matter of fact, my partner and I may have been among the last people to see her alive."

"Where?" Kendra asked.

"Downtown, at police HQ. She didn't think we were doing enough to search for the Morgan sisters." Breen rolled his eyes in a way that Kendra knew must have infuriated Paula. "That lady thought the girls might have actually cracked a case the police and the FBI couldn't make a dent in."

"Those women never gave up," Kendra said. "They were still at it years after everyone else threw in the towel. You know how details can shake loose after a few years. Maybe they found something no one else did."

Breen nodded. "Well, that's what the deceased kept trying to tell us."

Kendra winced. The deceased. Less than eighteen hours before, Paula Chase had been a vibrant older woman, passionately fighting to help those missing sisters. Now she was the deceased.

"Did you know her from before?" Metcalf asked.

"Nah, Detective Chase was a bit before my time," Breen said. "Some of the old guard have nice things to say about her, but I really wasn't fond of the way she implied I wasn't doing my job, you know?"

*Maybe because you weren't*, Kendra wanted to say. Instead she held her tongue for a change and just nodded. There was a reason why she was not popular with a number of officers, but she was working on it...sometimes.

"Are you working her murder?" Metcalf said.

"Nope, I'm not in homicide. Perry and Ellenshaw are on it. They're around here someplace. I got sent over because I've been working the Morgan sisters' disappearance, and there's now some thought this might be related, since the deceased had been squawking so much about it."

Squawking. Kendra shook her head, positive that there was no way she could continue to hide her dislike of the man standing in front of her.

Metcalf obviously saw she was about to lose it. He quickly gestured toward the back doorway. "Murder scene is in here?"

"Yeah. Knock yourselves out."

Kendra and Metcalf moved through the doorway, where Paula Chase's bloody body was sprawled on the floor beside her torn-up bed.

As difficult as it was to see, Kendra forced herself to keep looking. She'd never get used to the grisly and depressing sight of someone murdered in cold blood. The two latex-gloved forensics techs leaning over her obviously had no such issues, as they worked with clinical detachment.

Paula Chase wore the same cream-colored suit she'd been sporting at her and Kendra's one and only meeting at the Pacific Villas retirement community the day before. Her hands were bagged to preserve later evidence collection efforts at the morgue, and there were at least three puncture wounds on her torso. Her face was frozen in a horrible grimace, showing how excruciating her last minutes were for her.

"She definitely walked in on her intruder," Kendra said, trying to adopt the same steely discipline as the techs. "He continued tearing the place apart after he killed her."

"How do you figure that?" Metcalf asked.

Kendra pointed toward the mattress stuffing around the corpse. "Most of the stuffing and other debris is beneath her body, but some is on top. He killed her after most of the place had been ransacked, but finished the job after her murder."

"You're saying 'he.' Is there a reason for that?"

"Yes. In the living room, there's a faint partial heel print in blood. It's a large heel, probably a man's size twelve or thirteen. It was tracked in there after Paula's blood was spilled. There's a texture to it that suggests the print was stamped through a medical bootie."

Metcalf pointed to the bootie-clad feet of the evidence collection techs. "It could have been one of them."

Kendra shook her head. "Not likely."

"I agree," a strong male voice said behind them.

Kendra and Metcalf turned to see a police detective Kendra hadn't met before. He wore his badge and ID around his neck, identifying him as Detective Raymond Perry.

Perry nodded at Kendra. "The living room print is from an athletic shoe, which none of our people on this scene is wearing. Am I right?"

"Yes." Kendra extended her right hand. "Kendra Michaels."

Perry shook her hand. "I'm glad you're here."

"Really? It's more than your colleague would say."

"Breen? I'm not sure he wants to be here himself. Anyway, I'm quite confident of our ability to investigate this case without your help, Ms. Michaels. I was referring to the fact that you were among the last people to see Paula Chase alive. You're on my list of people I need to talk to."

"Of course." Kendra looked back down at Paula's corpse. "It's still so hard to believe. I'd just met her. She seemed like a special lady. She tried so hard to do the right thing for those missing women. I'm not sure she got the respect she deserved in the last days of her life."

Metcalf nodded. "My feeling is, she didn't get a whole

lot of help from the FBI." He looked up at Perry. "I'm Special Agent Roland Metcalf. She came to see us, too. Who found her?"

"We got a call from the next-door neighbor. The houses are close together here, and he had his windows open. He heard a lot of strange noises from here early in the evening. Breaking dishes, toppled furniture, that kind of stuff. Shortly after dark, he saw someone leaving the residence that clearly wasn't Ms. Chase."

"Did he see the guy well enough to give a description?" Kendra asked.

"Not much of one. Just that it appeared to be a man dressed in dark clothing. He walked down to the corner and turned right. The neighbor could see Paula Chase's car in the garage, so he knocked on the door to check on her. When there was no answer, he tried to look into the windows. The blinds were drawn all around, but there was one opening just big enough for him to see that the place had been trashed. So he called the police, and they came for a welfare check. They broke in and found her."

"Security cameras or webcams in the neighborhood?" Metcalf asked.

Perry nodded. "Two webcams on this block, a few more around the corner. After sunrise, we'll ask the owners for access and see if there is anything saved in the cloud we can use."

"Good." Kendra looked at the objects strewn all over the floor. "Any idea what the killer was looking for?"

"No. Her purse was emptied in the foyer. If there was any cash in it, that was taken. But credit and ATM cards are still there."

Kendra turned and knelt on the bedroom floor. "Even the tiniest drawers and cubbies have been searched. It could be something very small. And the pillows have been shredded. What could you possibly hide inside one of your bedroom pillows?"

"Something worth killing for," Metcalf added.

Something occurred to Kendra. "Did you find her dog?"

"He was locked in a hall closet. The doggy is fine. The next-door neighbor has him now. Her sister's flying in from out of state, so I guess she'll figure out what to do with the pooch."

"That's a relief."

Perry half smiled. "...you say as you stand over their owner's slaughtered corpse."

"I'm quite sure Paula would be even more relieved. She loved her dog."

"Judging from all the framed photos I've seen around here, I'd say you're right," Perry said.

Kendra looked at the smashed photo frames and papers spread over the floor. "You know...This may be nothing, but there is something that might have been of interest to whoever broke in here."

"What's that?"

"Are you aware of the Bayside Strangler case files that the Morgan sisters compiled?"

Perry wrinkled his brow. "They had a copy of the police file?"

"No. Well, that might have been part of it, but they've spent years interviewing witnesses and doing their own investigating. It never really led anywhere, but the sisters' aunt offered it up to the police after they went missing. I assume it was probably Detective Breen. Anyway, the offer was refused. I guess your department didn't think it had much bearing on the missing persons case. Paula took possession of the files to study them. There were thousands of pages."

"Huh." Perry glanced around. "I haven't seen anything like that around here. You think maybe they were taken?"

"No. Definitely not."

"How can you be so sure?"

"Because I have them. All of them."

Metcalf looked as surprised as Perry. "How did that happen?"

"Paula gave them to me. I told her I'd take a look and let her know if I thought there was anything I could do to help. They're in my condo."

Perry nodded. "Interesting. You really think there's anything in those files that could trigger this kind of mayhem?"

"I haven't had a chance to look at them yet, but Paula went through all those boxes page by page. She didn't see anything that jumped out at her."

"Maybe we should take a look. How about if I send someone by to pick them up later today?"

"Sure. Call first, and I'll make sure I'm around."

"Good. No problem. Will do. Thanks for cooperating."

---

Dawn was breaking when Kendra and Metcalf stepped outside Paula's house and walked together down the driveway.

"What do you think?" Kendra asked. "See anything that will make the FBI want to get involved?"

"Not sure. I'll write my report later this morning. The

files that those women pulled together may have more interest for everyone now. Sad to say, Paula Chase will probably have better luck attracting interest in the case just by dying."

Kendra made a face. Not only sad, totally tragic. "Unfortunately, I was thinking the same thing."

Metcalf glanced at his watch. "It's still early. Want to grab some breakfast?"

"I'm afraid I can't. I have to meet a client at my studio."

"Now?"

"In about an hour. I've been working with an autistic child a couple of times a week. She's fresher and more responsive in the mornings, so her mother brings her before school."

"Too bad. I'm thinking about chicken and waffles at Hash House a Go Go."

"Rub it in, Metcalf. You know I love that place."

"Or I might go for the pumpkin waffles at Cafe 222."

"Now you're just being cruel."

"It's what I do best." He shrugged. "Sorry you can't join me. It would be nice to catch up."

"Soon, I promise."

Metcalf nodded and held eye contact with her as he backed away. Most of Kendra's friends and colleagues, especially Lynch, insisted that Metcalf had a major crush on her, despite the fact that he never seemed to have any shortage of female attention. She'd refused to believe it until recently, when his long looks and sedated hospital proclamations finally convinced her they might be right. Face it, she hadn't wanted to believe it. She had enough problems with her career—and then there was Lynch, who was constantly on the scene and in her life.

But Metcalf was still lingering. "Let us know if you find out anything, Kendra."

"You know I will."

He slowly shook his head. "Not really."

"Point taken. Touch base with me if the Bureau decides to get involved. I promise I won't freeze you out, Metcalf."

He grinned. "I'll hold you to that."

"Good. See that you do."

---

Kendra drove straight to her studio in a medical plaza, where the large room was adorned with electronic keyboards, flatscreen monitors, and several other instruments, all in service of her music therapy practice. After a few minutes, eight-year-old Cecilia Barton arrived with her mother. The autistic child had been growing increasingly withdrawn in the years before they met, but Kendra discovered that she responded to a series of music games. Within months, Cecilia became more talkative and engaged in school and her other interpersonal relationships, and her parents and educators had given Kendra's exercises all the credit for her progress.

Kendra knew Cecilia could still slide backward, so she'd recently designed slightly more complex games that required even greater interaction. Cecilia had so far risen to the challenge, but this morning Kendra found herself distracted by memories of the murder scene she'd visited only hours before. She didn't think the girl or her mother noticed, but she hated not being completely present for her clients. Particularly when it involved a child. She concentrated and was able to give the girl her full attention.

"Good," Kendra said after seeing Cecilia correctly match three lengthy note sequences. "Try the next group."

The girl was getting better and faster with this game, but Kendra found it was herself that was finding it increasingly difficult to focus.

Damn. As long as the Morgan sisters were still missing and Paula Chase's killer was on the loose, sessions like this weren't going to get any easier.

The case had grabbed her and wasn't letting go.

---

Kendra said her goodbyes to Cecilia and her mother and was on her way out to her car when her text notification chimed.

She looked at her phone. It was a text from Lynch: HAVE FUN AT YOUR EARLY MORNING MURDER SCENE?

She leaned against her car and tapped out her reply: WONDERFUL. NOTHING LIKE A PRE-DAWN SLAUGHTER TO START THE DAY.

HMM. STILL QUESTIONING DECISION TO TIP YOU OFF. MAYBE SHOULD HAVE LET YOU SLEEP AND DREAM OF ADAM LYNCH.

She inserted a "rolling eyes" emoji and responded: AS ALWAYS, LYNCH HAS INSANELY INFLATED SENSE OF SELF.

MUST DISAGREE. SENSE OF SELF EERILY IN LINE WITH HIGH REGARD FROM WORLD LEADERS, LAWMAKERS, AND GENERAL POPULATION.

MORE IN LINE WITH NARCISSISTIC PERSONALITY DISORDER, PERHAPS.

CONVERSATION NOW TAKING MOST UNPLEASANT TURN.

She smiled and replied: MORE UNPLEASANT THAN GRUESOME MURDER SCENE?

FOR ME, PERHAPS.

SPOKEN LIKE TRUE NARCISSIST. WHERE ARE YOU? EXPECTED PHONE CALL, NOT TEXT.

His response came a few moments later: NOW SURROUNDED BY PARTIES TO A SENSITIVE NEGOTIATION. MAKING THEM BELIEVE CONCERNS ARE BEING TAKEN SERIOUSLY AND CAREFULLY RESEARCHED ON ENCRYPTED CELL PHONE.

INCREDIBLE. PERHAPS SHOULD TERMINATE TEXT CONVERSATION UNTIL LATER TIME.

NOT NECESSARY. TACTIC NOW GIVING NEGOTIATIONS ROOM TO BREATHE. BACK TO MORE PLEASANT MATTERS, WHAT IS THE STATUS OF YOUR INVOLVEMENT IN GRUESOME SAN DIEGO MISSING PERSONS/MURDER CASE?

Kendra crossed her arms in front of her while she thought about it. She knew the answer, of course. There was no way she could walk away from those young women or the heroic former police detective who may have given her life trying to save them. She tapped out her two-word reply:

ALL IN.

# CHAPTER 4

Kendra grabbed some croissants from Bagatelle on the way home. She figured she'd catch up on her emails and then see if Olivia wanted to come over after lunch. Then maybe she could have a long talk with her and find out what on earth was happening at the condo. After that, maybe she'd—

What the hell?

Kendra had opened the door of her condo to see that the place was a wreck. A repeat of Paula Chase's home, with almost every square inch of floor space covered with papers, silverware, and knickknacks from her emptied drawers, shelves, and refrigerator.

As she glanced over the mess, she saw that every item of value was present and accounted for.

TV? Check.

Laptop? Check.

Ridiculously expensive stereo system? Check.

She whirled around. One thing was missing.

The Morgan sisters' case files. Shit! There was no trace of them. The three file boxes and dolly were gone. It was clearly what her intruder was after.

Her hunch at the murder scene had been correct. Somebody really wanted to get their hands on those files.

But why?

---

An hour later, Detective Perry and a pair of uniformed officers were at Kendra's condo, trying their best to step around the mess in her foyer and living room.

Perry surveyed the scene. "After what happened to Detective Chase, I'd say you're lucky you weren't home."

"Maybe," Kendra said. "But now we've lost those files."

"We'll dust for prints, but our suspect probably wore gloves. That was the story at Chase's house." Perry looked at the three heavy-duty dead bolt locks on her door. "You're well fortified here. Good locks and a steel-reinforced frame. Difficult locks to pick, but that looks like exactly what happened."

"I think so, too. I was assured these were almost impossible to defeat."

"They usually are, at least to almost any sneak thief I've ever met. We work with a former burglar who speaks to neighborhood watch groups about the best ways to protect their homes. He recommends a couple of these same locks. You're pretty much doing everything right. If anything, this may be a bit of overkill. Three dead bolts?"

"I've had problems in the past. A couple of my investigations followed me home."

Perry made a face. "No wonder you're so reluctant to

take on these cases. Anyway, Detective Chase also had good locks and even an alarm. Whoever this is, they know what they're doing. A far cry from your typical residential burglar."

Kendra looked down at the floor. "This is strange."

"Your condo getting tossed? I guess 'strange' is one way of looking at it."

She walked from her living room to the front door. "No, I mean…That dolly with the files was heavy. The wheels would have made impressions on all the papers and photos on the floor between the living room and foyer. But I don't see a single mark."

He stared at the floor. "Neither do I. You think they moved the cart out and trashed your place afterward?"

"Why would they do that? It doesn't make sense." Kendra opened her door and walked down the hallway. Perry joined her. She pointed to the floor, where the fine carpet nap showed the path taken by the dolly's twin wheels. "It was rolled to the elevator."

"Yes. Then out the building's front door?"

She bit her lip. "There's a security camera in the main lobby. Why go that way when there are two other exits where it's easier to slip out unnoticed?"

"You said the dolly was heavy."

"Still not that difficult to roll down a step at a time. Our burglar seems too thorough to risk going out the front door."

"You never know. We'll look at the security cam footage. I'll talk to the building manager."

Something else occurred to Kendra. "Follow me."

"Are we going to the manager's office?"

"No."

Kendra led him into the elevator and punched the second-floor button. In less than a minute, she leaned out the door and looked down the hallway. "This is our stop."

"Are you sure?"

"Positive."

They followed the wheel marks on the carpet until they ended in front of a condo door.

"That's a surprise," he said.

"Not really." She knocked on the door.

After a moment, Olivia answered. "Good morning, Kendra." She cocked her head, obviously picking up Perry's breathing. "Who's your friend?"

"Detective Raymond Perry, SDPD," he replied.

"Oooh." She was still smiling. "Am I under arrest?"

"Only if you stole a dolly cart of files from my condo this morning," Kendra said.

"Guilty as charged." Olivia swung the door open wide to reveal the dolly and three boxes of files, with folders stacked all over the large wraparound desk that dominated the condo's living room area. A muscular young man stood in front of the desk, feeding a sheaf of papers into a scanner. "Though I don't think the charges will stick," Olivia said. "I have a distinct recollection that you wanted these to be scanned."

"Thank God," Kendra said, rushing toward the file boxes. "They're all here!"

"Of course they are," Olivia said. "I have some East Coast radio interviews today, so Zack came in early this morning. We went straight up to your place. You weren't home, so I let myself in with my key. I didn't think you'd mind."

"I'm overjoyed."

Olivia smiled. "That's a little extreme, but okay. We brought them up here and Zack started scanning everything. He's good. He's almost finished."

Zack smiled at them. "Only two folders to go."

"You are good," Kendra said. "When you two were down there, did you notice anything messy or out of place?"

"Like what?" Zack said. "It looked fine to me."

"What time was that?" Perry asked.

"About seven thirty," Olivia said. "Like I said, Zack came in early. What's this about?"

"Someone ransacked my condo this morning. I think they were after these files. The woman I got them from was murdered in her home last night."

"Holy shit," Zack blurted out. He looked apologetically at Olivia. "Sorry."

"Don't worry about it. You're learning. 'Holy shit' is entirely appropriate in an amazing number of workplace situations." She faced Kendra. "You're telling me that someone ransacked your place between the time we took these and now? And that person may be a killer?"

"Yes. You and Zack are probably the only reason they don't have these files right now."

Perry motioned toward the file folders. "We're going to take these. They may have some relevance to our murder investigation. We'll just gather them up, and—"

"After he finishes scanning," Kendra said.

Perry shot her an annoyed stare. "Did you just hear the part about this being possible evidence in a murder case?"

"I did." She turned to Zack. "Keep scanning."

"Do it," Olivia whispered to him.

Zack quickly fed another stack of file pages into the scanner.

Perry shook his head. "Look, I don't need your permission to take these right this moment."

"Maybe not, but you would need to get a warrant. It would be easier for all of us if you let Zack take a few minutes to finish his work. Then he'll repack each of those boxes exactly as he found them and send you on your way. That seems like a far more efficient use of your time."

Perry thought for a moment, the pause filled by the sound of Olivia's scanner whirring and drawing in pages from the feed tray. He finally smiled at Kendra. "My colleagues told me you were a pain in the ass."

"A compliment, Detective?"

"They didn't mean it that way."

"How would you mean it?"

"I don't know you well enough yet." He shrugged. "Okay, finish up here. I want to be out of here with those files in ten minutes."

Kendra glanced at Zack, who gave her a quick nod.

"Fine. We'll be ready."

---

As promised, Zack finished the scans in ten minutes, and Perry and the two uniformed officers carried off the file boxes.

"Come on," Kendra said. "You're not taking the big ugly dolly?"

"It's all yours." Perry hefted his box as he walked toward the door. "Thank you, Dr. Michaels."

And Detective Perry was gone.

Zack plopped down in one of the office chairs positioned around Olivia's large U-shaped desk. "Wow. I didn't expect this when I signed up to intern for a website."

Olivia pulled a USB memory stick from her desktop console. "Well, you can always go back to combing my mailing list for possible duplicates."

"Hey, I'm not complaining." Zack's square jaw and toothy smile gave him the appearance of an all-American quarterback. "I just didn't think I'd be helping out on a murder case." He looked at Kendra. "By the way, it's nice to meet you. I'm Zack Duffer."

"Kendra Michaels. Nice to meet you, Zack. I appreciate your help. You're a student at USC?"

"Yep. I graduate in May. I'm finished with my classes, but I need the internship to complete my degree requirements. Ms. Moore was nice enough to pick me."

"Nice had nothing to do with it," Olivia said. "I got your transcript. You could've had your pick of hundreds of internship programs."

Zack shrugged. "Maybe."

"See?" Olivia said. "He's not even going to try to deny it."

"I'm right where I want to be," Zack said. He turned toward Kendra. "I wanted to ask you...Have you actually looked at those files yourself yet?"

"Not really. I haven't had a chance."

"Olivia told me that they were put together by two women whose mother was murdered."

"That's right. They compiled these over a period of several years."

"There's some pretty graphic crime scene photos. Not

so much of their mother's crime scene, but of other Bayside Strangler victims. Those women must have somehow gotten them from the police."

"It's not that hard if you know which palms to grease. And these are obviously two very resourceful women."

Olivia extended the flash drive toward Kendra. "Well, you can now carry all their work around with you. Do you really think there's something in here that got that retired detective killed?"

"I don't know, but it's strange that my place got tossed just hours later. I'm just glad whoever it was didn't realize you had taken them."

"You and me both. Now get out of here. Unless you'd like to join Zack in observing my Zoom meetings with advertisers?"

"I'll pass on that, thanks. See you later."

---

After making phone calls in the morning and early afternoon, Kendra returned to her studio for a typical flurry of after-school appointments. As her last client left, Kendra pulled the USB flash drive from her pocket and looked at it for a long moment. She was sure Detective Perry and his colleagues were already studying the files they had taken. What could she possibly see that they couldn't? Surely no more than Paula Chase, who had worked the cases herself.

Well, might as well take a look.

Kendra plugged the flash drive into her main console, which displayed the file contents on three large wall-mounted monitors she used for her music games and exercises. She paced across the studio with the remote in her hand, paging through the files. She was amazed by the quality, quantity, and organization of the Morgan sisters' research. Many of the files were dominated by transcripts of interviews conducted by the women themselves. They had tracked down the victims' family members, witnesses, and even several law-enforcement agents, all of whom were surprisingly candid. Kendra supposed that the sisters' own tragic connection with the case made their interviewees more open and accessible than they may have been with the case's original investigators.

She raised her remote and paced around the studio as she perused the file's opening case summaries. Five women were murdered in a four-month period, all of them strangled. The first two were physically disabled; the last three were not, perhaps as the killer gained confidence in his deadly abilities.

The first victim, Donna Shetland, was a multiple sclerosis patient and used an upright walker to walk back and forth from her job as a luxury hotel events manager in the Gaslamp district. She lived alone, and no one had noticed she was missing until she failed to show up at work one morning. A police welfare check confirmed she wasn't at home, and area security cameras indicated that she'd disappeared on her way from work the evening before, somewhere in the vicinity of Eleventh Avenue and F Street. Her body was found three days later underneath a tarp behind a Little Italy restaurant, and her walker was recovered at a nearby homeless encampment.

Alyssa Morgan was the second victim, and although Kendra was familiar with her story after speaking with Paula Chase, the summary included details Paula hadn't given her. Alyssa's condition was the result of a ski accident that left her paralyzed from the waist down, and she raised her two young daughters alone after her husband left the family just months after her injury. She harbored dreams of participating in the Paralympics as a wheelchair racer, and the hiking path was one of her favorite training spots. She disappeared from there on a weekday morning, and inexplicably, her wheelchair reappeared on the path four days later. She was soon found hanging from a tree forty yards away. She'd been dead several days and most likely placed there the same time her wheelchair was returned.

As Kendra read the detached and almost clinical summary, she was amazed to think that it was written by one or both of Alyssa Morgan's own daughters.

*What in the hell happened to you, Chloe and Sloane?*

The third victim was Leah McLane, a thirty-seven-year-old waitress at the Hot Ribs barbecue restaurant in Ocean Village. She left work at ten on a Sunday night, but her fellow employees noticed that her car was still in the parking lot Monday morning. They followed up that afternoon, but she'd vanished. Like the others, her strangled body didn't appear until several days later, lying in the restaurant's back patio hammock. She was bound by the same green-and-white rope as the previous victims, with the same distinctive knots. Only then did law enforcement publicly concede that a serial killer might be on the loose.

Kendra pressed her remote repeatedly, flipping through scans of the newspaper stories. She had a faint memory of this period of time, but as a teenager living and attending school outside the city, the case had little meaning for her.

She stopped to scan the details of the fourth victim, Greta Waters. Greta sang and played piano at Zephyr's, a popular bar with a spectacular bayside view. She was apparently abducted as she left her apartment for work around 4:00 P.M. Her strangled body didn't appear until almost a week later, in the bed of a stolen pickup truck parked within sight of her apartment building.

The fifth and final victim, Katrina Burge, was last seen jogging near Ocean Beach, and her disappearance brought unprecedented attention from the local media. Hundreds of volunteers turned up to help search for her in the days afterward, and police kept a round-the-clock watch in the hope of catching the killer's return of her body to the local area. Despite their efforts, the killer still managed to surreptitiously return Burge's strangled and bound corpse to the beach four days later, hidden in a dilapidated lifeguard station marked for demolition. It had been searched by both police and volunteers literally dozens of times in the days before the corpse's appearance.

But here, for the first time, a vehicle and possible killer were seen in connection to one of the killings. A white Toyota FJ SUV was spotted on a security camera near the beach on the evening of the corpse drop-off, and the figure of a large, husky man was seen loading a shopping cart into its rear hatch. Wheel marks in the sand near the lifeguard station were clearly from a shopping cart abandoned just a few yards away, and the depth of the tracks made it clear that this was the probable means of transporting the victim's body to the location.

Kendra stepped closer to the screen to look at the grainy still image of the man loading the shopping cart. The vehicle's license plate wasn't visible, and it was barely possible to determine the FJ's make and model. Unfortunately, the video brought investigators no closer to finding the killer, even after it was widely spread online and on television news broadcasts.

There were apparently no more killings after Katrina Burge's, although some investigators and journalists tried to make the case that the murderer was still active and had merely changed his locale or modus operandi. But most concluded that the Bayside Strangler's reign of terror had come to an end because he was now dead or perhaps imprisoned for unrelated crimes.

Wishful thinking, Kendra thought. And Chloe and Sloan Morgan clearly didn't believe it.

She saved the files to her cloud storage account and pulled out the memory stick. There were hundreds of pages left to peruse, but this was a good introduction to the Bayside Strangler. She owed it to Paula Chase to at least—

"Kendra...? Kendra, can you talk?"

The disembodied voice came from the speakers suspended above her monitors.

What in the hell?

"Kendra?"

She knew that voice, of course. But why was it coming from her studio equipment?

"Lynch, what in the hell is going on here?"

The screensavers on her monitors gave way to a video image of Adam Lynch. There was a grimy, dirt-marred wall behind him, and the dim lighting left half his face in shadows. He raised a water bottle toward her. "Cheers."

"You can see me?"

"Of course. You use this system for teleconferencing, don't you?"

She bit her lip in anger. "You've crossed a line here. You think it's okay to hack into my work computer?"

"If it's to talk to you, why not?"

"Because I work with my clients here. They have a right to their privacy."

"I didn't start using your camera until you talked back to me just now. I know your office hours, so I didn't tap into your system until I was reasonably certain you would be alone."

"So you saw what I was doing on my system?"

"I did."

"Not cool, Lynch. If you want me to share something with you, just ask. It's not okay for you to spy on what I'm doing. Got it?"

"Point taken. I'm sorry. I actually peeked in to make sure you weren't in the middle of a session. Instead, I saw some fairly disturbing murder scene photos."

"So you saw everything."

"Yes. I assume it's the files that the Morgan sisters put together. Pretty grim stuff. I also heard that your condo was broken into. I'm sure it's occurred to you that it was probably the same person who ransacked Paula Chase's home and murdered her."

"Of course. They'd have had these files now if Olivia hadn't taken them and had her intern scan them all. The police have them all now."

"Good. For some reason, those files might have put a big target on your backs."

"But why? That's what I can't figure out."

He leaned forward. "When I get back there, we can figure it out together. Will you wait for me?"

Kendra raised her remote toward the screen. "I'm about two seconds away from switching you off."

He laughed. "That's a more frightening prospect than the bullets I was dodging this morning."

"I thought I heard gunfire. Care to enlighten me?"

"After I get back. Just another day at the office."

"Office? You look like you're in a hovel."

He glanced around. "Actually, I think it's a kitchen. Or at least it used to be."

"In any case, I'm not waiting for you. The Morgan sisters need all the help they can get right now."

He paused for a long moment. "You really think they're still alive?"

"I don't know. I realize that their odds get slimmer with each passing hour. But there's a chance, you know? Those women are heroes. After all they went through, you have to admire the way they've been working so hard to find their mother's killer."

"I agree. I read up on their case after we talked last. I figured their mother touched a nerve with you."

"What do you mean?"

"The husband and father who left his family when his wife's injury got too much for him to deal with. How could it not make you think of your own family?"

Kendra was silent for a moment. She hadn't discussed this subject with Lynch, and he'd never pressed her on it. Until now. "Like my father, who left his family after his child was born blind? You're thinking I might be identifying with them. I never knew the scumbag, and I never want to know him. I was only a few months old when he left. I know it was hard on my mom, but she never let on. If you ask her about it, she'd say it allowed her to flourish. I think it did. Just like I think Alyssa Morgan was flourishing before she was murdered. She wanted to qualify for the Paralympic Games, and she might have done it. She was a special woman."

"Obviously."

"So maybe I'm not just doing this for Paula Chase or the Morgan sisters, but for that gutsy mom who was only just starting to come into her own."

He nodded and stared at her in silence for a long moment. "I can see that. Whatever happened to her daughters, they're lucky to have you on their team."

She shook her head. "It's my honor. I just hope I can be of some help."

"Hey, I'm sure you will be." He finished his bottled water and tossed the empty container aside. "I really wish I could drop everything and be there to help. But I have a couple of days ahead of me here."

"Stop worrying about me, Lynch. I'm pretty good at taking care of myself."

"I've noticed." Lynch turned sharply as the sound of men's voices rang in the background. "Gotta run," he whispered. "Literally. I'll be in touch."

Before Kendra could reply, he grabbed his phone and cut the connection.

Kendra stared at her now blank bank of monitors. And Lynch was worried about her?

She shut down her system.

# CHAPTER 5

The next morning, Kendra rolled to a stop in front of the Carmel Valley home of Marlee Davis, the aunt who'd raised the Morgan sisters after her sister's murder. A telephone call to Detective Perry had given her the woman's address, along with the fact that she worked at home most days. Kendra took it as a good sign that a Honda CRV was parked in the driveway. It was an even better sign that a middle-aged woman waved at her from behind a gardenia bush next to the front door.

"Dr. Michaels?"

Kendra climbed out of her car and walked up the front driveway. "I didn't know I'd be expected."

The woman peeled off her gardening gloves. "Detective Perry told me that you might be coming. I'm Marlee Davis."

"Hi. I hope you don't mind if I ask a few questions."

"I'll talk to anyone who might be able to help bring Chloe and Sloane home." Marlee folded her arms in front of her. "I heard about what happened to Detective Chase.

I can't believe she's dead. Paula was a huge help to us after my sister was murdered. Even after all these years, she was available to talk to the girls about the case. I understand she reached out to you after they went missing."

"She did. I met her on the last day of her life."

"Well, if she thought enough of you to ask for your help, that's all I need to know. Would you like to come inside?"

"Thank you."

Kendra followed Marlee inside her pleasant two-story home, which was decorated with pictures and objects that showed a fondness for European travel. Many of the framed photos included shots of the Morgan sisters, Marlee, and a ruggedly handsome man.

"These are nice," Kendra said. "Is that your husband?"

"Yes. That's Keith. He passed away from lung cancer a few years ago. The girls were crazy about him."

"You obviously gave them a nice home."

Marlee gazed pensively at a photo of two girls with their mother. "My sister did a wonderful job in the short time she had with them, and I just wanted to do everything I could to make them happy. They've grown up into two amazing women."

"So I gather. I'm impressed by how dedicated they are to find their mother's killer. I've never seen anything like it."

Marlee motioned toward a loveseat and couch in her sunken living room. Kendra sat on the loveseat, but Marlee remained standing. "Chloe really started that. She was the older of the two, and she started asking questions about her mother's death when she was around thirteen or fourteen. My husband was uncomfortable discussing it with her, but I thought it was important to be as honest with the girls as we could. And who were we fooling anyway? Kids are better at finding stuff online than we ever were. Soon she was obsessed with finding out everything she could about Alyssa's case, and Sloane was right there with her, at least for a while."

"For a while?"

Marlee finally sat on the arm of the sofa. "Sloane started living life. She was very popular in high school and always had a lot of attention from boys. Chloe also had friends, but she was more academically inclined. She never stopped trying to find answers about what happened to her mother. Sometime during her college years, she started doing more than just digging up old newspaper and magazine articles. She started interviewing people connected with the investigation."

"Police detectives?"

"Police detectives, uniformed officers, FBI agents, witnesses who appeared in the police reports...It's when Chloe really started her own investigating. Almost everybody connected with the case was willing to talk to her. It was incredible. And when she exhausted all the leads in her mother's case, she moved on to the other Bayside Strangler murders. Sloane rejoined the investigation around this time. They were both out of college by then and doing well. Chloe is a coder with a software developer in La Jolla, and Sloane is a PR rep at a firm downtown. They talked to everyone they could about the case. They used dictation software to take their interview recordings and make transcripts that they just pored over. They were obsessed. To be honest, I think it got in the way of their personal relationships. Chloe never spent much time with any one man, and most of her friendships fell by the wayside. Sloane was engaged for a while, but her fiancé was never that supportive of what she and her sister were doing. He didn't like that it took her away from him so much of the time. I don't know if he actually made an ultimatum, but he made it clear he wasn't happy with things. So she left him."

Kendra nodded. "Did you ever feel they were in danger?"

"No. To be honest, for all the work and time they put into this, they never seemed to be particularly close to solving the case. I think they gathered a lot of information that even the police didn't have, but nothing that might make the killer feel threatened."

"That's probably why the police weren't interested in their files. Paula told me that, but she also said there was a recent development. Did you know anything about that?"

Marlee nodded. "I was just about to mention it. Their moods changed in the last month or so. Chloe and Sloane were excited about something they found. They wouldn't tell me what it was, but they became completely absorbed in their project, more than ever before. I found out later that Chloe had even started missing work, calling in sick when I knew she was fine. In all the years they had been investigating their mother's death, they've never shown this kind of urgency."

"You have no idea what they'd found?"

"I'm afraid not. No idea. After they went missing, I immediately thought of their case files. I talked to the police, but like you said, they didn't think that was an avenue worth exploring. That's when I spoke to Paula about it. She took their files and looked them over."

"Yes, she told me. She didn't see anything."

"She told me that, too. It's too bad. We thought there might be some hint there of what new lead they'd found."

Kendra nodded. Better not to tell her those case files might have been what got Paula Chase killed. "How often do you talk to them?"

"At least once every few days. They were here a lot after my husband passed away, but not so much lately. Life gets in the way, you know?"

"I know." Kendra made a mental note to call her own mother later. "Listen, do you happen to have keys to their homes?"

Marlee hesitated before replying. "Sure. We look after each other's places when we're out of town. Pick up mail, water plants, that kind of thing. Why?"

"I assume the police have looked their homes over, but I wondered if you might take me there."

Marlee was clearly mystified by the request. "Why? I've been to both of their places myself, and I didn't see anything out of order. Neither did the police."

"I know. I'd just like to see for myself. And I'd appreciate it if you would go with me in case I have any questions."

Marlee checked her watch. "Well, I'm free until dinnertime. We could do it now."

Kendra stood. "I was hoping you would say that. I'll follow you."

---

It took only fifteen minutes for Kendra and Marlee to reach Chloe Morgan's Pacific Beach residence, a one-story house just a few blocks from the community's boardwalk and popular surfing spots.

Kendra walked around the sporty red Audi parked in the driveway next to the house. "This is Chloe's car?"

"Yes. It's been here since she went missing."

"Keys?"

"In her purse, on the foyer table. Along with her wallet, cash, ATM and credit cards. No activity on any of them."

Marlee led Kendra to the front door and let her into the house. It was immaculate, and many of the walls featured framed art prints of surfers and beach scenes. Two colorful surfboards hung on the wall over the living room sofa.

"Chloe surfs?" Kendra asked.

"Oh, yes. Since college. After several hours of writing software, she grabs a board and goes to the beach to clear her head. It's why she lives here."

"These are her only two boards?"

"She has another in her garage. It's in there, I checked. She didn't drown, Dr. Michaels."

Kendra nodded. Marlee had obviously considered all the possibilities. Kendra turned and glanced around the living room. Like Marlee, she'd packed her home with family photographs. An area above a low bookshelf was dedicated to her mother, and also included several shots of her sister and Marlee. She looked away. "Does Chloe work at home often?"

"Yes. Her company doesn't really care where she does her coding, as long as she's productive. She goes up to La Jolla for meetings, but most of her work is done here. I'll show you her office."

Marlee led her into a small room in the back of the house. The walls were dark, and most of the illumination was provided by lengths of neon tubing on the walls and ceiling. Track-mounted window shades sealed off any trace of sunlight. A long desk, free of papers or any other clutter, faced the door.

"Wow," Kendra said. "It's like a cave."

"That's the way she likes to work. She says it helps her focus, but you can see why she likes to get out in the sun during her breaks."

"Do you know what she's been doing at work?"

"Yes, she's lead coder on a new scheduling system for the University of California schools. But like I said, she's been distracted lately. Chloe is the best at what she does, but she's been so preoccupied with her mother's case that I've been afraid she might lose her job."

Kendra backed out through the door and looked down the hallway. "Her bedroom's down here?"

"Yes, but there's not much to see."

Kendra walked down to the next door and leaned inside. Marlee was right: Aside from a bed and a pair of night tables, the room was empty. The windows were covered with the same track-mounted blackout shades as in the office, but they were wide open in this room.

"Chloe sometimes works around the clock, so it's not unusual for her to sleep during the day. She likes these shades to give her total darkness whenever she needs to grab a few winks."

Kendra pulled open the night table drawers. One held an open box of condoms, the other remotes for the shades and room lights. The closet was filled with an assortment of wet suits, casual wear, and a few dressier items of clothing. The master bathroom was spotless, with only a few bottles of skin care and hair products in the shower and on the counter.

"Very sparse," Kendra said. "It almost looks a place that you might find for rent on Airbnb."

"No, she doesn't do that. She just never liked clutter. A minimalist through and through."

"I can see that."

Kendra walked back through the bedroom and froze. She cocked her head as Marlee walked behind her. "Go back."

"What?"

"Go back and walk toward me again."

Marlee wore a puzzled expression. "You want me to—?"

Kendra knelt on the floor. "Go back a few steps, then walk back toward me. Please."

Marlee walked toward the bathroom, then turned and stepped toward Kendra.

"Stop!" Kendra stared at her feet. "Did you hear that?"

"Hear what?"

"The floor." Kendra knocked on the floor, moving her hand around to isolate a single ceramic tile that sounded slightly hollower than the others. "Right here."

"Maybe...Your hearing must be better than mine."

"I doubt that. I just grew up paying more attention to what I hear." Kendra knocked on the floor again, then ran her fingernails along the grout line surrounding the tile. She tried prying it at several points, but the tile didn't budge.

"What are you trying to do?" Marlee asked.

"I'm not really sure." She moved her fingers to the other side of the tile. "I thought if I could just—"

The tile separated from the floor and flipped upward.

Marlee gasped. "Look!"

Kendra leaned over to see an opening under the floor,

its sides carved in the same dimensions as the tile she'd just removed.

"Is it a safe?" Marlee asked.

"Safes usually have locks. This was glued shut." She pulled her phone from her pocket, activated the flashlight function, and shone it down into the opening. "There's something down here. Get me some tissues from the bathroom."

Marlee ran to the bathroom, pulled a few tissues from the box, and brought them to Kendra.

Kendra used them to reach inside and pull a worn object from the opening. She laid the object on the floor.

It was a foot of electrical cord tied between two wooden handles.

Marlee leaned close. "What is it?"

"It looks like a homemade garrote. The Bayside Strangler's victims were strangled by what was thought to be extension cords. Pretty much just like this one, but none were ever recovered." They stared down at it for a long moment. "Marlee, do you know why Chloe would have something like this in her house?"

"She was thorough. She might have made that herself to figure out the kind of weapon the killer might have used against her mother and all the others."

"Reasonable enough. One thing, though."

"What's that?"

"Look closer." She moistened her lips. "I think there's blood on it."

# CHAPTER 6

Less than twenty minutes later, Detective Ronald Breen was standing alongside Kendra and Marlee in Chloe's bedroom, staring at the garrote resting next to the square-shaped hole in the floor.

Kendra crossed her arms. "I'm guessing you walked right over this."

Breen scratched his short mustache. "You guessed right. But I'm a bit curious about how in the hell you knew how to find it." He looked at Marlee. "You told her about this?"

"Nope. I didn't have a clue."

Kendra smiled. "It's a twelve-by-twelve-inch hole in the floor, Breen. It sounded like a bass drum when we walked across it. In my experience, your officers don't pay nearly as much attention to their ears as they do their eyes."

"You may be right about that. I probably walked over this thing half a dozen times." He knelt and stared at the garrote. "It does look like blood on this thing. Though I'm not sure if the Bayside Strangler actually drew blood from any of his victims."

"Two." Kendra read from her phone screen. "Leah McLane and Katrina Burge. The others just showed bruising."

Breen squinted at the gory photos on Kendra's phone. "Wow, those are police crime scene photos. Did you get those off the Web?"

"No. Courtesy of the Morgan sisters. Scans of their work that your colleague carted off yesterday afternoon."

"Oh, yeah. Perry's taken over an entire conference room with that stuff." Breen was still staring at the garrote. "You're not suggesting that this contraption is the actual murder weapon, are you?"

"I have no idea. I just think it's strange that it was so carefully hidden in the home of someone who devoted her life to finding a killer who murdered his victims with a cord just like this one."

"I won't argue with that." He produced a clear plastic evidence bag. "You didn't touch that thing with your bare hands, did you?"

"Please."

"I had to ask." He scooped up the garrote and sealed the bag. "I'll have it tested, and if it's blood, we'll run DNA."

"Good."

He looked between the two women. "You find anything else I should know about?"

"Not yet, but the day's still young. We're about to head over to the sister's place. Sloane Morgan's house." Kendra smiled. "Of course, you've already gone over it with the same fine-tooth comb you used to search this place. No way I could ever find anything there, right?"

"Very funny. Now I can see how you've earned that 'pain in the ass' rep."

"Aw, come on. It was given purely out of affection."

"Keep telling yourself that, Dr. Michaels."

"Trust me, I will. Sometimes it's the only way I can make it through the day."

Breen chuckled as he left the room and walked toward the front door.

Marlee turned toward Kendra. "Now I see why Paula wanted to bring you in to this. You found something a whole army of cops couldn't find."

Kendra shrugged. "Still no telling if it's anything worthwhile."

"We'll know soon enough." Marlee checked the time on her phone screen. "Listen, we lost time waiting for Detective Perry to get here. I'm afraid you're going to have to go to Sloane's place by yourself."

"Are you sure?"

"Sorry. I have a business dinner, and the client is only in town this one night." Marlee fished the key from her pocket and handed it to her. It was attached to a penguin-shaped keychain. "You can give this back to me later. There's an alarm there, but I left it off in case the police want to go back in. If Paula trusted you, I can trust you. If you have any questions, call me. Okay?"

"Sure."

"Thank you, Kendra. Please let me know if you find anything."

"I will."

---

Kendra drove to Golden Hill, a downtown neighborhood that possessed a decidedly artsy vibe. Within easy walking distance of the Gaslamp district and Balboa Park, the community featured several recording studios and art galleries. It was also home to one of her favorite restaurants, the Turf Supper Club, where she and her friends often gathered around an indoor cooking pit, grilled their own steaks, and consumed craft cocktails.

Kendra almost laughed when she realized that Sloane's address was a building she'd noticed many times since its groundbreaking two years before. The six-story structure was constructed to look like an old factory that had been repurposed to hold a collection of artist's lofts. The design was obviously in the interest of attracting hipster tenants who populated the area. It was marketed as studio space, but the sidewalk signs also noted that the units were zoned for residential use.

Kendra took the large industrial elevator to the fifth floor, amazed at the extent to which the builders made the new structure appear to be over a century old. Unbelievable. It was almost like a Disneyland attraction.

Kendra exited the elevator and found Sloane's unit at the end of the hallway. She inserted the key, entered, and locked the door behind her. It was a spacious apartment with floor-to-ceiling windows, wood floors, and exposed ceiling pipes and HVAC ducts that continued the industrial theme. The lights of the city sparkled outside, and the lack of any window treatments gave her the feeling of being in a fishbowl.

Kendra looked at the artwork on the walls. They were modern mixed-media pieces that combined oils with time-lapse photography, and all appeared to be Sloane's work. Very impressive.

A purse and keys were on the kitchen counter. Kendra assumed Sloane's phone had been taken by the police in the hope of gleaning some useful info from it.

Kendra looked in the bedroom and bathrooms, and saw little of interest except indications that Sloane was dating two men and possibly one woman. None probably knew about the others, judging by her elaborate attempts to hide certain toiletries in the back shelves of her linen closet.

All in all, the place had a more relaxed and easier vibe than her sister's house, better decorated and arranged for entertainment and relaxation. But still no indication of what had happened to her. And, as far as Kendra could tell, no hidden bloody weapons.

Thump.

The sound came from the front door.

She listened. Someone was working on the lock. After a few seconds, the lock was thrown, and the door swung open.

Footsteps. A man, probably, with long strong strides. A cop? A boyfriend of Sloane's?

She called out. "Hello?"

The footsteps stopped.

"Hello?" she repeated.

All the unit's lights shut off.

What the hell…? She reached for the bedroom lamp and hit the switch. Nothing. The main power breakers must have been thrown.

She heard the rustling of fabric in the next room. The intruder was taking pains to be quiet out there. She could play that game. She slipped out of her shoes and inched toward the doorway. She reached for a Salvador Dalí bust she'd remembered seeing on a low shelf.

Damn, it was lighter than it looked. Couldn't inflict too much damage with this thing. Maybe if she—

BAMM!

The bedroom door flew into her and knocked her off her feet. Before she could regain her footing, a strong pair of hands gripped her back jacket collar and tossed her into the living room.

Ouch.

"Find anything?" The intruder spoke in a low rasp. "Did you?"

He grabbed her again and tossed her against one of the tall windows. It cracked as she struck it. Damn. Did her head just do that?

In the next instant she found herself picked up and hurled back at the fractured pane. This time the glass shattered and rained down in pieces on the sidewalk far below.

Shit. She was inches away from raining down there herself.

Cool wind blasted through the apartment, and traffic sounds echoed from the street.

She rolled over and took her first look at the attacker. As she'd surmised from his footsteps, he was indeed a tall man. He was dressed entirely in black and wore a black hoodie with ski mask attached with gold-colored snaps.

He leaned down and grabbed her. "What did you give the cop? Tell me!" He slid her closer to the window's edge.

"What are you talking about?"

"Don't play dumb. I know who you are, Kendra Michaels. I know what you're doing."

"At least one of us does."

"Enough!" He thrashed her back and forth, scraping the back of her neck over the broken windowpane.

"Okay! Just tell me what you want."

The man leaned close. "What did you give him?"

Kendra took a deep breath. She wasn't going to get a better shot at this. She swung her left arm upward, still gripping the Dalí statue.

Contact!

Blood and a single tooth flew from the man's mouth as he screamed and fell backward.

Guess that bust was heavy enough after all.

She struck him again. His howl was even more bloodcurdling this time. Good.

She rolled away and ran for the door. He was a heartbeat behind. She pulled down a tall bookshelf and a shorter one next to it, listening with relief as she heard him stumble over them.

She ran into the hallway. Shit. What now?

Three studios in the hallway had light leaking from beneath their closed doors.

She tried the first door.

Locked.

The second door.

Also locked.

Movement behind her. He'd pulled himself to his feet and was on his way.

She ran toward the third door and grabbed the knob. It turned! She opened it, slid inside, and closed and locked it behind her.

"Hey!"

Kendra spun around and put her finger to her lips, shushing

a young man in a goatee chopping vegetables at his kitchen island. He was standing in front of a camera and tripod.

"I'm recording a YouTube video here! You just ruined a take."

"Shhh!" She hit the wall switch and turned off the lights.

"Come on!"

"Shhh!" Kendra pressed her eye to the peephole. She saw her attacker half staggering, half running past the door and down the hallway. He was heading toward the stairs, just as she'd hoped.

But then he stopped.

Shit.

He turned. Still wearing his ski mask, he appeared to be looking right at her. Could he tell that she was blocking light from the peephole?

Another long moment. He turned and ran for the stairs.

She faced the YouTuber, who still held up his knife as if he might have to use it as a weapon. "Relax. The bad guy was on the other side of this door, and now he's gone." She flipped on the lights and pulled out her phone. "I'm here looking into your neighbor's disappearance. Sloane Morgan. Know her?"

"No. To be honest, I'd never heard of her until she went missing. I already talked to the police about her."

"I'm not a cop, but I'm about to call one. Mind if I hang here until they show up?"

He finally lowered the knife. "Uh, okay. But after you make your call, I need to finish up here with my cooking demonstration. My fans are expecting it by midnight."

She wasn't sure she had heard him correctly. "Your—"

"My fans."

"Right. Thanks." She punched the number.

---

Kendra only had to endure three takes of the young man's food prep demonstration before Detectives Perry and Breen appeared with a pair of uniformed officers in the hallway outside.

She flung open the door. "Did you get him?"

"Not so far," Breen said. "We have ten officers downstairs, but no one matching that description is anywhere around. Of course, all he would have to do is ditch the jacket and mask, and he could be standing on the sidewalk drinking a caffe latte and we wouldn't have any idea."

Perry's gaze was examining her forehead. "You're bleeding."

She lightly rubbed the wound. "Head versus plate-glass window. Neither one of us did well against the other."

"You should have that looked at."

"No, it's pretty much clotted. I'd rather you look at Sloane Morgan's apartment. I drew blood and, I believe, a front tooth from our guy. Maybe we can get a DNA hit from it."

Perry smiled. "Well done. Let's go see."

They walked back down to the apartment. The wind from the broken window was colder and more intense than before. Two uniformed officers were already on the scene, and they had restored power to the unit. Kendra crouched next to the twin puddles of blood next to the shattered pane. She pointed to one. "Okay, this is mostly his blood, and you'll find even more on that Salvador Dalí statue."

Perry looked around. "Which way did the tooth go?"

"Look toward the kitchen."

One of the uniformed officers shone his flashlight on the floor near the small dinette set. "Sir?"

Perry bent over a bloody object. "That's it. I think you may have ripped out a piece of his gums along with it. Wherever he is right now, he's not feeling too good."

"Glad to hear it."

He bagged the tooth and used a Sharpie to mark the label. "I'll make sure forensics swabs the blood in here."

"Thanks. But there's something else." Kendra looked out the window, knowing that her attacker could be on the street below, watching their every move. She backed away. "This guy knew who I was and what I've been doing. He knew I gave you something."

"The files?"

"It seemed more specific than that, but he didn't quite know. He kept asking what I gave you. I think he may have been referring to that garrote I found at Chloe's house and gave Breen right before I came here."

"You think you may have been followed today?" Breen said.

"I'm not sure. But I don't see how else he could have known that. Or that I'd be coming here."

Perry nodded. "Well, thanks to you, he gifted us his DNA. Did you find anything else here?"

"No. It's funny, but there's something that this place has in common with her sister's. There's absolutely no evidence, no scrap of paper, nothing, that they were investigating the

Bayside Strangler murders, even though we know it has consumed their lives for years."

Perry shrugged. "Maybe it all went into the files."

"Maybe."

"In any case, maybe you shouldn't go anywhere you might ordinarily be expected."

"Like my home? My job?" She shook her head. "I can't just walk away from my entire life. Certainly not my career."

"I understand. But until we know who this is and what he's after, you need to be careful. Do you need a ride?"

"No. I'm parked on the street."

"Let one of our men walk you to your car." Perry gestured toward one of the uniformed police officers. "Can't be too careful..."

---

Can't be too careful.

Detective Perry's warning was still ringing in her ears during the short drive back to her condo. Lynch would certainly concur, she thought wryly. Paula Chase was dead, the Morgan sisters were missing, and she'd almost been thrown out a fifth-story window. Yeah, a little caution was in order.

Kendra received a call from Olivia two hours later. She was obviously not pleased. "I believe you'd better come home," she said curtly. "I don't know if I can handle this mess."

"Mess?" Kendra stiffened. "What kind of mess? I don't remember any mess in your life that you haven't managed to handle since we met as children at the academy. What's different about this one?" Then her thoughts were immediately flying to the death of Paula Chase. "Where are you? Are you safe?"

"I'm not the issue here."

"Then what *is* the issue?"

"You. Were you just not going to tell me that you were attacked tonight?"

"How in the hell did you know about that?" It suddenly dawned on her. "It was Lynch, wasn't it? I can't believe he called you."

"It wasn't Lynch. It was your police sketch artist friend."

"Bill Dillingham?"

"He's here in the building. Some of his buddies on the force told him about what happened to you tonight. He's feeling guilty about getting you involved in this case. I think he wants to stand watch in front of your door. He went to your unit, and when he found out you weren't home, he looked for you here at my place."

Kendra shook her head. Between Lynch's sources and Bill's, she couldn't make a move without everybody knowing about it.

"Olivia, I'm fine."

"How do you know? You didn't even go to the hospital."

"You know that, too? Jeez, I may as well walk around twenty-four seven with a Ring camera strapped to my head."

"Not a bad idea." She added crossly, "And where is Lynch?"

"Lynch is in Switzerland saving the world," Kendra said. "And he doesn't owe me anything. I keep telling you that. We both run our own lives. I'll be back at my condo in thirty minutes to handle your 'mess.' Which I can't see can be laid at my door. Never mind. I'll see what's going on when I get there. Okay?"

"Okay," Olivia said. She was silent a moment. "It's only a mess because I care about you and I felt helpless to do anything for you. See you when you get here." She hung up the phone. Which left Kendra frustrated and confused and tempted to call her right back and make her explain in detail. This wasn't like Olivia at all. Her friend was one of the most clever and capable people Kendra knew, and she'd had to be. She'd had to cope with being blind since she was a small child and had still managed to set up and run a successful business. Olivia made sure everyone knew that there was nothing she wasn't capable of handling. She would never admit to a weakness unless it was one she could overcome. So it might be that she had another agenda in mind and was using the excuse as a subterfuge. There had to be another reason Olivia was so upset. She had mentioned Lynch specifically, and that might be one key. Olivia liked Lynch, and she appreciated his protectiveness and expertise.

But Lynch had his own life and career. What did Kendra know? Maybe they hadn't even sent him to Switzerland this time. Lynch was a one-man army when he chose and wrote his own rules. The last thing Kendra wanted was for him to know about her being hurt this evening. Olivia was entirely too protective and thought she always knew what was best. Kendra just had to make certain that Olivia's problem didn't become her own problem. And to do that she had to clarify what the hell that was right away.

The next moment she was dialing Olivia's condo. "Okay, what the hell is happening? And I don't want any bullshit about messes and how ineffectual you are. Talk to me."

"I was wondering how long it was going to take you," Olivia said. "I was disappointed in you."

"Talk to me," Kendra repeated. "I'm ready to strangle you. Tell me you didn't talk to Lynch about anything that's going to make me have to explain."

"You should have told him everything yourself." She hesitated. "But I didn't know where he was. So I couldn't reach him. You weren't being fair. I do have some respect for your privacy. Lynch had nothing to do with the problem I'm having. Now I have to go talk to security. Come to my condo when you get here. We probably need to talk."

"That's why I'm calling you now. I'm not going to run home unless it's vitally important. This Morgan sisters disappearance case has gotten...complicated."

"Yeah, well, a dead body and your attempted murder does seem pretty complicated."

"It's nothing to worry about."

"I'll be the judge of that," Olivia said.

As always, Olivia was perceptive as hell.

"I have one more stop to make," Kendra said, "but I'll be there as soon as I can unless you tell me that it takes precedence."

"Over a bloody corpse and possible bodily harm?" Olivia asked. "Never where you're concerned. I was just hoping to distract you. I should have known it wouldn't. Just promise me to be careful and get here as soon as you can."

"That goes without saying. I'll just do my job. I'll see you soon."

But Olivia had already hung up again.

"It took you long enough," Olivia said as she opened the door of her condo when Kendra rang the bell. "I almost gave up on you."

"No, you didn't," Kendra said. "You never give up when you make up your mind. So give me a cup of coffee and let me sit down and get my breath. I've had a rough day."

Olivia pulled Kendra into the living room and pushed her toward the coffee bar. "No leads?"

"A few but far between." She poured herself a cup of coffee and dropped down on the sofa. "And I respected and liked Paula and she shouldn't have ended up a victim. It makes me angry."

"I've heard she was a very giving person. You were bound to feel that way," Olivia said. "It goes with the territory."

"Now I wonder how you came to that conclusion?" Kendra murmured. "And who you've been talking to." She held up her hand as Olivia started to protest. "Don't bother. I ran into Bill Dillingham as I was driving into the parking garage. He looked very sheepish. What a shock and surprise." She made a face. "Not. I can see why you would be so concerned about him. Even when he was in his prime, I don't think he ever drew his service revolver. Now he's in his eighties and much more at home in his luxury retirement community, charming all the women standing in line to have their portraits drawn by him. Did he offer to draw you, too, Olivia?"

"Certainly not. I just like him, and he told me how badly he feels about involving you in something dangerous. I thought it wouldn't hurt for you to let him talk to you and maybe recommend a friendly policeman to keep an eye on you."

"I don't want one of his buddies to keep an eye on me, and I certainly don't want Bill feeling guilty about introducing me to Paula. It was entirely my decision." She put her cup down on the coffee table. "And now I have to go and find Bill and have a very difficult conversation with him. Thank you very much, Olivia."

"You're welcome," Olivia said. "You do know there's a perfectly simple way to settle this? Only you won't accept it."

"Because it's not my solution." Kendra was heading for the front door. "Back off."

"As if I'd get in your way. But after you have your talk, be sure you invite Bill to come back for a late dinner. I want to make certain he has a solid meal before you throw him out in the street. He told me that he was looking forward to it." She smiled. "Be gentle to him. After all, he's not in his first youth."

Kendra gritted her teeth. "I'll try to restrain myself."

"I know you will," Olivia said. "How could you not? He's such a sweet guy and only wants to make things easier for you. I'm sure you'll come to an understanding. I'll start cooking."

"You do that." Kendra closed the door behind her and headed for the elevator.

Bill was waiting there for her, smiling mischievously, eyes twinkling, leaning against the wall next to the elevator. "Am I in trouble?"

"Maybe a little." She sighed. "Because Olivia didn't start all this commotion on her own. You had a hand in it. What are you doing camping out in the hall?"

"Trying to keep a low profile." He reached out and

touched the bloody bruise on her temple. "Nasty." His lips tightened. "Are you okay?"

"Of course I am. The bastard just wanted to take something I wasn't prepared to give him." She shrugged. "Not that I have any idea what that was."

"Which reinforces the reason why you should let me protect you," Bill said. "I felt guiltier than ever about introducing you to Paula when I found out what happened. Maybe we should team up. It's not as if I wasn't a police officer first before I was an artist." He opened his coat and showed her his holstered automatic. "You can see I'm prepared to do that."

"I'm afraid I prefer the artist persona, Bill," Kendra said gently. "You look a little odd toting a gun."

"You could get used to it." His voice was wistful. "I kind of like the idea of protecting you. Think about it. I do get a little bored occasionally. It seemed something that would be worthwhile."

"My sincere thanks," Kendra said. She meant it. She could see how Bill would have moments when life would seem a little dull. Didn't everyone? "Maybe we can set up something when life isn't quite so hectic. But Perry seemed determined to keep me on his radar after what happened. Check with me tomorrow or the next day. And please don't tell Olivia anything more about what happens to me."

"Ah, an undercover assignment," Bill said. "It would be my pleasure to spare her that worry."

"I don't believe *pleasure* will be the correct word," Kendra said. She linked her arm in his and said cheerfully,

"But in the meantime, let's go eat one of Olivia's wonderful dinners before I walk you back to your car this evening."

"I look forward to it." Bill was frowning a little. "If you're certain Perry is going to furnish you with an armed escort to keep you safe..."

# CHAPTER 7

NEXT DAY
SAN DIEGO POLICE DEPARTMENT
DOWNTOWN HEADQUARTERS

Detective Perry was waiting for Kendra when she stepped off the elevator at the police department's third floor. The downstairs desk sergeant had made her wait almost fifteen minutes before reaching Perry and permitting her to go upstairs.

"What brings you here, Dr. Michaels?"

"You called me this morning, didn't you?"

"You could have just called back. That's how it's usually done."

"I like the personal touch. Or maybe I was moved by your concern for my welfare."

"Well, when you left us last night, you were sporting a

big bump on that blood-drenched head of yours. I wanted to make sure you woke up today."

"Still here, still in the fight. I hoped you were calling with something more important, but I guess it's a little early for DNA on that sample I helped collect for you."

"Afraid so. But I thought you'd be interested in some news on that garrote."

"Uh, maybe a little."

"That is human blood on it."

The news took her breath away. "Any idea how old?"

"Not yet. But they're running DNA on it."

Kendra nodded her approval. "Definitely worth a phone call, Perry. Thanks. Breen tells me you already started digging into the Morgan sisters' case files."

"You could say that. Want to see what I've been doing?"

"Sure."

He motioned for her to follow him down the corridor. "I've mostly been trying to get a handle on what those women were doing and the leads they were following. There's about ten years of work to wade through."

"Impressive, isn't it?"

"Trust me, a lot of the case files I see around here aren't nearly as thorough. I was looking at the dates on some of the transcripts, and those girls were seventeen and fifteen when they took their first witness statements. They could give a seminar."

"Find them, and maybe they will."

Perry pursed his lips and looked slightly pained. He clearly didn't believe the sisters would be found alive. "I'd love to sit in the front row for that."

"You and me both."

They rounded a corner, and he gestured for her to enter a doorway ahead of him. "Welcome to my makeshift command center."

Kendra entered a long conference room where every square inch of wall and table space was taken up by the Morgan sisters' files. Perry had neatly separated the files according to each of the Bayside Strangler's victims, with photographs and newspaper clippings higher up, and interview transcripts down where they could be more easily perused. Each of the written records was color-coded with strips of removable tape, though Kendra couldn't immediately discern his coding system.

"Nice," she said. "I flipped through my scans, but sometimes it's easier to grasp when you can look at them this way."

"Well, my boss is going to want this conference room back soon. Especially since these cases aren't active. Right now, we can't even prove they're a relevant part of our investigation."

Kendra looked at photos of the last two murder scenes, which for some reason were especially vivid and disturbing. "Has anything jumped out at you?"

"Rather than look at the facts of these cases, I've just been trying to follow the chronology of the sisters' investigation. That's what the colored tape is for. Ever since the Morgan sisters started this project, they've been focused on adding to their body of knowledge by interviewing new subjects and finding new and different evidence and written material." He pointed to an interview transcript with green tape placed on the upper-right-hand corner. "That all changed here, last August. For the first time, they doubled back and re-interviewed someone they'd spoken with years before. For the past six months or so, that's pretty much all they've done."

Kendra followed the green-tape-marked transcripts down the length of the room. "You're right. That's a cold-case technique, isn't it? Re-interviewing the witnesses years later to see if the stories have changed?"

"Exactly. Once again, those sisters knew what they were doing. In the intervening years, people may die, relationships might fall apart, witnesses could have guilty feelings about things they withheld...There are all kinds of reasons why a round of fresh interviews might shake loose some new information."

"Did it work for Chloe and Sloane?"

"I'm still studying that. You might follow up in your files. They definitely got more information. At first glance, it seems like there's less of a tendency to place the victims on a pedestal, but that's not uncommon with the passage of time. At least two of the victims' acquaintances now admit to a sexual relationship with them, where they didn't before."

"Seriously?"

Perry tapped the green-coded transcripts. "Victims three and five, Leah McLane and Katrina Burge. One guy knew that the significant other is always the number one suspect and didn't want the heat. And the other guy was married at the time, so there's that. There's no reason to think one of them is our guy. It's just the kind of thing that shakes loose when you re-interview so long after the fact. But there may be something else here, I don't know."

"Good work, Perry."

"Thanks."

She turned and walked out of the conference room.

"What happened to you?"

They were the first words out of Marlee Davis' mouth when Kendra turned up at her front door. Kendra had been trying to fool herself into believing that her forehead wound was barely noticeable, but that clearly wasn't the case.

"Oh, this." She waved her fingers over her forehead. "I'm afraid Sloane is going to need a new window." Kendra handed her Sloane's door key.

"What?"

"My visit to your niece's condo was…eventful."

Marlee opened her door wide for her to enter. "Get in here." She motioned toward her sofa. "Can I get you anything? Water? Cold compress? Paramedic?"

"It looks worse than it is."

Marlee made a concerned face. "Are you sure?"

"Well, that's been my story since the moment it happened, so I guess I'm sticking to it. But seriously, I'm fine."

"If you say so. Do you plan to tell me what happened?"

"Yes." Kendra gave her the blow-by-blow of her visit to Sloane's condo, making sure to repeat every word that came from her attacker's mouth.

"Damn," Marlee said when she finished. "You have no idea who it was?"

"He didn't leave his card. At first I thought it might be a friend of Sloane's being overly protective, but when he said that stuff about wanting to know what I gave the detective, it was pretty clear he'd been following us."

"Yes. Scary."

"That's why I thought you should know. It seemed very clear I was the main target, but you should be careful, too."

"I will be. Thank you."

"But there's something else I wanted to ask you about. You said Sloane had a fiancé who was completely unsupportive of her and Chloe's investigation."

"Yes. Charlie. She was crazy about him. Things were going well between them until Chloe drew her back into the case. He never understood the obsession that both sisters had with their mother's murder."

"Have they stayed in touch?"

"I'm not sure. If they have, she never talks about him. If anything, she seemed relieved that he wasn't around to fuss at her about the case."

"I'd like to talk to him. Do you have a phone number or email address for Charlie?"

"I'm afraid I don't. But he's a car mechanic. He owns a garage that specializes in exotic foreign cars."

"Do you know the name?"

"I think his name is on it. Charlie Davenport. It's in Chula Vista."

"Thanks."

Marlee made a face. "I'm not certain that you have anything to thank me about. You've evidently been taking quite a bit of punishment since we came together."

"But we're making progress, and I may have come close to the man who killed Paula. We might still have valuable clues from that encounter, and the authorities are keeping an eagle eye on me. In any case, you should be careful and stay aware of your surroundings."

"You think I might be in danger?"

"I don't know. It depends if the killer thinks Chloe and Sloane told you about whatever lead they discovered."

"But they didn't."

"The killer may not know that. Just keep an eye out. If there's any indication you're in danger, we may be able to arrange protection. You've been very helpful. If you think of anything else, please let me know."

Marlee nodded doubtfully. "I guarantee I intend to watch my back. You do the same."

"Absolutely." Kendra smiled and headed for her car in the driveway. "Thanks again for your help. I'll let you know if I learn anything from this Charlie person…"

---

It took Kendra all of two minutes on Google to find Davenport Exotic Auto Service and Repairs in south San Diego County, and only another fifteen minutes to drive there from Marlee's house. A few questions later, she was standing in front of a tall, slender man wearing a protective face mask as he leaned into a McLaren Spider's engine compartment.

"Can I help you?" He didn't look up from the car.

"Are you Charlie Davenport?"

"If you want an update on your car, the guy at the inside counter can help you with that."

"I'm not here about a car. I'm here about Sloane Morgan."

He finally looked up warily. "And who are you?"

"My name is Kendra Michaels. I've been asked to look into her disappearance."

He stepped toward her. "It isn't just Sloane, you know."

"I know. Chloe, too."

He still didn't pull off his mask. "What does this have to do with me?"

"It wasn't that long ago that you and Sloane were going to be married. You didn't keep in touch with her? She didn't talk to you about the case she was investigating with her sister?"

He muttered a curse under his breath. "I heard enough about that damn case. It's all she wanted to talk about when we were together. I knew about her family history when we started dating, but I had no idea it was still such a big part of her life, you know? Sometimes I wanted her to just leave it behind for a while. She wouldn't do it."

"Did that make you angry?"

He glared at her over the mask. "You think I had anything to do with what happened to her and her sister?" He cursed again. "I was frustrated that we couldn't just live our own lives. I was pissed that this killer still had so much power over her and our relationship. And yes, I felt sorry for her, too. But it wasn't a recipe for a great marriage, so I finally broke it off."

"I think most people could understand that." Kendra stepped back, knowing that the next words out of her mouth could royally piss him off. "But tell me…at what point did you start sleeping with her sister?"

His eyes literally bulged. "What?"

"When did you start dating Chloe? Before or after you broke up with Sloane?"

"After!" He spoke so loudly that he felt the need to repeat it again in a quieter voice. "After. No way I would've cheated on Sloane, especially not with her sister."

"Then why the big secret? Nobody seems to know anything about it."

"Sloane wouldn't have understood. How could she? She probably never would have forgiven Chloe or me. It's nothing we planned. It just...happened."

"Relationships are rarely that simple."

He nodded. "Okay, maybe it wasn't. Chloe reached out to me after Sloane and I broke up. I think she felt guilty."

"Guilty? Why?"

"Because of how she got Sloane so involved in their case again. They were like a couple of addicts. Nothing else in their lives mattered to either one of them. When Sloane and I split up, I think Chloe felt it was partially her fault. She called me a couple of times, and we started spending time together down at the beach. One thing led to another."

Kendra said slowly, "You do know how bad this looks? You were involved in something of a romantic triangle in which both women are now missing. And it's something you've kept hidden."

Charlie was looking down and away from her. For an instant he appeared ashamed. "I didn't think it mattered."

"That's up to the police to decide."

"To be honest, I didn't think anyone would find out about me and Chloe. It's the last thing she would have wanted, and I sure as hell didn't tell anyone. I was too embarrassed. Who told you?"

"No one. As far as I'm aware, you and she are the only ones who knew."

He stared at her for a long moment. "Then how the hell did you find out?"

"I've been to Chloe's house."

"Yeah?"

"I saw the bottle of Gojo skin cleaner in her shower. It's very popular among mechanics, pumice-based, and it has a distinctly orange scent. That's what is coming off you right now. I guess you scrubbed with it here before lunch."

"A lot of people use that. How do you know it wasn't Chloe's?"

"I didn't, although I never saw any indication that she got her hands dirty enough to use a product that could scrape her skin raw. But more than that, I could smell what I presumed to be a hair product on one of her pillows. It wasn't a product I could recognize. It wasn't a common one, whatever it was, but you're wearing it now. Some kind of mousse?"

His glance sidled away. "Conditioner. I buy it online. It doesn't hold the grime from this place like a lot of the stuff out there."

"When was the last time you saw her, Charlie?"

He thought for a moment. "I was there two nights before she went missing. After Chloe and I started up, we almost never talked on the phone. I usually just swung by after work. If I saw her car, I'd go in and we'd hang out. She was spending more time at her sister's, though. They really thought they were onto something lately."

"Any idea what?"

He was quiet as a co-worker in a jumpsuit walked past. "Chloe went out of her way not to talk to me about that stuff, especially after she saw what it did to my and Sloane's relationship. But I did overhear some things when they were talking on the phone."

"Like what?"

"I'm not totally sure what it meant, but Chloe seemed pretty intense when she was talking about 'the bomb place.'"

"The bomb place?" Kendra frowned. "As in explosives?"

"Yeah. That kind of grabbed my attention. I even asked her about it after she got off the phone, and she told me not to worry about it. She said it wasn't what it sounded like."

"I don't know. It sounds pretty clear to me."

"Yeah, I thought so, too. I know. And of course, after she went missing, I wished I had followed up with her more. But in those last few weeks, she didn't talk about it to anybody but her sister."

"So I keep hearing."

"It's the truth," he said defensively. "None of this would have happened if she'd have talked to me. I loved her. Maybe if I hadn't been so impatient, she wouldn't have left me. I did love her."

"I think maybe you did," Kendra said quietly, her gaze on his glittering eyes. His face was twisted with pain, and there had been no hint of a threat in his demeanor when confronting Kendra. He seemed almost relieved to tell her about his affair with Chloe. "You wouldn't by any chance have an alibi that would explain what you were doing on the night those women disappeared?"

He shrugged. "I don't remember. I think I spent at least part of the night at a bar in town getting drunk as a skunk. Someone might remember me. Why?"

Wow. This guy was pretty dense, she thought impatiently. "Look, it's my duty to notify the FBI of what you told me, and I will do it. But I'll give you three hours before I make the call. I want to give you time to make a few arrangements before they haul you into the interrogation room." She stared at him for a long time, studying him. "I won't be the last one who will be questioning you. If I were you, I'd call the cops and the FBI right away and tell them everything you've told me. All of it. It will be better if you tell them yourself. Get yourself a lawyer. If you can present alibis for the time when those women disappeared, try to do it before you turn yourself in."

"I guess you're trying to help me." He frowned. "Thanks. I think. But I don't know why you're doing it."

"I'm not sure, either," Kendra said. "But maybe it's because both those women had it pretty rough in one way or another. Though both of them seemed to care about you for some reason. Since they were both smart, it could be you're actually worth it. But it's going to be a very short leash. So do what I told you, do you hear?"

He nodded. "Whatever you say."

"But do me one more favor. Will you pull down your mask for a second? I need to see your face."

"What?"

"You have a similar build and eyes to someone I met last night. Would you mind?"

He pulled down his protective mask, flashing a disbelieving grin. All front teeth present and accounted for, she noticed. Cross that off the list.

"Thanks. Had to check." She turned and headed out of the parking lot.

---

As Kendra walked down the sidewalk toward her car, a text appeared on her phone screen.

JUST RECEIVED EXTREMELY DISTRESSING NEWS. WHAT THE HELL IS GOING ON THERE?

It had to be from Adam Lynch.

That's all she needed—an input from Lynch after the morning she'd had.

She typed her reply. REALLY NOT YOUR BUSINESS. NOT MUCH GOING ON. JUST ANOTHER DAY IN THE LIFE.

WHICH INCLUDES ALMOST BEING THROWN OUT OF A SIX-STORY BUILDING? I KNEW I SHOULD HAVE FOLLOWED YOU BACK HOME TO THE STATES.

STOP BEING DRAMATIC. ATTACK WAS ON FLOOR FIVE.

His response was immediate. SUCH A RELIEF. IN THAT CASE, SIDEWALK SPLATTER SLIGHTLY SMALLER.

Kendra leaned against her car and tapped out another message. MOST UNCOMFORTABLE WITH POLICE SOURCE REVEALING MY EVERY MOVE TO GLOBE-TROTTING SOMETIME COMPANION.

She waited a long moment. No response.

She finally typed: STILL THERE?

STILL HERE. JUST SLIGHTLY WOUNDED BY "SOMETIME COMPANION" DESIGNATION.

DESIGNATION MORE A PRODUCT OF COMPANION'S FREQUENT OVERSEAS ADVENTURES.

M'LADY WOULD BE WELCOME AT ALL SUCH EXCURSIONS.

She smiled. SINCERELY DOUBT THAT.

SOMETIME COMPANION SINCERELY MISSING YOU.

She was about to type something glib, but she found she was touched by his display of vulnerability. Before she could decide how to respond, another message came from him: IMPRESSED BY YOUR INSISTENCE ON SEEING AUTO MECHANIC'S FACE. NOT YOUR NOW TOOTHLESS ATTACKER?

Shocked. Her hands tightened around her phone. WHAT THE HELL? ARE YOU USING MY PHONE TO EAVESDROP ON ME?

WOULDN'T VIOLATE COMPANION'S PRIVACY IN SUCH A CONTEMPTIBLE WAY.

SURE YOU WOULD.

OKAY, POSSIBLY. BUT NOT THIS TIME. TOO CAPTIVATED BY TIGHT-FITTING NAVY-BLUE SLACKS AND SUEDE PUMPS.

"No way!" She said the words aloud.

There was laughter behind her. She turned and saw Adam Lynch standing on the sidewalk five feet behind her. His blue eyes were gleaming with mischief as he tapped his forehead mockingly at her and put away his phone. "Sorry, I couldn't resist."

"What the hell are you doing here?" she asked as he strolled toward her. Dear God, how much she had missed him. She wanted to run to him. But his presence here had been totally invasive and the fact that he had just shown up with no advance notice made her want to shake him. "And what source did you tap this time?"

"Breen." He was close to her now. "I figured he'd be able to give me the most info in the shortest time. I was in a hurry. I didn't like what I was hearing." His lips tightened as he moved even closer. "I like it even less now that I see what you've been going through." His hands were ultra-gentle as they moved caressingly over her throat and cupped her face. "Would it have hurt you to tell me what was happening to you?" he asked roughly. "I told you I couldn't leave right away." His fingers were gently probing the wound on her temple. "This is nasty. But you knew I'd be there if you needed me. All you would have to do is let me know. I've been wanting to reach out and kick ass ever since Breen told me about the attack on you."

"And that was what I didn't want you to do." She was instinctively leaning into his touch. It wouldn't hurt to stay like this for a few minutes more. He felt so good...It had been so long. "I took care of it. It's not as if I need you to watch out for me. I've told you before that I know what my place is in your life."

"Do you? I've been thinking and I'm not at all sure that you have any idea." For a moment his grip tightened on her throat. "I believe you'd better reexamine that belief. Because we might have to have a discussion about it."

"It wouldn't be necessary." She forced herself to step back away from him. "It's not as if we don't know that we're two independent people going our separate ways. Because we're also friends, you feel a certain responsibility when you see that there might be a certain weakness in my vicinity. That's also perfectly natural."

"How logical you are," Lynch said caustically. "But you also said that you wouldn't mind if I stepped in if I discovered a way to find those two women who had disappeared. You were quite explicit where that was concerned. I'm sure you'll recall."

"I was upset. I would never have insisted you interfere with my business. Any more than I would believe I was capable of going after that crew you were dealing with when you talked to me last. That would annoy you big time if I decided to get in your way."

"Not necessarily. I can remember a few times that you stepped in to help when I've been in trouble."

So could Kendra. "That was rare, and most of the time we were working together."

"Too late. The fact remains. You did ask me for help." He grinned. "I refuse to take it back. You'll just have to find a way to keep me around. I promise I'll be gentle with you." His hand fell away from her face. "Now, the first thing I want to do is go to your condo and search it. I'm very angry about what happened to you while you were wandering around San Diego and getting in trouble. I can't believe that Breen and Perry didn't find any decent leads."

"They've found a good many. So have I. We're waiting on DNA right now. You're not irreplaceable, Lynch."

"No, but I'm boundlessly useful on occasion. Admit it."

"You're...okay."

"Oh, that hurt." He looked back at her. "I'm not going to push you or get in your way. I just want to help you get whatever makes you happy. That's all I ever wanted." He was getting into his glossy red Lamborghini, parked just a few feet behind her Toyota 4Runner. "I'll follow you back to your condo and we'll have a cup of coffee. I'll look around and see what I can find that's interesting. Would it be all right if we invited Olivia up for a drink? I've missed her."

"You know it would be," Kendra said curtly. "You're one of her favorite people. Olivia hasn't been very content with what's been going on around here. Unlike you, she trusts that I know what I'm doing, but she doesn't think much of the authorities. She always believes you could handle anything better than they could. She tried to call you a few days ago. She was disappointed you weren't available."

He met her gaze as he started the Lamborghini. "Was that before or after you got that nasty bruise? We both know that I would have made myself available if she'd gotten through to me. All you would have had to do was send word."

"That I needed you? Take you away from your assignment?" She shook her head. "That's not the way we've ever handled our relationship. That's the last thing I wanted." She shrugged. "And I made sure that Olivia didn't find out about that little tap I got. She wouldn't have understood." She made a face. "As it was, she was constantly trying to set me up with Bill Dillingham as my bodyguard."

"Bill?" He started to chuckle. "He's a good man. However, you might say that his qualifications are a little lacking in that area."

"He wouldn't agree with you. And I admire his willingness to try to help me." She lifted her chin. "I even told him that when the situation got a little more on an even keel, I might call on him."

"Which pleased him, I'm sure," Lynch said. "And if that's what you want, I'll go along with it. Even if I have to keep an eagle eye on him. Anything you want, Kendra."

"You're being very agreeable." Kendra's lips twisted. "Not like you at all, Lynch."

"It's sheer terror. Did it occur to you that you scared the shit out of me when Breen told me about the attack on you?" He added teasingly, "You've got me where you want me, even if it's acting as old Bill's guardian."

"That's not where I want you." She was scowling. "Haven't you been listening to me?"

"You want your independence. You want me to go away," he said quietly. "But I can't do that, Kendra. Not until I know you're going to be safe. I don't like the company you're keeping. So you'll have to put up with me. I'm not going to cause you any trouble or get in your way. But it's too late to send me packing. So take me to your place and give me a cup of coffee. Then we'll talk and you can fill me in on everything you know about the case. It's nothing different than we've done before."

"It's different," she said. It was always different when she was with him. It had been different from the first time she had met him.

"Okay, maybe it is," he said. "But like I said, it's too late to send me packing. You'll just have to put up with it until we bring the bad guys home."

"I don't have to do anything I don't want to do," she said jerkily.

"No, you don't. But you will. Because I promised to help you find those two women who might have given their lives to find their mother's killer. You'd think that would be worthwhile."

"Yes, I would."

"My promise is still good, Kendra. I don't break my word."

"I know you don't." Her voice was shaking. "You've never broken your word to me. That's not what this is all about."

"No, it's about you being damnably stubborn and not letting me help you. I've already given you my word, now let me run interference until I get you safely inside your condo. Is that too much to ask?"

"No, only completely unnecessary and annoying." His chin was hardening and she'd seen that expression before.

*Give it up for the time being.*

"Oh, for heaven's sake." She turned and walked toward her Toyota. "Just follow me to the condo and I'll tell you what I know about the case. But it's my case, Lynch."

"It's your case," he repeated. "I'm not arguing that point. I wouldn't dare."

"Don't tell me that. You'd dare anything," she said. She climbed into her Toyota, started it, and tore off down the road toward the freeway.

# CHAPTER 8

Kendra was already sitting in her usual parking spot when Lynch's Lamborghini took center stage a few minutes later. Kendra jumped out and headed for the elevator. "I'll see you up at the condo. If I remember correctly, everyone in the parking lot has to swoon over that blasted Lamborghini of yours after you park it."

"No problem." He threw his keys to Pauley, the garage attendant. "Take good care of it. I'll be up in the condo."

Pauley grabbed the keys eagerly. "You bet I will, Mr. Lynch. Okay if I wax it?"

"Carnauba paste?"

"Of course. Nothing but the best for such a fine piece of machinery."

"Thanks, Pauley. I'll reimburse you." He was already getting in the elevator with Kendra.

"You made his day," Kendra said as she gazed at Pauly's eager face. "You know, it took him months to learn my name. For you, it took all of one visit."

Lynch smiled. "Roll up in a car like mine, nobody will ever forget you."

Kendra shrugged. "I told you I'd go up ahead of you."

"Well, I wasn't going to let you go up to the condo alone," Lynch said as he punched the button. "Not a good idea considering what happened the last time that scum decided to raid your place."

"I wasn't hurt. Nothing was stolen here."

"Pure luck."

"No, I was careful to make sure Olivia had the documents safe. No luck about it."

"I stand corrected." Lynch was grinning. "Forgive me."

She grinned back at him. "I'll think about it."

"You do that." Lord, she loved his smile, and she was suddenly back to the time when it was so very natural for them to be together.

"It's going to be fine," he said softly as they exited the elevator and walked toward her condo. He watched her unlock her front door. "I told you I'd go slow. No rush. But I go in first to look around. Okay?"

Her mouth dropped open. "The hell you do." She threw open the door and stepped to one side as she entered the condo. "In your dreams, Lynch. My condo. My assignment."

"Whatever." He sighed resignedly and yet somehow he'd suddenly managed to get ahead of her, using his own body to block her as she moved through the condo. "I thought there was no way it was going to be that easy." He gestured ahead of her into the living room. "By all means, guide me. Show me…everything. I'm at your disposal."

"You bet I will," she said crisply. "The documents first… Those women managed to find virtual treasures that no one else in the case had discovered." Kendra pulled her iPad from her leather satchel and pulled up the Morgan sisters' files that Zack had scanned for her. "I'll explain as I go along."

She explained in detail as he sat on the couch, his intent gaze fixed thoughtfully on her face, only asking a question now and then. But there was no doubt that he was paying attention to every word she said. She knew him well enough to be able to read his every expression, and when she finally started to put the iPad away, she tilted her head and asked curiously, "Well, do you believe I've missed anything?"

"You know you haven't." Lynch's eyes were twinkling. "You were reeling off those facts as if you were quoting the encyclopedia. However, there's a distinct possibility that I might have missed something. But I'm certain you can take care of that as well."

Kendra frowned. "I thought I was being very clear. What do you think you missed?"

"Why, you promised me a cup of coffee. So far I haven't seen a drop." He reached for his phone. "But I'm certain Olivia will take care of me."

"She always does," Kendra said. "Did it occur to you to ask me?"

"Of course. But I'm trying my best not to be a bother. Haven't you noticed?" His smile was almost blandly innocent. "I guess I'll have to try harder."

"I believe I got the point." Yet she'd be relieved to have Olivia as a buffer in the hours to come. She listened to him chatting with Olivia, and then a few minutes later Olivia was at the front door and Lynch was acting as if he owned the condo as he welcomed her.

*Patience*, Kendra thought.

Then she saw Lynch wink mischievously at her as he handed her a cup of coffee and was tempted to throw it at him.

*Patience*, she thought again.

---

"Isn't it time you made your move, Lynch?" Olivia lifted her glass of wine to her lips. "Personally, I'm getting a little bored with this game you're playing. You took too long, and you let Kendra get hurt before you showed up on the scene. I always thought you knew what you were doing, but I had to make a few moves myself before you got around to showing up. I shouldn't have to tell you how that pissed me off."

Lynch turned toward the hallway that led back to the home office, where Kendra was adjusting her client appointments. He turned back to Olivia. "I can't tell you how upset it makes me to hear that. Particularly since I dropped everything and rushed back here when I heard that she'd been attacked by that scum."

Olivia shrugged. "Perhaps I was playing a few games myself. I got very tired of worrying about Kendra this time. She's my best friend, and she can be very stubborn. I didn't see why I should take a chance on losing her because you didn't move fast enough. I decided that wasn't going to happen." She took another sip of her wine. "I thought you might understand."

"Oh, I do," Lynch said. "That prospect is totally unacceptable. I can see why you decided to use desperate measures. Only I wasn't quite as desperate as I might have seemed. I was doing a little investigating of my own while I tied up a few loose ends. I did get here as quickly as possible, Olivia."

"Then you'd better tie up these particular loose ends here, too, Lynch." She handed him her empty wineglass. "Because I've been watching Kendra since I came here today and I'll bet she's becoming impatient, too. She's used to working with you and she wants those women found. I can see the signs. If you handle it right, we can get this show on the road."

Lynch grinned. "Then by all means let's get you out of here and I'll stroll over to her and see if you're right."

"I am," Olivia said as she headed across the living room. "Just don't blow it."

"I promise I'll do my very best to please you." He waited a few minutes before he followed her and then gave Olivia a kiss on the cheek. "Thank you. I believe I can handle the situation now, Olivia."

"See that you do."

Kendra emerged from her home office. "Is everything all right?"

"It will be now," Olivia said. She quickly changed the subject. "Listen, I've been wanting to talk to you about those files I had Zack scan."

"Oh, thank you again. He did a fantastic job."

"He did. His scans were very easy to import into my text-to-speech app. I've been going through the files, and I've been amazed at the work those young women did. But one thing stuck out: In the past few weeks, they've been re-interviewing so many people connected with the case, and their files reflect this. Pretty much everyone connected with the case has their own file, but not former detective Todd Williams."

"Really?" Kendra said.

"Yes. Which is strange, because along with Paula Chase, he was lead investigator."

"Maybe he didn't cooperate with the Morgan sisters," Lynch said.

"But he did. In the section summaries, he appears a lot. There are recent quotes and information only he could have provided. I think he must have had a file devoted to him, and it was recently removed. Did you find a file like that in Paula Chase's house or in either of the Morgan sisters' homes?"

"No," Kendra replied. "And not in their cars or anywhere else."

Olivia shrugged. "It seems like it should be there."

"I agree. Wow. Good work, Olivia."

"Thanks. I'll keep listening to the files when I'm running or taking an Uber somewhere. I'll let you know if anything else jumps out at me." Olivia hugged her. "I'll see you tomorrow." Then she left the condo.

Kendra turned toward Lynch. "That was fantastic. I didn't even catch that."

"Neither did I. Not much gets by her. Something we should definitely keep in mind."

Kendra plopped down on the sofa. "So...I have a feeling I missed something while I was out of the room."

"Yes. Unlike you, she was very angry with me for not showing up on the scene sooner. I had to apologize to her. She considered it an act of betrayal."

"It was none of her business," Kendra said. "You'd think she'd listen when I try to explain our relationship."

Lynch shook his head. "She cares about you. And I totally understand her attitude. It was the one thing about which we were in complete agreement. No, there was one other thing. She told me that she thought you were ready to ease off and give me a break and let me help you find those two women. Is that true?"

Kendra didn't speak for a moment. "It might be."

He shook his head. "That's not good enough, Kendra. I have to be in all the way. I'm not going to put up with the thought of letting some lowlife beat you up because I'm not around to stop it. Screw your independence. We'll work something out."

"Not with an attitude like that." She started to turn away.

He whirled her back toward him. "We'll work something out," he repeated. "Unless you want it all to come to an end. Do you?"

She could feel the tears sting her eyes as she looked up at him. Dear God, she loved him. "I didn't say that."

"Then tell me we'll work it out," he said softly. "I'm not going to be unreasonable. I realize how lucky I am to have you. Let's just go out on the terrace and let me hold you for a little while and talk about plans and how we're going to go after those bastards and find those two women. All I want to do is help. Okay?" His arm slid around her waist and he was leading her toward the French doors.

"You never want to just help," Kendra said. "You tend to take over."

"I suppose I do, but it's probably because I grew up an orphan, working in Hell's Kitchen, and developed a passion for order. I learned very young that you eat more and considerably better if you have organization on your side."

Kendra nodded. "Though I imagine it also helped you in getting your own way."

"True. But I always work hard at making certain you're happy, don't I? I never leave you out in the cold?"

She shook her head. "I have to admit, there's nothing cold about you, Lynch."

His eyes narrowed on her expression. "But is there an implied *but* in that sentence?"

"Perhaps," Kendra said slowly. "No one can be more charming or entertaining and the sex is wonderful, but you're so many-faceted that sometimes I'm not sure I really know you. You just told me about growing up an orphan in New York, but I don't remember you mentioning it before. I know you're a great cook. Is Hell's Kitchen where you learned it? What else don't I know about you, Lynch?"

"Probably a good many things, but it's not because I'm intentionally keeping secrets from you. Ask me and I'll tell you anything you're interested in knowing. I've just never been generous about sharing the more seamy side of my life with you. Some of it's not been easy or pretty. But I'll even go down that road if you choose."

"I don't choose," she said jerkily. "I don't have the right. Forget I asked."

He chuckled. "And now you're feeling guilty? I don't care, Kendra. If you want to explore, step into my world. Just don't go too deep. I don't want to have to dive after you."

"You won't," Kendra said. "But now you know how I felt when you were running around thousands of miles away, possibly getting shot at, and there was nothing I could do to help."

"Yes, I know how you must have felt," he said quietly. He was no longer smiling. "My worst nightmare."

But she was no longer wanting to think of nightmares. She wanted to take a step forward where hopefully no nightmares existed. "But I should have been grateful that you wanted to be there for me this time. Because it's not only me that you're helping now." She suddenly turned and gave him a swift, hard kiss. "I am grateful. I wasn't at all gracious. Please forgive me. I won't be that way again."

"You probably will." He was laughing as he gave her an affectionate hug. "But I'm just happy that you decided to be gracious this time. I'm sure the occasions will be few and far between."

Her lips were suddenly twitching. "And that was bordering on rudeness, Lynch. I didn't deserve it since I was being exceptionally polite at the moment."

"Then I'd better make amends very swiftly," Lynch said. "Any suggestions?"

"Maybe," Kendra said. "And if those sisters are still alive, I might have found a way to help them."

His eyes narrowed. "What are you up to, Kendra?"

"It's a big if, I know. But I have to try."

"We have to try."

She turned to face him. "Yeah?"

"I'm in this with you to the end." His hand tightened on her waist. "I thought I made that very clear. Now what's your play?"

She drew a deep breath. "Detective Perry has the Morgan sisters' files spread out over a conference room at police headquarters. It was interesting seeing them that way. Chloe and Sloane were excited about something they found in the last month, just around the time they started re-interviewing witnesses."

"Interesting. Was there anything special in those new interviews?"

"Not really. But seeing everything reminded me of what Olivia noticed...about how there was no file for Detective Williams, even though new material from him appears elsewhere."

"Right, so he's obviously still alive."

"I looked him up. He retired from the force four years ago, but he's still local. I believe I should talk to him."

"When?"

Kendra felt the excitement begin to soar. They were together again. It was going to happen. This was how it was supposed to be. "How about right now?"

Lynch nodded. "Let's do it." He was already heading for the front door. "I'll drive."

---

"I'd forgotten how ridiculous this car is, Lynch." His new Lamborghini was attracting more than its share of attention in Williams' middle-class suburban street.

He smiled. "There's nothing ridiculous about pure automotive perfection."

"I think a guy back there gave your car an actual catcall."

"Maybe he just saw you."

"He was screaming something about 'sexy wheels.'"

"Not the first time that's happened. The man probably couldn't help himself. And who could blame him, really?"

"I definitely could."

"Aw, come on. I caught you giving an admiring glance or two when we climbed inside."

"We've discussed this before..."

"And we will again, if you keep dissing my ride."

"Far be it from me."

They rolled to a stop in front of a one-story Spanish bungalow at the end of the street. The yard, obviously designed with an eye toward water conservation, was tastefully landscaped with rocks and desert plants. Kendra and Lynch walked to the front door and rang the bell. A trim, handsome African American man in his sixties answered.

"Todd Williams?"

"Yes, ma'am."

"My name is Kendra Michaels. I've been helping out with the Morgan sisters' disappearance case. I was brought in by Paula Chase."

Williams winced at the mention of Paula's name.

"I know who you are, Dr. Michaels. Paula told me she would be talking to you. Please come in." Williams opened the door wide for them to enter. "We can talk out back."

As they walked through his living room, Kendra took notice of several hand-painted portraits, most picturing different dogs. "Did you do these?"

"As a matter of fact, I did."

"You're very talented."

"Well, I have to admit I had some help." Williams smiled. "You can send a photograph to companies out there, and they'll send back a paint-by-number set. These are pets we've had over the years. My friends want me to try doing it freehand, but I haven't found the courage yet. Maybe someday."

He led them out a sliding back door to a table next to a small swimming pool. They sat down, and Williams gestured toward Lynch. "And you are...?"

"Adam Lynch. Former FBI. I've been working freelance for a few years now."

Williams gave a low whistle. "I've heard of you, too."

"Really? I'm quite sure your former partner didn't mention me."

"No, but a lot of other law-enforcement officers have. You have quite a reputation, Lynch. You move in very unique and specialized areas. I'm impressed by what I've heard."

"Good things, I hope."

"It depends on who you ask. Not many local FBI agents leave the Bureau and become black ops agents-for-hire for the DOJ."

Lynch shrugged. "Just one of my employers. I'm kept fairly busy."

Williams regarded him for a long moment. "I'm sure you have some interesting stories to tell, Mr. Lynch."

"Some interesting, some not so interesting. I guess it's like being a cop."

"Indeed." Williams sat back in his patio chair. "Now, what can I help you with?"

"Well, as you may know," Kendra began, "I met with Paula Chase on the last day of her life. She was extremely concerned about Chloe and Sloane."

"We all are," Williams said. "Paula and I knew them since they were children. We were with them the day we found their mother's corpse near that hiking trail. It isn't something you easily forget."

"You and Paula stayed in touch with them over the years?"

"On and off. They've been kind enough to invite us to some of their big events. High school and college graduations, that sort of thing."

"They reached out to you several times, isn't that right? That's unusual."

"Very. But those are two extraordinary young women. Most families of murder victims retreat into their grief and just learn to live with it. Not Chloe and Sloane. I'm sure you've seen the lengths to which they've gone to investigate their mother's murder over the years."

"Of course. Did you ever do anything to discourage that?"

"Absolutely not. It's how they chose to deal with it. I've met the families of many murder victims in my career, and everyone deals with these things in their own way. If this helped them feel that they had some control over their world, who was I to take that away from them?"

"I get it," Lynch said. "But did you ever feel that their investigation might put their lives in danger?"

"Never." Williams seemed annoyed by the suggestion. "If I believed that, I never would have encouraged them. I know Paula felt the same way."

Kendra leaned forward. "Paula was trying to figure out what they were doing in these last few weeks. She didn't have much luck. Did she talk about it with you?"

"Only after they disappeared. Chloe and Sloane were in the process of re-interviewing witnesses, and somewhere in that process, they apparently found out something that put their investigation on a whole new track. Paula thought I might know something about it, but I didn't. I hadn't seen either one of them in years."

"Really? I would've thought you would be one of the first people they re-interviewed," Kendra said.

"We exchanged a few emails, but I honestly didn't have anything new to give them. I'd already been in touch with Chloe and Sloane several times over the years. I just tried to be of help."

"Was there anything about their questions, anything at all, that gave you even the slightest hint about what leads they may have been pursuing?"

Williams flashed a pained smile. "Paula asked me the same thing. I'll tell you what I told her: I'm afraid not."

"I can tell that Paula Chase's death hit you hard," Lynch said. "It hurt Kendra, too. The minute she heard, she was on her way to find out how she could help. I had to be the one to break the news to her. I'm sorry for your loss."

"You have no idea," Williams said. "I'm still in shock about it. She was my partner for over nine years." Kendra could see tears welling in his eyes. "She was a better cop than I ever was."

"Did you keep in touch with her after you retired from the force?" Kendra said.

"Not as much as we said we would, but I guess that's normal. I retired first, and she left a couple of years later."

"Any theories at all about what happened to her?" Kendra asked.

He shook his head. "I leave the theorizing to the cops working her case. But of course, it's suspicious that this happened just as she was investigating this old case of ours. Yet I don't know what to think."

"One more question," Kendra said. "And I know this is going to sound strange. Did Chloe and Sloane say anything to you about 'the bomb place'?"

He cocked his head as if he may have heard her incorrectly. "I beg your pardon?"

Kendra repeated herself. "The bomb place."

"That's what I thought you said. No, they didn't mention anything like that. Really? 'The bomb place'? I have no idea what you're talking about."

"Neither do I," Kendra said. "I have no idea what it means. Or if it even means anything at all. It just came up during the investigation."

Williams shrugged. "Sorry."

Kendra stood, and the others followed her lead. "Thank you for your time, Detective. I appreciate it."

He smiled and shook her hand. "I'm not a detective anymore. I'm just Todd. If there's anything I can do to help bring Chloe and Sloane home, please let me know."

---

Kendra and Lynch didn't speak until they were back in the car and pulling away from Williams' house.

"Chloe and Sloane did communicate with him in the last few weeks," Kendra said. "But there's no written report. All the others they did were in their file. Why not his report?"

"I have no idea," Lynch said. He was silent a moment. "Also, he seemed slightly suspicious of my government work."

Kendra shot him a glance. "Half the world has probably heard about the way you're hired to bring down governments. That might be entirely justified. I certainly wouldn't fault him for that."

"Hmm. I'm not sure what to think of that."

"Let me ask you this: Did you kill anyone this week?"

"Kill?" He pretended to think about it for a moment. "No."

"Did anyone try to kill you?"

"Well...Yes."

"I thought so. I was certain that was going on during one of our calls. Considering...Then it might be wise to drop the subject."

Evidently Lynch wasn't quite ready to let the subject go yet. "They don't appear to understand my methods. By all means, though, let's move on, shall we?"

"Let's do," she agreed quickly. "It's been a couple of days since I checked in with the police and I have a few questions I want to ask them. Wanna go downtown?"

"If you like. But as I said, sometimes I have difficulty with the locals."

"Gee. And you wonder why an ex-cop might give off negative vibes toward you?"

"Good point." He asked solemnly, "Then do you suppose I should look at this as my opportunity to mend a few fences?"

She could tell he was teasing her. But she was enjoying it, so what the hell? "Let's not get carried away. I'd consider it a success if you just managed not to step on any toes."

Lynch grinned. "Then suppose we see where the day takes us."

---

Detective Perry had only three words for Kendra and Lynch when he approached them in the headquarters' fourth-floor lobby.

"The bomb place?"

"I see you've spoken to Charlie Davenport."

Perry nodded. "You put the fear of God into him. I think he broke a land speed record getting here after you talked to him. He told us about his affair with both Morgan sisters, and his overhearing something about 'the bomb place.' Which is just vague enough to be almost completely worthless."

"For now. Maybe there's just a piece we haven't seen yet."

"Well, I hope you're close to finding it, because I don't seem to be getting closer."

Perry looked at the name printed on Lynch's visitor's badge. "Mr. Lynch. I was told that Dr. Michaels' participation in our cases occasionally brings you as part of the package. I was beginning to think that wouldn't be the case this time."

"I'm here mostly as an observer." Lynch shrugged. "Kendra puts on a good show. I always enjoy it."

"So I've seen."

"So, what did you think of Charlie Davenport?" Kendra asked Perry.

"He didn't give us any reason to disbelieve him. He seemed to genuinely care for both sisters, and his alibi checks out. The 'bomb place' bit he overheard sounded a bit wonky, but he was helpful in another way."

Kendra wrinkled her brow. "What way?"

"Chloe and Sloane's phone PIN numbers. He watched them each using their phones and tapping in their unlock codes. And what's more, he remembers them."

"Good man," Lynch murmured.

"Naturally you would think that's an admirable thing for a boyfriend to do," Kendra said.

"Not admirable as much as fortunate. Fortunate for us, and maybe for Chloe and Sloane."

"Exactly," Perry said. "It's one thing to get a warrant to search someone's phone, but another thing entirely to get one of the big tech companies to help bypass the encryption for you. It's almost impossible. That young man saved us weeks."

"What did you find?" Lynch asked. "Texts? Emails?"

"All that, of course, though those weren't really of much help to us. But our computer forensics team were able to take advantage of Google location tracking history on those phones. Both women spent a lot of time at one location in the past month. Come look."

Perry led them past a row of desks to his workspace, where a printout was resting on top of a short stack of papers. Perry picked up the printout and pointed to the thousands of tiny red dots on it. "Each of these dots represents a stop that these phones made. If you look at the clusters, you can see a concentration of visits that we've tracked to likely destinations: workplaces, gyms where they held memberships, favorite lunch spots." Perry's finger traced another cluster on the other side of the page. "But both women also made frequent visits to this area."

Kendra leaned over the printout. "Where exactly is this?"

Perry turned the page over. "We're checking it out now."

She gazed at him in disbelief. "May I remind you that I'm the one who gave you Davenport? You wouldn't even have this if it wasn't for me."

"Which is why I showed you what I did."

Kendra stared at the overturned page on Perry's desk. "A

geographic map with a bunch of dots and no street or neighborhood names. Come on, Perry."

"We've had a couple of officers there all morning on a canvas, waving around pictures of Chloe and Sloane. I'll fill you in after we're done." Perry picked up a stack of files and dropped them on top of the overturned page.

Kendra shook her head. "It looked like the other side of the bay. Where was that? Coronado?"

"We'll talk about it later. By the way, our lab is confident they'll be able to get usable DNA off that blood and tooth you extracted from your attacker at Sloane's apartment. That could be a big help."

"Good. I fought hard for that lead."

"I know you did. And good work getting Davenport to fess up to his affair with both sisters. It gave us something to work with."

"All in the spirit of cooperation, Detective. Try it sometime."

Kendra turned and walked out of the squad room.

---

Kendra swore as she and Lynch stepped onto the sidewalk outside police headquarters. "That son of a bitch. I was starting to think Perry was a decent guy."

Lynch shrugged. "He is a decent guy. He was much more forthcoming than a lot of cops you've dealt with."

"Not forthcoming enough."

"He didn't need to be. We got everything we needed from him."

"How can you say that? He totally shut us out on that tracked location."

Lynch smiled. "He tried."

"Whoa whoa whoa." Kendra stopped and turned to face him. "What are you saying?"

"We have our own copy of that printout." Lynch raised his phone. "Right here."

"You didn't."

"Of course I did. Chalk it up to my usual trust issues with local law enforcement. And our friend Perry should beware any man crossing his arms in front of him while holding a phone. It's far too easy to squeeze off a few dozen photos or even videos without being detected." Lynch pulled up a perfect copy of the printout Perry had quickly showed them.

Her eyes widened. "How long will it take you to zero in on that location where Chloe and Sloane went?"

"Thirty seconds, give or take." He flashed her his best movie-star smile. "Still wish I'd stayed in Switzerland?"

"You're not out of the woods yet. Show me."

"Sure." His fingers flew across his phone screen. "It's just a matter of pulling up a street map of the San Diego area, rendering a translucent copy, and superimposing it over the geographic map that Perry so cruelly dangled in front of you. It's easy to line up the Coronado Bridge and the coastlines on each map..." Lynch used his thumb and forefinger to size and rotate the image until the two maps matched perfectly. He pointed to a cluster of red dots. "This is where they went. You were right when you said that it was across the bay in Coronado."

Kendra looked at the superimposed maps. "It looks like all their visits were on or near Flora Avenue."

Lynch nodded. "That's where the officers must be doing

their canvas today. We could either join them, or hang back someplace and wait for Perry to call with their results."

"You're joking, right?"

"Of course I am. I know we're going there right this instant."

She grinned. "Damn straight."

# CHAPTER 9

"There's nothing here!"

Kendra stood in the middle of a residential street, surrounded by charming little houses that were probably valued at four to six million dollars apiece. Star Park, a postage-stamp-size park made up of a few sidewalks, green space, and benches, was the area's only point of interest.

"Maybe they know someone here," Lynch said.

"Could be. But it's funny that they started coming here around the time they got so hot on a new lead in their investigation."

Lynch pointed to a few of the front doors. "It looks like the police have already been here with their flyers. Maybe Perry will have something to tell us after all. Might be worth a call."

"That won't be necessary."

"Why not?"

Kendra was looking up the street. "Perry's here."

Lynch turned just as Perry finished parking his SUV and

climbed out. He smiled politely as he walked toward them. "Guess we should've carpooled."

Kendra shrugged. "Guess you should have been more generous with your information."

"I had a feeling you two would find your way here."

"That's what made you jump in the car after us?" Kendra asked.

He nodded. "You gave up far too easily when I wouldn't give this location to you. I figured one or both of you had a line on it. Mr. Lynch's government connections are legendary, and you've racked up quite a list of law-enforcement officers who feel they owe you one for the help you've provided over the years."

"Your instincts serve you well," Kendra said.

"A detective's hunch. Just curious, how did you two zero in on this place so quickly? It was someone in the forensics lab, wasn't it?"

"There are some secrets and methods we'd rather keep for ourselves," Lynch said.

Perry nodded. "I guess I deserve that. Anyway, I talked to one of my officers on the way over. Only about half of the residents were home. The ones that were here didn't identify Chloe and Sloane as anyone they'd ever seen."

Kendra walked down the street, and Lynch and Perry kept pace with her. She looked at the well-tended lawns and gardens. "I can't figure out what brought Chloe and Sloane here. It's nothing that appeared in any of their files."

"Remember, it could be nothing," Perry said. "An old mutual friend, a distant relative..."

Kendra stopped. She was staring at a pleasant two-story house across the street from the park.

"What do you see?" Lynch asked.

"The Wicked Witch."

"What?"

"And Toto, too." Kendra nodded toward the house. "There's a picture of the Wicked Witch in the upstairs window. And there's a statue of Toto on the front porch."

"I see," Lynch said. "And aren't those ceramic ruby slippers by the mailbox?"

Kenda gasped and pulled out her phone.

"What is it?" Lynch asked.

"Just one second." Kendra typed in the street address and read the search results. "Wow."

"Time to share," Perry said. "What did you find?"

"Chloe and Sloane weren't talking about 'the bomb place,'" Kendra said.

"Then what were they discussing?" Perry asked.

"The Baum place."

"What?"

"The Baum house." Kendra smiled broadly. "L. Frank Baum wrote three of his Oz books in that very house over a hundred years ago. That's what Chloe and Sloane were talking about. Not the bomb place, but the Baum place!"

"Bingo," Lynch said softly. "By George, I believe she's got it."

"Well, you're the one who pulled this location out of your hat," Kendra said. "Now we've got to figure out what it means." She hugged him impulsively. "You might just be as brilliant as you think, Lynch."

"I tried to tell you." Lynch was grinning. "But I'm glad you finally came to see the light on your own. That's always inspirational."

Perry stepped closer to the house. "The Baum house…Is it a museum?"

"No." She looked at the Tripadvisor write-up on her phone. "Just a private residence, as it apparently always has been. Now occupied by a family that obviously appreciates its place in literary history."

"I'm still not sure why Chloe and Sloane suddenly appreciated it," Lynch said.

"Me neither. And judging by the flyer we tucked into the front doorjamb, no one has been home to answer any questions."

"It's not just the police flyer," Kendra said. "There are two restaurant take-out menus and a local coupon book on the porch. I'd say the residents have been out of town for at least a week."

Lynch stared at his phone. "By residents, you mean Ted and Lucinda Nichols, and their children Mark and Sasha."

Kendra looked over at his screen. "You found that already?"

"Real estate records, then a quick trip to the last census. They've lived here for nine years. I'm sure Detective Perry could have just as easily pulled this up from his police databases."

Perry chuckled. "Mine are a bit more sluggish than the ones you're using. I usually end up calling someone and waiting for them to get back to me."

Kendra couldn't just stand here. She stepped closer to the house. "Up for a little bit of trespassing?"

Lynch smiled. "Sure. Coming, Perry?"

"Why not?" Perry made a wry face. "It'll give me a chance to count up all the other Oz-related clues that my officers probably totally missed."

Kendra, Lynch, and Perry opened the side gate and walked down the length of the yellow house. The backyard was just as beautiful as the front, with stunning pops of color coming from the flowers and lawn ornaments. Dozens of ceramic winged monkeys dangled from the two lemon trees, and stone pavers had been painted to give an approximation of the Yellow Brick Road.

"They're really leaning into the whole Oz thing," Lynch said.

"It's nice." Kendra ducked to avoid a winged monkey. "I'd love to talk to the owners and see if they had any contact with Chloe and Sloane."

Perry jotted something into his notebook. "We'll track them down, maybe through their workplaces. I'll let you know what we come up with."

Kendra definitely felt uncomfortable relinquishing control to Perry and his officers, but she nodded anyway. Oh, well, she'd decide what to do later. Then she realized Lynch was watching her, and he suddenly chuckled. Sometimes it was like the bastard could read her mind, she thought crossly. Was it possible that what made him so infuriating was the exact same thing that made her miss him so much when he was away for weeks at a time?

Probably.

Dammit.

---

"I'll let you know as soon as we track down the owners of that property," Perry said as he walked Kendra and Lynch toward the Lamborghini. "It shouldn't take more than a day or two at most."

"Thank you," Kendra said. "I'd appreciate knowing as soon as possible. It may open the entire case if we can trace what the sisters told the owners of this house. I know you want that as much as we do."

"Of course I do." But his answer was absentminded as he gazed at the Lamborghini. "That's quite an automobile. I bet it gets a lot of attention." He turned to Lynch and said wistfully, "I've always wanted a car like that. But I guess everyone does."

Kendra had had enough of car worship for one day. She jumped into the passenger seat. "Thanks for everything, Perry. We'll be in touch."

"My pleasure," Perry said. "You've been a great help."

"She always is." Lynch hurriedly jumped into the driver's seat and started the car. "If there's anything I can do, let me know." Then he was roaring out of the driveway. He shot her an amused glance. "I wasn't sure if you were going to let me get in the car. Did he annoy you that much?"

"Not really. I just wanted to get away from the automobile cult so we could get to work. It was obvious he wasn't going to be all that helpful." She turned, looked over her shoulder, waved at Perry, and smiled sweetly. "While he tracks down the current owners, I'd like to go deeper."

"Meaning?"

"How about the residents of that house fifteen years ago, when the Bayside Strangler murders were happening? That's what Chloe and Sloane may have been interested in. How fast can you get us that info?"

"Ah, so you're going to use me? I admit I do like to be needed."

"We'll see," Kendra said. "You managed to get the info we needed here. How fast, Lynch?"

"If you drive so I can concentrate, I'll get right on it. I regard it as a challenge."

She made a face. "Pull over. Much as I hate to be associated with your blasted fan club, I regard it as my duty to help get this information as quickly as possible."

"Nah." His eyes were dancing with mischief as he pulled over to the side of the road. He then exchanged seats with her. "You're just using it as an excuse to get the chance to drive this beauty. I know you've been secretly lusting after it."

"You're crazy," she said as she started the engine. "Just give me directions and I'll show you how eager I am to drive the damn thing. How are you going to get me this info?"

"Probing. Trial and error. I'll find it."

She hadn't the slightest doubt that he would search until he did. His intensity was incredible as he went through databases with speed and accuracy.

"How is it coming?" she asked after ten minutes.

"Good enough. I'm bringing up real estate records now," Lynch said. "Fifteen years ago, that house was owned by a property management company." He pulled up an address. "They're still around, on Bankers Hill."

"Next to Little Italy?"

"Yep. We're going the right way now." He looked at his watch. "And we're right on schedule. I just sent a text to June Adcock, co-owner of the company, and asked if we can drop in and ask a few questions. Another few minutes..."

June Adcock was a woman in her sixties with brick-red hair and a brisk but smart demeanor. But she appeared to be willing to talk about the Baum place. According to her, it was more a tourist attraction than anything more dangerous.

"I can't tell you much more about it," June said. "The Baum place was a popular rental property for vacationers, especially Wizard of Oz fans."

"We're looking for renters from a certain period," Kendra said. "It's been a while. Fifteen years ago last summer." Kendra pulled up the Notes app on her phone and displayed the date range of the Bayside Strangler murders. "Do you think you can give us a list of the renters of that house during this time?"

"Well, it would be an extremely short list."

"What do you mean?"

"I happen to remember that the house was occupied by only one renter for that entire year."

"You remember that off the top of your head?" Lynch asked.

"Only because it was so unusual." June leaned back in her desk chair and sipped from a tumbler of iced tea. "The house was rented by a corporation. Sometimes companies will rent places when they know their employees will be in town for extended periods of time. It's less expensive than a hotel. But this corporation paid their rent a year in advance, plus another fifty-five-hundred-dollar security deposit, all in cash."

"Cash?" Kendra asked.

"Yes. And a couple of months before the end of the rental period, they dropped off the keys at our office in the after-hours box. The house was spotless. It was as if no one had ever been there. I tried to contact the corporation to return their deposit, but there was no valid address or working phone number. We tried every search we could think of, but the corporation just didn't exist anymore."

"What was the corporation's name?" Lynch asked.

"That's one thing I don't have at the top of my mind." June leaned forward and typed on her desktop keyboard. "We normally protect the confidentiality of our clients, but since this one doesn't exist anymore..." She squinted at the screen. "It was called the Dayton Group."

"Never heard of it," Kendra said.

"Nobody has, before or since."

"Do you happen to remember anything about the person who signed the rental agreement?" Kendra asked.

"No, sorry. That was handled by someone who hasn't worked here for years. But I believe it was a gentleman." June looked between the two of them. "If you don't mind me asking, why are you so interested in this place?"

"Two women took an interest in that house last month," Kendra said. "We don't know why. The women have gone missing."

June's eyes widened.

"We don't know if it has anything to do with that house," Kendra quickly added. "Just covering all the bases."

"Interesting. Well, we don't own it anymore. Our company sold off most of its properties around ten years ago, when the housing market spiked. We concentrate more on property management these days." She stood. "Speaking of which, I have to go look at a place right now."

They thanked her for her time and left. On the sidewalk outside, Kendra walked in silence for a moment while she processed what they'd just been told.

"Just plain weird," she finally said.

"The vanishing corporation, you mean?"

"Yes."

"There could be any number of reasons why it was done. Both crooked and legitimate. After all, a corporation could be a conglomerate or a single person. Any industry you can imagine. An energy company, a drug dealer, a classical violinist, or someone who sells watercolors along the Embarcadero."

"You're really reaching now, Lynch," Kendra said.

"Maybe not. You've just got to harness your imagination and then give it free rein."

"Suppose you do that, Lynch," Kendra suggested and added slyly, "Or is it too much of a challenge for you?"

"Not at all." He met her gaze. "You really want to find this guy?"

"Of course I do. He's a strong lead."

"Possibly. Or he might be another victim. We'll have to take a look and see." He grinned. "But I'll do my best to track him down for you."

"And then prove how clever you were to do it?"

"I'd hate to deprive you of a challenge."

"I could survive it."

"But I'd have problems with it. I did give you my word that I'd try to find the sisters. I have to keep my word to you."

"We seem to have gotten along fine with me driving you here."

He shook his head mournfully. "I'm afraid we didn't, Kendra. Maybe if I'd had more time to coach you about the eccentricities of driving such a magnificent car. I'll keep it in mind next time."

"I'm not worthy of driving that damn car?"

"I told you I'd coach you."

"I may murder you, Lynch."

He smiled. "But I could probably do that better than you, too. It's all in the practice, Kendra. First, you have to have the knack, then you have to practice, practice, practice."

"Any other suggestions?" she asked.

"You have to learn how to duck really well when confronted with irate motorists."

"I've got that down pat."

"And you have to let me feed you dinner tonight. At Juniper and Ivy while we discuss the case. Their Wagyu short rib can't be beat, and I insist you try their yodel for desert."

"I'll work on it."

"Then you're a shoo-in." He got behind the wheel. "I knew you could do it!"

---

"Yodel?" Kendra scanned the dessert menu at the Juniper and Ivy restaurant. So far the décor had proved to be absolutely charming and the food as good as Lynch claimed. "I believe I'll pass on yodeling for dessert. It's a bit on the exhibitionist side and not really my thing."

"Nonsense. You're a music professional and I've heard you sing with your students. You do a great job. Actually, it's really good practice and I was going to suggest you bring some of your students here for an occasional lunch. The entire table could become a guest of the proprietors if your party does a good enough job of the yodel. But it must be loud enough to resonate off the other tables in the restaurant. Your students would love it."

"They might at that. It could be fun for them. And I might be tempted to do it if I was sure that it was for their benefit and not to amuse you, Lynch."

"Well, part of it would be for me." His grin was puckish. "But I'll try to persuade you again when you have a more welcoming audience for your yodel. I'm sure it will be an astounding success."

"I thought so." She was shaking her head and trying to keep from smiling. "You're a very wicked man, Lynch."

"Just trying to help you with your students," he murmured. "I guess we'll have to choose something more boring to keep you entertained. Let me think about it."

Kendra's phone vibrated in her pocket. She pulled it out and looked in surprise at the caller ID notification. "It's Metcalf."

"Metcalf? I didn't think the FBI was on this case."

"They're not. He probably just heard about my run-in at Sloane's condo." She answered the call. "Metcalf, my head is fine. Nothing to worry about."

"Uh, glad to hear it," he replied. "But that's not why I'm calling, whatever that's about."

"Oh."

"I'm on my way to a crime scene. Kendra, I guess you haven't heard..." She could hear the stress in his voice.

"Are you okay?"

"Yes. Listen, this is related to the case you've been working. I knew you'd want to know right away."

Lynch's phone chimed on the table in front of him. He looked down at the screen and whispered a single swear word.

"I guess Lynch just found out," Metcalf said.

"Found out what?"

"Kendra..." He hesitated and then just came out with it. "The Bayside Strangler is back."

# CHAPTER 10

It was completely dark by the time Kendra and Lynch approached the taped-off police line surrounding Pepper Park, a small plot of land in the National City neighborhood south of downtown. Helicopters were circling the area, and Kendra could see at least three harbor patrol boats keeping watch from the adjacent bay.

A uniformed officer moved to stop Kendra and Lynch from ducking underneath the line, but Perry waved them through before it became an issue.

"Who invited you to this party?" he said.

"The FBI. I understand they may be taking over this investigation."

"In negotiation as we speak. If this is what we think it is, that could very well happen."

"The victim?" Lynch asked.

Perry looked at his notebook. "Anna Mae Robinson, age twenty-eight. She worked as a customs manager at the Port of San Diego. They have an office a few blocks from here.

She went missing after she left work three days ago, then tonight her body turned up on a slide in that play area over there."

Kendra looked at the cluster of work lights on the other side of the park. "That's a familiar pattern, but what makes you think it's really the Bayside Strangler after all these years?"

Perry lowered his voice. "Something that wasn't released to the media back then. Each of the victims' hands were bound behind them in a specific way."

"I remember seeing it in one of the photos in the Morgan sisters' files," Lynch said. "A handcuff knot reinforced by an overhand knot."

"Exactly," Perry said. "I saw it there, too. The sisters shouldn't have had that picture. They must have bribed someone for it. And the strangler always used the same kind of rope: a green-and-white triple-braid bamboo-and-cotton blend. That's what this looks like."

Kendra nodded. "Wow. That's his MO, all right." She looked around the park. "Any security cameras here?"

"No such luck, but we've already started combing the surrounding area. There are a hell of a lot more cameras in this city than there were fifteen years ago. We'll come up with something."

Kendra took a deep breath, steeling herself for the sight she knew was waiting for her under the work lights. "Take me closer."

"Of course," Perry said. "I know how to show a girl a good time."

He motioned for Kendra and Lynch to follow him across the park to the brightly colored children's play area, which felt oddly incongruous with the grim centerpiece of all the activity. As police officers, FBI agents, photographers, and forensics techs moved around the scene, Kendra caught her first glimpses of the victim, lying upright on the playground slide, eyes open and staring up to the heavens.

This part never got easier.

This poor woman probably started her last day like any other, showering, walking her dog, making breakfast for her kid, or some other mundane task she'd never do again. All of it taken away by some monster who had already caused so much pain in the world.

Lynch squeezed her arm. "Are you okay?"

"Yes." She tried to toughen her facial expression. "I need to see this."

She stepped closer. A few of the investigators on the scene probably recognized her, and others saw her with Perry and just assumed she belonged there. She finally stopped about six feet from the corpse.

The victim looked younger than twenty-eight; she could have passed for a teenager. Kendra had long ago given up trying to guess anything about a murder victim's final state of mind from their facial expression. She had no doubt that young Anna Robinson's last moments were spent in agony, but no one would ever know it from the serene expression on her lifeless face.

There was something particularly disturbing about that expression, Kendra thought, a reminder of how every thought, every emotion, everything this woman would ever be had been so completely erased.

"Who found her?" Kendra asked.

"Someone called it in shortly after dark," Perry said.

"She was probably placed here just after sunset." He pointed to the nearby office buildings. "It would be tough to bring her here during daylight hours without someone seeing."

Kendra stepped closer to examine the bruising on her neck. "Strangled by the same rope used to bind her?"

"That's how it looks, just like the others. It appears she was killed around the time she disappeared, but the medical examiner hasn't weighed in on an approximate TOD yet. The killer kept the corpse for a couple of days before delivering it here. No evidence of sexual assault. Every detail lines up with the Bayside Strangler killings."

She heard a grim voice behind her. "I told you. He's back."

She turned to see FBI Special Agent Roland Metcalf. He was on the scene with Michael Griffin, head of the San Diego FBI regional office. She knew Griffin from several prior cases, and although he often seemed to resent her presence, she knew he was the one who usually enlisted her aid in the first place. Confusing.

Lynch smiled. "Hello, Griffin. I thought you were done trudging around crime scenes in the dark of night."

Griffin shrugged. "And I thought you kept busy collecting exorbitant paychecks from our government while barely skirting international laws."

"I still like to mix things up."

Perhaps sensing the tension between the two men, Metcalf stepped forward. "Special Agent Griffin worked the Bayside Strangler case back in the day. He knows more about the case than just about anyone at the Bureau."

"It wasn't for long," Griffin said. "The FBI had only been involved for a couple of weeks when the killings stopped. We barely had time to get up to speed on the work that SDPD had done before it was all over." He looked at Kendra. "Did the police ask you here?"

"No." Griffin obviously didn't know Metcalf had tipped her off. "I'm investigating the Morgan sisters' disappearance. My focus will stay there."

"Obviously, you're considering the possibility that this case may have suddenly become part of yours."

"Difficult to say."

"You have to admit that it's strange that the Bayside Strangler is back after fifteen years, just days after the daughters of one of his victims have gone missing."

Metcalf nodded. "Daughters who appeared to have discovered something while investigating his murders."

Kendra stepped a few yards away, and the others followed her lead. She lowered her voice. "But what could have possibly caused him to resume his spree so many years later?"

Griffin crossed his arms in front of him. "Believe me, our profilers are going to start addressing that question within the hour. But if I was to take a stab at it, it could be that he's been in prison."

"And he just happened to get out now?"

"No. But maybe the jail time broke his rhythm. He's older now, and murders like this take strength and energy. Maybe he's been free and itching to get back in the game for years, but he's had doubts he could pull it off. But then something happened that finally flipped his switch."

"He knew Chloe and Sloane were getting close?"

"Maybe. Or maybe it wasn't that at all. It's possible that the media reports about their disappearance woke something inside him. The Bayside Strangler was back in the news again, and maybe he…liked it."

Kendra thought about it. "Actually, either could be the case. That's pretty good, Griffin. It makes sense."

"Just a possibility."

Griffin cocked his head back toward the corpse. "Your turn. What did you get from that?"

Kendra took a deep breath. "First of all, instead of referring to this poor woman as 'that' or 'it,' how about 'she' or 'her'? Or maybe her name?" Kendra looked at Perry, who had been keeping a low profile since Griffin and Metcalf's arrival.

"Anna," Perry said. "Anna Robinson."

She turned back to Griffin. "See? That isn't so hard."

Griffin sighed. "Fine. What did you get from her?"

"She was stored in a walk-in cooler. But not a freezer."

Griffin stepped closer to her. "Only two of the five original victims were refrigerated between the time they were killed and when they were finally dumped."

"So I understand. Anna Robinson is another one. Though I hesitate to use the word 'dumped' when the killer so carefully brought out and posed his victims for display."

Griffin shrugged.

"She was held in an older building, somewhere near the waterfront," Kendra said. "When you look for security camera footage, concentrate on the bay. I think she was brought here on a small boat and literally carried the fifty yards from the water. Our killer is as physically strong as he ever was, so I don't believe we're looking for a geriatric."

Metcalf was smiling. He always enjoyed these displays. "Surely that can't be all."

"Well, did anyone find a pair of eyeglasses?"

Perry cocked his head. "Eyeglasses?"

"Yes. She wore glasses, and the perp took the time and trouble to refrigerate her with her glasses on after he killed her. That's why it's so strange she's here without them. He may have kept them as a souvenir, or they may have just fallen off while he was bringing her here. Hard to say, but it's something to look out for when you start talking to suspects."

Griffin shared a quick glance with Perry and Metcalf. "Good. But before we start searching old waterfront buildings, I'm going to need to know how you arrived at all this."

"Sure. Well, she's obviously been refrigerated. There's skin discoloration but no decomposition odor, which I'm sure I would have picked up."

Griffin nodded. "You don't need to convince me of that."

"But I did pick up a faint whiff of ammonia on her. A lot of older walk-in cooler systems used almost pure ammonia in their pipes as a refrigerant. But as they age, the ammonia can start seeping out in small quantities."

"How on earth would you know that?" Perry asked.

"Hamburgers. There was a restaurant near where I went to school that had an ancient walk-in cooler. The lettuce and tomatoes had a slight off-taste that drove me crazy. It was from ammonia leaking from the refrigeration system. It's not a smell, or a taste, you ever forget."

Perry grimaced. "I guess not."

"There are also a few rust flakes in her hair, which I'm guessing came from that cooler or the old building where he kept her until he was ready to bring her here."

"Good," Griffin said. "But what makes you think she was brought here by boat?"

"First of all, it just makes sense. It's half the distance from the waterfront to the playground by boat than it would be by car, with much less chance of being seen and getting caught. But the cashmere sweater she's wearing is a magnet for the chipping paint we can see on the sidewalk and railings along the waterfront."

"How about the eyeglasses?" Metcalf asked.

"Another effect of the refrigeration. There's more discoloration on either side of her nose bridge, and even more behind each ear. Marks left by eyeglasses. I didn't see them anywhere around there."

"We'll comb the entire park," Perry said. "But I pulled up her driver's license photo a while ago, and she was wearing a pair of cat's-eye glasses. I suspect those are the ones we're looking for."

Kendra nodded, and she suddenly felt a wave of sadness cascading over her. She'd wanted to be here, she reminded herself. But now she just wanted to get the hell away.

"Ready?" Lynch asked.

"Yes." She took a deep breath. "Let's go."

---

Another helicopter!

Rod Wallace reached into his pocket to bring out his binoculars. He knew he was taking a big chance by staying this close. But that was part of the thrill. Anyway, he had it all planned. All he had to do was get to the next street and then move onto the boat he'd left down at the dock.

And the risk was worthwhile. How he'd missed this

heady feeling of power as he'd reached out and taken life after life. It had been stolen from him and he bitterly resented it. No one had the right to take that power from him.

He was getting a text message. He was tempted to just ignore it when he saw that it was Victor Krebb, who was probably going to whine at him. But he decided he'd better reply because this area was crawling with cops and Feds and he might need him to help him to escape. "I'm okay, Victor," he said when he took the call. "One more block. Just have the boat ready."

"Are you crazy?" Victor was almost screaming. "I warned you against doing anything like this. Another murder? How can I keep you safe when you show up as if you'd never left here? The last thing we want is to have them all looking for you again. What in the hell are you thinking?"

"I'm thinking I needed this. I deserve it," Wallace said simply. "I've missed the feeling it gave me. It's really quite exhilarating. Now stop yelling and find me a safe house where you can whisk me away from my acquaintances from the FBI. So sad I can't consider them friends any longer."

"Don't get near them," Victor muttered. "You'll end up at Leavenworth. Just get the hell to the boat."

"I'm on my way." Wallace glanced at the sky. Another helicopter overhead. One more block and he'd be on the boat and making plans to go after that final victim who had been getting in his way since she'd appeared in his life. Did she actually think she could bring him down?

*Don't worry, it won't be long now, Kendra...*

# CHAPTER 11

Kendra jumped into the passenger seat of Lynch's car and immediately looked at her phone. "Sorry, I may be on a call for a while."

"Problem?" Lynch asked.

"Olivia tried to phone me three times while we were at that crime scene. She finally texted me. She wants to know if I'm okay. I think that the word is out about the Bayside Strangler's return. I texted her back, but she wants to talk to me. She insists we stop at her condo as soon as we get back."

"Uh-oh." Lynch chuckled. "It sounds like she's in a demanding mood."

"Yep. She's the most loyal friend you could ever ask for, and you've already seen how protective she can be. When Paula Chase was killed, you'll remember she encouraged an eighty-eight-year-old retired police sketch artist to grab his gun and leap into action."

Lynch nodded. "I had a few problems with her choice of a bodyguard at the time."

"Well, if she knows the Bayside Strangler is back, she might be calling in the National Guard. I grew up with her, and you have no idea how hardheaded and determined she can be when the notion strikes her."

"Yes, I do. I got a taste of it when she was reading me the riot act telling me that I wasn't doing everything she expected of me. I fully expect to have a similar experience when I see her tonight." He sighed. "But I'm willing to suffer through it."

"Well, I'm not," Kendra said flatly. "For the most part you've been very helpful today. You don't deserve that kind of flak."

"Really?" He smiled. "And it only took the emergence of a genuine monster to make you see me this clearly?"

"It's a question of comparison. Don't let it go to your head."

"Too late. I'm filled with confidence now. I might even be able to handle our Olivia."

"Don't count on it."

"I have to count on it." Lynch shot her a glance. "Because I have to prove I'm worthy of your trust. You've officially already declared me to be worthy of battling with monsters. I think that's something like being a knight in armor. Now I only have to go and face the dreaded magician Olivia. That will be another battle, but I'll find a way to win her to my side."

Kendra was shaking her head. "Lynch, you're a complete idiot." She had to stop laughing.

He nodded gravely. "But one in whom you have total confidence?"

She nodded. "You might say that. I'll let you know after I see how Olivia handles you."

"That will go well," he assured her. "Because I already know a few of her magician's secrets. Now lean back and relax and I'll whisk you to Olivia's stronghold. Don't worry about anything before we get there."

"Whatever you say." She obediently leaned back on the headrest. "But I have to warn you, Olivia often manages to concoct new and more powerful magic at a moment's notice."

"Then you might have to help me. I'll look forward to it." He smiled down at her. "It's always more fun if we do it together." He covered her hand with his own. "Isn't it, Kendra?"

She was quiet for a long moment. "In most cases." She forced a smile. "As long as it has nothing to do with monsters or things that go bump in the night. I'm afraid I'd draw the line at either of those. No magician's castles or knights in armor. The minute you start going after the monsters is when I bid you goodbye and take over the job myself. Because that's the way it should be from the beginning. I don't believe I could bear the thought of causing you or anyone else to become a victim for my sake. It would hurt too much." She blinked hard. She was not going to cry, dammit. "So make up your mind about all that nonsense. I couldn't stand it."

"Then we'll have to make certain it doesn't happen."

He reached out and gently wiped the tears from her cheek. "No big deal. Heaven forbid I inconvenience you. We'll just go forward as we intend to go on. Okay?"

"Sounds good to me." She adjusted herself in the seat and looked straight ahead. "Now get me to Olivia's condo so we can find out if the FBI has found out anything more since we left the park."

---

The minute Kendra left the elevator as they reached Olivia's floor she knew what Olivia probably had in mind when she asked her to come here. And by the time they had reached the door of her condo she knew definitely. She grabbed Lynch's arm. "Hold on to your hat. The magician is starting to work her magic."

Lynch gazed at her inquiringly but a minute later he heard the howl and he understood. Another howl and he flinched as Olivia threw open the front door. Olivia's huge sandy-colored dog with his big ears and one brown eye and one blue was immediately on Lynch in an ecstasy of greeting, with his paws on Lynch's shoulders and licking his ears. "Hello, Harley." Lynch fought him off and gave him a pat as he gazed at Kendra. "I was wondering why Harley didn't show up last night when Olivia came to your condo."

"He's been in the country at the trainer's," Olivia said as she pulled Harley down and gave him a pat. "But he always loved you, Lynch, and you were excellent with the training. I thought you might as well be useful at something since you're obviously being fairly inept when it comes to keeping an eye on Kendra."

"Now, that hurts," Lynch said.

"Then find a way to get rid of that damn strangler," Olivia said. "And keep Harley with you all the time. He's probably smarter than you are. His trainer says he's very intelligent."

"I believe you. And I'll keep Harley by our side whenever possible. I'm not taking any chances, Olivia."

"See that you don't," she said sternly. "You can start by taking Harley up to Kendra's condo tonight. But right now I want you both to tell me all the details of what happened in the park tonight. I can't understand it. Why did that beast just suddenly reappear on the scene after all this time?"

"We don't know that yet, Olivia," Lynch said quietly. "I wish we did. I'll search every avenue I have to find out. But you can bet that we'll know very soon. The only thing we can be certain of so far is that something appeared on the scene that wasn't there before, triggering the killing," Kendra said. "Maybe if we talk about it we might find a clue."

Lynch reached out and took Olivia's hand. "I realize I disappointed you, but I promise I'm going to find out. Right now, we're going to take Harley up to the condo and get him settled for the night. Is HGTV still his favorite TV network?"

Olivia nodded. "Yes. I have to turn on the TV for him every afternoon. And now he barks and runs around the room every time *Property Brothers* comes on. You spoiled him rotten. It took weeks for the trainer to put him back on the right track the last time I let you puppy-sit when I went out of town."

"I'll watch it this time," Lynch said. "Kendra will keep an eye on me. But a little spoiling doesn't do any harm. He was missing you. The two of you are a team, and he needed a little pampering."

"Kendra," Olivia said, "I'm relying on you."

Kendra was already pulling Harley toward the front door. "We'll see you in the morning. Everything is going to be fine. We'll talk and maybe we'll come up with something."

"You'd better," Olivia said. "I'll see you in the morning and I want answers." She gave Harley's throat a final pat. Then she brushed a kiss on Kendra's cheek. "Tomorrow," she said again. "No excuses."

"We hear you," Kendra said as she pushed Lynch out into the hall. "So much for confronting the magician," she continued as they headed for the elevator. "But you didn't do all that bad. You sounded sincere. That's important to Olivia."

"I couldn't have been more sincere," Lynch said as she unlocked her condo door. "Every syllable." He watched Harley running around the condo for a moment before the dog stretched out lazily on the couch. "But you've had a bit of a rough time tonight and you should rest." He gave her a light kiss. "I'm going to do some research and see if I can put all this together." He turned toward the French doors. "But first I believe I'll search the terrace and make certain we don't have any visitors."

She stiffened. "Do you want company?"

"No." He smiled. "I want you to go to bed and let me work on finding the solution I promised Olivia. I really did mean it when I told her I'd do everything I could to keep you safe."

She was disappointed. They had spent most of the day working and talking together and she felt a little sense of abandonment. "Would you like a glass of wine before you go hunting for the bad guys?"

He shook his head. "Stop trying to take over. I have a duty to perform that the magician decreed."

"Whatever." She headed for her bedroom. "May you and Harley be very happy together."

"I'm just trying to please your best friend." He followed her to the bedroom. "Though I might be persuaded to change my mind."

"I wouldn't think of inconveniencing you." She kicked off her shoes and pulled off her clothes. Lynch smiled, but she made a shooing motion. "Go forth and conquer. I'll join you for breakfast with Olivia in the morning. If that won't get in your way. Heaven forbid that happens." She climbed into bed, reached over, and turned off the bedside lamp. "Go do your duty to Olivia. But you damn well better come up with an answer by morning. I'm tired of being left out in the cold while you take over the action. I thought we already had that discussion."

"Kendra..."

"Out," she said and turned over in bed. "You'll have to be a good deal more persuasive the next time we come together."

"I promise I will. Evidently I couldn't be worse. And I won't make the attempt until I'm on solid ground."

"Good thinking."

He gave a low whistle as he closed the door behind him.

---

Damn. Damn. Damn.

Kendra's hand clenched on her pillowcase as she saw the lights go on in the living room. She wanted to go to Lynch and make things right again as they had been all evening.

She'd been difficult and a bitch and she knew she wasn't going to sleep tonight. Why couldn't she be like other women who could accept being softer and less demanding? She knew the answer. Because it wasn't her nature. Because she had fought too long and hard to become who she was, and Lynch was part of who she had become. She pounded the pillow one last time and then drew a deep breath and closed her eyes. Tomorrow was another day and she would probably never be what he wanted her to be. But maybe she could be what she wanted to be, accomplish all she wanted to do. Throw in a little more patience and kindness and that would be good, too. That might be enough. Yes, that might be enough...

---

The first thing Kendra heard when she woke was Lynch's shower pounding in the guest room next door. The second thing she heard was her door opening and then Lynch was on the bed beside her. "It's time to get up." His lips were buried in her throat. "I'm heading for the shower but I want company."

Her fingers instinctively went to his hair and began stroking it. "You didn't want it last night."

"I wanted it. When the hell have I ever not wanted you? You're an addiction. I was being noble and trying to please the magician and still making sure you had a good night's rest."

"And did it do any good? Was it worth it?"

"No, not worth a damn. I'm not good at noble. Especially not after I watched you get naked and slide into bed just a few feet away. So do you want to take a shower with me? We have time before we go down to breakfast."

She couldn't think of anything she wanted more at this moment. "Too late," she said regretfully. "I was restless and took my shower in the middle of the night."

"Do you want another one?" He was grinning mischievously. "I promise to make it worth your while."

"I know you could, damn you. But I just can't stop thinking about those sisters. I want to know what you discovered last night."

He leaned back slightly. "I've been thinking about Olivia's observation about there being no file for Detective Williams. I decided to research him."

"Good idea. What did you find out?"

"A very good record, in the police department and before that as a naval recruit. His navy career was undistinguished, but he found his groove with the San Diego Police Department. By all accounts, an outstanding detective, and he even received a meritorious service award shortly before he retired. He's divorced and has a daughter who lives in New Mexico. There's nothing in his background that suggests he can't be trusted."

Kendra nodded. "I want to talk to him again."

"We will. In the meantime, my shower offer is still open."

"I'll think about it."

He bent and gave her an especially sweet kiss. "Think hard. I'll be waiting." Then he was heading for the door. "But I do take rain checks."

Which made her want to run after him. Of course.

She sighed and got up and headed for her bathroom. If she didn't change her mind, she'd finish getting dressed so that she'd be ready to leave the condo when he came out of the shower. If she did change her mind...

---

She was fully dressed and was brushing her hair when her phone buzzed on the counter. The caller ID number looked familiar, but it wasn't one listed in her directory. She answered it. "Kendra Michaels."

"Dr. Michaels, it's Pauley, down in the garage."

"Pauley...Is everything okay?

He sighed. "Well, some idiot whipped into the garage and clipped your car's left rear taillight and bumper."

"Just to get things straight, we're talking about my car, not Lynch's Lamborghini, right?"

"Oh, God, no, not the Lamborghini." Pauley seemed happy and relieved that it was her car, not Lynch's, that was damaged. "This guy has his phone out, and he's taking pictures all around. He's making noises like some of the damage was already there."

"Seriously?"

"Yeah, he's a jerk. You should probably come down here and swap insurance info. I already snapped a pic of his license plate in case he decides to take off."

Kendra muttered a curse. Just what she needed. "Okay. Keep him there. I'll be right down." Kendra cut the connection and immediately called Olivia. "We may be a little late for breakfast. Pauley said someone dinged my Toyota and I need to exchange insurance info. But it's my car and not that Lamborghini, thank heavens. Pauley would have had a nervous breakdown if it had been Lynch's car. I'll call you as soon as I find out when we'll be down. This shouldn't take long."

"Let me know if I can help," Olivia said.

"Just keep breakfast warm. I haven't even let Lynch know yet. He'd probably want to give the guy the third degree. See you later." She put down her phone and grabbed her keys. She took the elevator down to the building's main floor, then took the rear hallway to another elevator that took her to the parking garage.

Just go soothe Pauley, exchange insurance info, and then go back and get Lynch. Not a terrific way to start a day, but the early part hadn't been bad at all. And she still had those rain checks if she wanted to collect.

She stepped out onto the second garage level, where she expected to see Pauley standing behind her car.

He wasn't there.

"Pauley?"

No answer.

All the garage lights shut off.

What the hell?

"Run! For God's sake run!" Pauley's voice. Then there was a low curse and gasp of pain.

And Kendra ran! Pauley's voice called weakly from the other side of the garage. "Kendra, get the hell away! The guy's a—"

Pauley's voice cut off in mid-sentence.

She ducked behind a car. The guy's a what? Kendra thought. A random psychopath? A chill went through her. It could be something even worse, she realized. Something much worse.

She turned back toward the hallway door, just in time to see it slam closed.

Shit.

Where would he be expecting her to go? Back toward Pauley's voice? It's where she wanted to be, helping him…

No, this guy would know that. She couldn't do what was expected. It could be fatal.

She heard a single footstep, then the rustling of fabric. He was trying to be quiet, forgetting that his nylon jacket gave him away far more than his athletic shoes.

Kendra crouched even lower and rolled under the black Humvee next to her. She froze. Had he heard her?

She didn't think so.

She rolled again, toward a minivan. She curled underneath. She needed to put more distance between herself and that creep, whoever he was. But she'd lost track of him.

Was he being still, waiting for her to reveal herself?

She listened.

Not a sound.

*Come on, you bastard. Give me something…*

There!

He'd brushed past a car nearby, his jacket zipper striking a side panel.

But still too close for comfort. Damn.

She rolled again, moving two cars over. All well and good, but she needed a plan.

She heard jagged breathing on the other side of the garage. Pauley was alive! But there was no way in hell she could get to him.

"He's seen my face, Kendra."

The voice sliced through her. It was barely louder than

a whisper, but she heard every word. He couldn't have been more than ten feet from her.

"I can't let him identify me," the voice continued. "I'm not going to let myself get caught by some greasy garage attendant. Pity. I'm afraid he needs to die."

He was trying to draw her out, to panic her.

And doing a damn good job of it.

*Don't panic. Close your eyes. Concentrate.*

What could she figure out about this guy?

He spoke with a slight northwestern dialect; Oregon or maybe even Washington State. He pronounced *caught* like *cot*, which was always a giveaway.

What else?

His gait and his breathing sounded different from the man who had attacked her at Sloane's condo the other night. *Another* psycho?

"I want you to know you weren't part of the original plan, Kendra."

He was now on the other side of the garage, close to Pauley. *Gotta draw him away. Make him talk.*

"What plan?"

She heard him turn.

*Keep him coming.*

"Where have you been all these years?" She spoke in an almost taunting manner.

He paused before replying. "Waiting."

"Waiting for what?"

Another long pause. "The time wasn't right."

Kendra cocked her head. He was on the move again, away from where she thought Pauley was. She listened for the sound of that rustling nylon. He was creeping along the edge of the garage, trying to make a long arc toward her.

*Do you think that's going to keep me from hearing you, you asshole?*

She moved closer to the wall.

Wait a minute…She'd seen something earlier in the week, something that had annoyed the hell out of her. It was in front of a white work truck, cluttering this corner of the garage. Kendra crouched low and crept toward the truck. Were the offending objects still there?

*Keep him talking. Make it harder for him to listen.*

"I never knew there was ever a good time to start killing innocent people," she said.

"You'd be surprised, Kendra."

"Then go ahead and surprise me. I'm listening."

His icy chuckle cut through the darkness.

"I'm serious. Tell me."

"It's a long story, Kendra. I was…interrupted."

"You were in prison."

He laughed again. He was closer now. "Prison? Have I done anything to make you think I could be so hopelessly inept?"

Kendra knelt in front of the truck. He wanted to talk. Good. "Where are Chloe and Sloane Morgan?"

"I'm afraid I can't help you with that."

"Can't or won't?"

"Let's just say I've never been afraid of them. They were always going to remain on my list."

Kendra's hand closed around something on the dark floor. It was cold and heavy, and it scraped across the concrete as she picked it up.

The man froze. Shit. Had she given herself away?

After a long moment, he started moving again.

Good.

She gripped a piece of rebar, a long slender length of iron used to reinforce floors and walls in construction sites.

"Then you must be afraid of me," she said. "Why else would you be here?"

He didn't respond. Suddenly, she was having a difficult time hearing him. He'd shed the jacket. He'd obviously realized it was giving him away.

She turned her head and listened. Where in the hell was he?

She heard his breathing. Quiet, measured.

In the next instant, he rolled out from under the truck and leaped to his feet. Before she could react, his arm snapped around her neck!

He whispered into her ear. "I'm not afraid of you, Kendra. But others are. That makes it much more exciting for me."

Kendra swung the rebar upward and struck him on the head. He grunted in pain, but his grip remained strong. He twisted her around and slammed her head against the truck. She swung the iron bar toward him again. A miss.

She swung again. Another miss.

His grip tightened, cutting off her airway. She was losing consciousness. She swung at him again. Contact! He released her and staggered backward.

The door flew open on the other side of the garage. "Kendra!" It was Lynch.

Thank God.

She held the rebar in front of her. "Over here! Hurry!"

Her attacker was gone…

"Kendra!"

"Watch out!" she shouted. "He's here!"

Lynch slid over the hood of a car and was suddenly beside her. He held his automatic in front of him. "Which way?"

She pointed toward the ramp up to the garage's main level. "There."

"Are you okay?"

She felt her bruised throat. "Yes. Let's go."

They bolted up the ramp and stopped. "How many exits are there up here?"

"Three, plus the main gate."

"Are the doors locked?"

"Yes, but only from the outside. He could've gone out any of them."

Lynch cursed and lowered his gun.

Kendra turned and headed back down the ramp. "We need to check on Pauley. He's been hurt..."

They ran back to the garage's lower level. "Pauley?" Kendra called out.

No answer.

Dear heaven.

"Pauley?"

"Any idea where he is?" Lynch asked.

"Somewhere on the far side."

Still holding his automatic, Lynch held up his phone with the other hand to light their way across the dark garage. Finally, between two parked cars, they found Pauley's blood-stained body.

"No!" Kendra knelt beside him. He was alive. Bleeding and struggling to breathe, but alive. She turned back toward Lynch. "Call 911! Now!"

Lynch was already on it, she realized. He finished the call and cut the connection. "There's a first-aid kit in the trunk of my car."

He bolted for his Lamborghini.

She made a face. "Of course there's one in the Lamborghini. What did I expect? Doesn't every luxury car have its own first-aid kit to take care of the needs of its owners?"

"No." He scowled. "Only the ones whose guests don't check in with me and tell me that there might be a problem requiring it."

Considering her situation, she decided it was the better part of valor not to argue the point. Instead she started to bandage Pauley's shoulder.

She could hear the ambulance sirens now. "I should have let you know before I came down here. But it seemed perfectly safe. It was Pauley..."

"And after all, no one else could be down here waiting for you." He held up his hand as he added caustically, "At least no one you couldn't handle? Let's not talk about it right now. I'm a little irritated. I just want to make sure Pauley is okay." His lips tightened. "And I want to get that wound on your neck taken care of so I don't have to look at it any longer. It's a very potent reminder that I should have been here with you. It can't happen again, Kendra. Not like this. It hurts too much." He raised his phone light and waved it toward the EMTs, who were approaching with their work lights. "But let's get Pauley taken care of and then go after the bastard who did this to him. Then I'll worry about the brand-new wound that murderer gave you." He helped her to her feet and then pushed her gently over to the EMTs. "I'll find the garage lights, then stay with Pauley until you get to the hospital. But you should give Perry or Breen a call while you're in the ambulance. They're going to want a report on this little incident. I'll meet you at the ER. Okay?"

"Of course it's okay," Kendra said curtly. "I was going to call Perry the minute I got the chance. You should have realized that. I've been a little busy lately."

"I've noticed." He turned away. "All the more reason to have that talk I mentioned as soon as possible. But get that wound taken care of first. I'm going to ask for a report on it as soon as I arrive at the hospital."

"Is that a threat?" Kendra's brows lifted as she got into the ambulance. "It had a few uneasy overtones of that."

"No, the threat is over for the time being," Lynch said. "I believe both of us have had enough of that today. As far as I'm concerned, I've had enough for the next decade." He was heading for his car. "I'll see you at the hospital."

# CHAPTER 12

Lynch didn't arrive at the ER until over two hours later and Kendra was filled with relief when she saw him get off the elevator and come toward her. "Pauley is going to be fine," she told him quickly. "Though they're not going to let him leave here for a few days. I tried to reach you but you weren't answering your phone."

"I was doing a little research," Lynch said. "Something occurred to me that I'd run across a couple of times in the past and I decided I had to check it out."

She was frowning. "That had to do with what happened to Pauley?"

"Probably not. But one thing led to another." He took a step closer and examined the bandage on her throat. "And this?"

"Just a bruise."

"You've been taking a beating on this case."

"I'm still standing."

"Has Perry or Breen been here?"

"Yes, I called Perry as soon as I got here and gave him a complete report…just as I told you I would. That garage should be crawling with the police as well as FBI by now."

He touched the bandage. "What did Perry say when he saw this?"

"What could he say? I survived it, didn't I?" She shrugged. "Did you expect him to assign one of his men to permanently follow me around? He's already gone that route. Not at all practical." She suddenly grinned. "Much more reasonable for us to bring the bastard down ourselves, don't you think?"

"Do you expect me to disagree with you?" Lynch asked.

"Anyway, Perry is here right now. I'm giving him a few minutes alone with Pauley before I go in."

"Good. I saw a coffee machine down the hall. I think we could both use some." He went to the machine and got them each a cup of coffee. "Shall we go for a stroll?" He handed her a cup. "Because I was dead serious about not being able to go through a day like this again."

She took a sip of her coffee. "So you're all set to give me hell?"

"I'm all set to find a way to stop that agony in its tracks no matter what it takes. As you know, I can be very innovative."

"Yes, you can. I've seen you in action." She took another sip of coffee. "But you told me there would be no more threats and I trust you. So it would be interesting to see how you're going to accomplish it."

"With a good deal of trepidation." He was scanning her face. "And I'll have to be very clever."

"More than you know. But you're lucky I'm feeling very mellow at the moment. If you'd have let me speak rather than jumping into battle, you wouldn't have had to go into all this stern crap. I fully intended to talk to you. When I was crawling around in that garage, I thought I might not ever see you alive again." She looked down into her cup and said simply, "And I thought that if I didn't, it would break my heart. You might have noticed I have a few problems with maintaining my independence."

"What, you?" he said gently. "Say it isn't so."

"I don't promise I'll change. I don't know if I can. I don't know if I'll even want to." She stared him in the eye. "But I'll never do anything that will put you in danger or do anything that will give you reason to come after me as you did today. That's all I could think of. When I was trying to get away from that bastard, I realized you'd probably come after me. I should have thought longer and harder before I went down there without calling you. It won't happen again because I won't risk your life as well as my own. That's as much as I can promise you. Is it enough?"

He brushed his lips across her nose. "That was very generous. Yes, for the time being. We'll work on the rest later."

She looked teasingly up at him from beneath her lashes. "I thought it was exceptionally generous. Don't be selfish, Lynch."

He sighed. "Never satisfied." He took her hand. "Take me to Pauley's room. I know he'll be glad to see me."

"Maybe." Her hand tightened on his. Together. And he felt so alive that she didn't ever want to let him go. "We'll have to talk about that bastard who hurt him after he sees that I'm safe and sound."

"Kendra! Lynch!" Pauley was elevated in his hospital bed and looked surprisingly spry considering what he'd just been through. His face was bruised, and his neck was wrapped in a white bandage much like Kendra's. His face fell when he saw her throat. "Oh, God. I'm so sorry. I didn't know what I was bringing you into."

She approached the bed and rubbed his arm. "Are you kidding? You're a hero, Pauley. You warned me about that psycho, and you almost got yourself killed doing it."

Perry stepped out from a corner. "That's what I told him. I haven't been able to get much from this guy. All he wanted to talk about is you and how you were doing."

Kendra's hand went to her neck bandage. "I'm fine, Pauley. I'm already up and around, and they're letting me go home."

Pauley clicked his tongue. "Which is more than I can say. I'm stuck in here for another couple of days, at least."

"We heard. I'm sorry, but this is the best place for you right now."

Pauley turned toward Lynch. "I'm glad you're here to look after her, Mr. Lynch."

Lynch smiled. "You know Kendra. She's pretty good at looking after herself. She got in some licks with that rebar leaning against the wall of the garage."

Pauley chuckled. "I've been on those construction guys to get that stuff the hell out of my garage. I'm sure glad they didn't."

"Me and you both," Kendra said. "Listen, Pauley...you're the only one to have gotten a good look at this guy. This could be a killer that's been wanted for over fifteen years. I'm sure Detective Perry has told you all this."

Pauley nodded. "He did. It scares me to think what could have happened today."

"We're going to make sure it never happens again. Can you give us a description?"

Perry raised his notebook. "I got one from him. Dark hair, brown eyes, bushy eyebrows, full lips, chiseled cheekbones, dimple in his chin. He says he's sure he can ID the guy if he ever sees him again. A sketch artist is already on the way."

"I've got a better sketch artist," Kendra said.

Perry put away his notebook. "Are you talking about Bill Dillingham? He's, what, a hundred years old now?"

"He's eighty-eight. Don't be ageist. I guarantee you that he's a better sketch artist than whoever you're bringing in."

"Well, our department is going to want our guy to do a sketch no matter what."

"Fine." Kendra turned to Pauley. "You won't mind working with my friend after the police officer comes up with a sketch, will you?"

"Nah, it's fine. Not like I got anything else to do in here."

"We don't want to tire him out," Perry said. "The FBI may want to have their own sketch artist come here."

"No, they won't." Kendra shook her head. "Not after they've seen Bill's sketch. They'll know they can't do any better."

"You're pretty sure of yourself," Perry said.

"I'm sure of Bill Dillingham. And you should be, too. But in the end, it may be tough to get a usable sketch no matter who draws it."

"What makes you say that?" Lynch said.

Kendra stepped back so she could speak to all three men at once. "The guy in the garage was wearing a disguise."

"How do you know?" Perry said. "You said it was too dark for you to see him."

"It was."

He smiled. "I'm starting to get the hang of this now. I take it that you heard or smelled something."

"Smelled."

"And what, exactly, did you smell?"

"Ben Nye prosthetic adhesive. When he had me in that choke hold, I was close enough to get a good whiff. It's used by everybody from high school drama clubs to Broadway stars to attach fake noses, chin pieces, ears, you name it. That guy was wearing a facial disguise, and it was good enough that Pauley saw him from a couple of feet away and couldn't tell." She turned back to Pauley. "Could you?"

He shook his head. "No."

"Do your best with the sketch artists anyway," Kendra said. "Bill is especially good at coming up with alternatives that account for disguises the perps may have used."

Pauley looked slightly dazed. "Will do."

She patted his knee. "Take care, Pauley. We'll be back to visit you soon."

---

Kendra and Lynch hadn't quite reached the elevator when Perry called from down the hall. "Kendra?"

They both turned.

"There's something else I wanted to talk to you about," he said. "We extracted a good DNA sample from that tooth you knocked out, and we ran it through CODIS."

Kendra looked at him excitedly. "Did you get a hit?"

"Of sorts."

"What does that mean?"

Perry glanced around to make sure they were out of earshot of the workers and visitors. "The sample came back as 'expunged.'"

"Expunged? As in deleted?"

"Yes. It happens occasionally."

Lynch nodded. "Often for juvenile offenders who have finished their sentences, or for innocent suspects in closed cases. Sometimes law-enforcement agencies remove it automatically, sometimes people have to petition to have their DNA samples removed from the database."

"Well, who pulled it?"

Perry shrugged. "We have no way of knowing that. We tried running it again, and this time it didn't come back at all. So it looks like someone just deleted the record in the past few days. Our people did some searching to see if any petitions for removal were filed and executed recently, but so far we haven't come up with anything. We'll keep looking, though."

Kendra bit her lip in frustration. "Thanks, Perry."

"Sure. I'll be in touch." Perry headed back to Pauley's room.

Kendra turned to Lynch. "That isn't the news I was hoping for."

"Well, there's still hope. The vast majority of our citizens don't have a DNA record at all. This guy, whoever he is, has one somewhere."

"Who do you think would be able to pluck it out of the database?"

Lynch thought for a moment. "Someone in law enforcement would have the easiest time. There are all kinds of ways that DNA and biometric records can be erased. When I worked for the FBI, my DNA and fingerprints were on file. But when I started doing my special projects..."

"That sounds so much nicer than *black ops assignments*."

"Thanks, I'm glad you approve. Anyway, my DNA and biometric records were immediately deleted from every database. There are all sorts of reasons why it can happen. But I'm willing to bet they're still on file somewhere at MI6 and Mossad. I'll ask around and see what I can find out about this DNA profile that was just deleted."

Kendra nodded. "Listen, maybe we can go talk to Todd Williams again."

"You think he has more to say?"

"Maybe. Let's tell him about this and see if it shakes any more thoughts loose."

"One thing," Lynch said. "We'll have to do something with Harley."

"What do you mean?"

"I picked him up on the way to the hospital."

"He's here?"

"Yes. It's cool out, so I figured there would be no harm. There's something vaguely sacrilegious about a hundred-pound dog slobbering in the backseat of a Lamborghini, but I promised Olivia we'd take him with us as your personal protector."

"Hmm. I guess she thought you weren't enough."

"Apparently not."

They walked to the hospital parking garage, where Harley seemed perfectly content in the backseat of Lynch's car.

After Kendra and Lynch climbed inside, the dog happily lapped up the fresh water Kendra poured for him. Kendra then called Williams. After a one-minute conversation, she hung up and turned to Lynch. "He wasn't exactly cordial, but he didn't seem to be surprised to hear from me. I told him we'd be bringing Harley and be knocking on his door within fifteen minutes." She turned to the backseat and patted Harley's head. "You remember your manners, young man. I'd like to make a good impression. He's been trying to help us find the sisters. We definitely need some answers." She glanced at Lynch. "And we may need all the help we can get. When I mentioned I was bringing Harley with me, Williams said it sounded like an excellent idea."

Lynch nodded. "Another person who probably thinks this animal will help keep you safe."

She nodded. "Well, a man with Williams' contacts should have an idea what was going on in the local law-enforcement community."

"Perhaps not only in this city," Lynch said. "Do you want me to do the questioning of Williams?"

She shook her head. "When we spoke to him, I had a feeling that Williams trusted me. I think I'd have a better chance of getting information. But you're welcome to come along and chime in if you like."

He shook his head. "I've never been good at chiming." He grinned. "But it was a generous offer and I'm duly appreciative."

She made a face at him. "At least I'm making the effort to keep my promise."

He nodded gravely. "And with practice it might even come naturally to you. I look forward to it. But until that happy day, I don't want to put any undue stress on you. So Harley and I will sit on his front porch and wait until you finish your discussion with Williams while keeping a watchful eye on you in deference to our Olivia. Okay?"

She nodded. "Except I think you're enjoying this a little too much."

"Possibly."

They parked in front of Williams' home, and Lynch sat in a porch rocking chair and pulled the dog down beside him. "I feel I deserve this considering the morning I had. What do you think?"

She nodded slowly. "Don't rub it in. I told you it's not going to happen again."

"Absolutely not. So run along and grill Williams. Harley and I will be fine dozing here on the porch."

"I shouldn't be long." She was already heading for the front door. "I'm sure Harley will keep you entertained. But neither one of you really likes to do much dozing, do you?"

"Life's too short," Lynch said quietly. "I hate to waste the time. But then I've noticed, neither do you." He waved her toward the door. "Let's get this over with. Harley is getting restless."

"Heaven forbid," she said as she knocked on the door. "We wouldn't want that to happen."

Apparently it wasn't going to happen, because Todd Williams was impatiently throwing open the door. "Ah, there's the dog," he said as he peered out on the sunporch. "Rather strange-looking creature, isn't he? One blue eye and one brown eye? Is he a competent guard dog?"

"My friend believes he's very competent, and I haven't

heard any complaints," Kendra said. "He's very loving, and that's what is important to her."

"But it might not be the most important thing for you to consider," Williams said grimly. "In the brief time I've known you, you've appeared to be surrounded by violence. That was why I asked a few of my friends in the police force to keep me informed if you appeared to be having any more problems. I admit I was relieved when you told me about the dog."

"Relieved?" Kendra repeated. "Lending me Harley was my friend's idea, but it's not as if I go around asking for trouble. It's just been a very upsetting time in all our lives. But while we're talking about it, when I first met you it was clear that even you were frightened by the fact that Chloe and Sloane Morgan were missing. Isn't that true?"

He didn't answer for a moment. "I can't deny I was concerned."

"Why should you deny it?" Kendra asked. "You cared about them. They seemed to be wonderful young women. I wanted to do everything I could to bring them home to the people who cared about them. I thought we were on the same page."

"We were," Williams said. "But you can understand that I didn't want to involve anyone else in my personal business. I certainly didn't want to involve you in that madness, too. Particularly when you were displaying signs that you might be a little too impulsive for my taste. I was beginning to feel guilty."

She shook her head in bewilderment. "Why? I'm a professional. I've made it my job to try to find them. My problem was that I wasn't sure you were telling us all we should know about their disappearance." She looked him in the eye. "Were you?"

Williams hesitated. "I tried to keep you safe just as I always tried to keep them safe. I learned from experience that that sometimes means not telling quite everything I know. It's not always safe." He shrugged. "Because it's a world full of secrets and you don't want to try to look too deep into them. You can never tell when you'll stumble over one that's particularly dangerous."

"That's not really an answer."

"That's all you're going to get from me right now." He smiled. "I'll let you know more when I believe it's safe. I like you and I trust you. I promise you'll be one of the first I'll go to."

"I don't like this." She was frowning. "I want to know more and I don't like the fact that you're not really telling me anything." She had another thought. "Will you be safe?"

He chuckled. "I've spent most of my life taking care of myself. Yes, I'll be safe."

"One more question."

"Yes?"

She told him about her attacker's deleted DNA file, and he suddenly became very quiet. "What do you think of that?" she finally asked.

"Don't know," he said, obviously still thinking about it. "That might be something for your friend Mr. Lynch to look into."

She wrinkled her brow. "What makes you say that?"

He opened the front door. "Now go out on the porch and collect your dog and Lynch and take care of both of them. That's the only thing you have to worry about at the moment." He gave her a gentle push toward the porch. "And tell Lynch to keep an eye on you and not rely solely on that huge dog."

"This isn't the end," she said impatiently over her shoulder. "I'm going to get those answers, Williams. It's not fair for you to keep silent. Once you think about it, I hope you'll agree with me."

"Well, I know you'll persist until I don't have a choice." He added gently, "Be safe, Kendra." He shut the front door.

# CHAPTER 13

Kendra sat silently in the passenger seat of Lynch's Lamborghini with her fists still clenched. Lynch looked over at her as he turned off Williams' street. "No good?" he asked quietly. "You look a bit frustrated."

"In spades." She looked out the passenger side window. "He knows something. He probably knows a lot but he gave me some balderdash about not revealing secrets and taking care of the people close to him. He even included some protective nonsense about taking care of me. He wouldn't listen when I told him I was a professional and didn't need his help."

"Imagine that." He smiled. "So are you going to try again, or are you going to let me help?"

"You know what I want to do." She turned toward him. "But that's not fair to you. So I'm going to tell you everything that he said to me and we're going to work on it together."

"Amazing," he said.

"And you will not try to shut me out. Or protect me."

"That I won't promise. That might be self-destructive," he added. "We'll see how it goes. But we'll work on this together and I'll do my best to keep you firmly in the loop." He shot her a glance. "I'll find a way to get Williams to tell us what he's been hiding. I have a few ideas in that direction. Is that a good start?"

"It's a good start," she said. He knew it was and he wasn't trying to make it difficult for her. Nothing he'd done today had been anything but helpful. "Do you want me to begin telling you what Williams said now?"

He shook his head. "It will wait until tonight. Relax and take care of the pup."

She suddenly chuckled and reached to pet Harley in the backseat. "That's what Williams said. He told me taking care of the pup and you was all that was necessary."

"Then he's even smarter than I thought. But I still think we can go back and lean on him," Lynch said. "I can be extremely persuasive when the situation demands it."

"He's a retired police detective, not some thug you can threaten within an inch of his life."

"I know several police detectives who are thugs. And a few heads of state who fall into that category, too."

"I'm sure you do, but I have a more civilized idea."

"It won't be nearly as fun."

"Reserve that fun for third-world dictatorships. Right now, I need to know if you still have Chloe Morgan's phone location map for the last couple of weeks."

"I do. And not just a photograph of it."

"What do you mean?"

Lynch shrugged. "The police sent a copy of her phone map data to the FBI in Washington."

"Ah. And once it went there, of course it was just a hop, skip, and a jump back to you."

"Is it so bad that I have friends in high places?"

"In this case, no. Because I'd like you to use it to see if she visited Todd Williams in the past couple of weeks. I'm still suspicious of the fact that there isn't an updated file for him when she created one for everyone else she and her sister were recently in touch with."

Lynch pulled over, parked his car, and picked up his phone. "Let's see what this can tell us." His fingers glided over the phone screen. "Just a matter of superimposing the tracked locations over the map again..." He concentrated on the screen. "Okay, it looks like Chloe may have made a stop in Todd Williams' neighborhood three days before her disappearance."

"At his house?"

Lynch looked at the phone screen a moment longer. "Afraid not. A couple blocks away."

"Where?"

"Looks like a commercial building. I'll look it up." Lynch transposed the image over a map app and held up his phone to show Kendra. "Zeke's Coffee. I've never heard of it."

She squinted at the map. "Off the beaten track for Chloe. Not really her beat, if these other map stops are any indication. But this place does happen to be a favorite of Todd Williams."

Lynch stared at her. "How do you figure that?"

"We walked past his car on the way up his driveway.

There were at least six empty Zeke's coffee cups in the cup-holders and on the floor. I'd say it's a place he visits fairly often."

Lynch nodded. "And a place he might feel comfortable setting up a meeting." He put down his phone and shifted his car into gear. "Let's go."

"Wait. I don't think this is enough to start working your powers of persuasion on him."

"Neither do I. My powers will be far more useful somewhere else right now."

"Where?"

"Zeke's Coffee, of course."

---

A few minutes later, Kendra and Lynch walked into Zeke's Coffee, a charming neighborhood shop with well-worn furniture that looked as if it could have been purchased second-hand. Lynch glanced at Kendra and nodded his head toward a camera mounted high in the back corner.

Lynch immediately went to work, charming the barista and her manager with small talk. Kendra could hardly believe it as she watched him coax those workers into giving him what he wanted. She'd always been aware Lynch could be as hypnotic as a snake charmer when he made the effort, and he was definitely making the effort at the moment. It took him only another five minutes before the supervisor ushered them back to the office to show the security camera video files on a laptop.

Lynch gave the manager the day and time as noted on Chloe's phone's tracked location. Fortunately, the video files were stored for thirty days before being automatically erased, so it only took a minute for her to scan back to the exact moment that Lynch had requested. There, on the laptop screen, was a clear image of a young woman sitting at a round table near the door.

"That's Chloe," Kendra whispered.

A moment later, a tall figure entered the shop, momentarily silhouetted by the bright sunlight outside. As the door swung closed behind him, the figure came into view.

It was retired detective Todd Williams.

He joined Chloe at her table as he looked at some documents she had spread in front of her. After a few moments, he folded up the papers and leaned close and spoke to her again, as if whispering. He stood and quickly left the shop.

Kendra and Lynch stared at the screen for a moment longer, watching as Chloe made a quick phone call, then stood and walked out the door.

Lynch turned and thanked the coffee shop employees for their assistance. He leaned toward Kendra. "I think we're done here," he murmured. "Unless there's something else you want to see."

"No," Kendra said. "Let's get out of here."

They left the shop through the same door they'd watched Chloe and Williams use. "I have a feeling that your reality distortion field is already starting to wear off on those people. They're realizing they've been conned. Is that why you didn't ask for a copy of the video?"

"Have you no faith?" Lynch asked. "My phone interfaced with their laptop and downloaded the video file as we were watching it."

"Naturally," Kendra said.

"And as far as their willingness to help me goes, you've

just seen a prime example of a citizen trying to maintain her basic freedoms with our humble help."

"Humble?" Kendra repeated. "There was nothing humble about that display. It was pure camp and bull."

"But effective," Lynch said. "It showed us that Williams was lying when he said he hadn't seen Chloe or Sloane in years." He led her toward his Lamborghini. "However, it's only fair that you do your share to help out on the next bit of business. In the name of our partnership, of course. It's the way that we should handle this."

"What bit of business?" she asked warily.

"To Williams' house for a pointed discussion with him."

"I thought you were confident that your powers of persuasion—or bullying—would work with him."

"Part of that ability is knowing the best approach to apply in any given situation. And I could see that you made a much more favorable impression on Williams than I did. You're clearly the best one to talk to him about his rather obvious lie. I'll wait outside again." He tilted his head. "Make sense?"

She sighed. "Yes. I'll talk to him. But I still think the staff of that coffee shop is already seeing through your bullshit."

---

Five minutes later, Kendra left Todd Williams' house and walked toward Lynch.

"That was quick," he said. "Did Williams throw you out on your ear?"

"No. He isn't there. I spoke to a very nice maid who cleans his house once every two weeks. She said he packed his bags and left town about an hour ago."

"What?"

"You heard me. He left behind a note saying he wouldn't be needing her services until his return at some unspecified future date."

"Suspicious timing," Lynch said. "This leaves us with zilch, unless you let me go and take a look around and see if Williams might have left something in the house that gives us a helpful clue. Naturally I'd be careful not to disturb anything that might fall in the category of evidence tampering."

"And end up in jail? There are laws, Lynch."

"And you desperately want to find those sisters before they end up victims."

"Yes, I do. I'll think about it. Maybe I can persuade Williams to talk to me when he comes back home."

"My way would be much more efficient," Lynch said.

"No, it wouldn't," she said absently. "Actually, if someone was going to break in and look around, it should be me. I'd be much better at it than you. I'd see more."

"No," Lynch said definitely. "Hell, no. I'm sorry I even mentioned it. Never. Get it out of your head. If that's possible. Never you. Understand?"

"I understand." She shook her head and smiled faintly. "I'm wondering if you do. Since you see nothing wrong with bringing down governments and yet you won't let me do a little minor burglary."

"Which you were horrified to contemplate when I was doing the breaking and entering."

"I had to get used to the idea. First, I'd have to work around the concept to make it both palatable and maybe even virtuous."

He shook his head. "Never. But we might be able to

track him through his phone. I'll reach out to one of my connections."

"Good." She thought for a moment. "In the meantime, we might have something even better."

"What's that?" Lynch said.

"You said you had appropriated a copy of that coffeehouse security camera video."

Lynch nodded. "I did. It's in my phone and my cloud account. But I don't know if it shows us anything other than that Williams actually met with Chloe in the days before she went missing."

"It might show us more."

He cocked an eyebrow. "What do you mean?"

"When I first got my sight, one of the most amazing things to me was seeing how the movements of lips, tongue, and teeth corresponded with the sounds of speech I'd been hearing all my life. It fascinated me. So I've gotten to be a pretty good lip-reader."

"I've seen you do it. But do you think you can read their lips on that?"

"I'm not sure. It needs to be on a much bigger screen for me to even try."

"How big?"

"Well, I have those big monitors in my studio."

"Those are, what, seventy inches?"

"Yes. Shall we go take a look?"

"Actually...I just had the system in my house upgraded. I have a hundred-inch 8K monitor in my basement. It's connected to a state-of-the-art video processor to enhance anything I play on it. Maybe we can go there."

"A hundred inches? You play Xbox on that thing?"

"I could, if I ever had the time. Anyway, it's very impressive."

"I have no doubt. Okay, let's give it a shot."

---

They drove to Lynch's large Tudor-style home in an upscale neighborhood north of the city. As beautiful as the house was, Lynch had it built as a steel-reinforced bunker of sorts, with bulletproof windows and walls that could withstand a grenade blast. Lynch had made many enemies over the years, both domestic and foreign, and he often said that his house was the one place on Earth where he could totally relax.

Kendra's eyes widened at the sight of his backyard, visible through a row of floor-to-ceiling windows. The yard seemed to be four or five times its former size, with a gargantuan pool and several elaborate rock formations. She stepped outside through the towering back doors. "When did you do this?"

"Just in the past few weeks. I like to have my renovations done when I know I'm going to be out of town."

"Unbelievable...But where did all this extra space come from?"

"I bought a few of the lots around mine."

"And tore down the houses? Those weren't exactly tear-downs."

"They were when I got through with them."

"Amazing. This is like...an incredible resort. I could go on a two-week vacation here."

Lynch smiled. "I wish you would. But I had more work done downstairs. Come see."

Kendra followed Lynch downstairs to a large room that

had completely changed since the last time she'd seen it. Before, she had teased him about having an upscale sports bar in his basement, with half a dozen televisions and a mahogany-trimmed pool table dominating the room. Now there was the massive flatscreen monitor, a long table, and several leather chairs.

Kendra laughed out loud. "Now it looks like the White House situation room."

Lynch smiled. "I can't win with you. When I'm being briefed on assignments, I find it very useful for teleconferences, graphics, and satellite imagery."

"I was joking. So this *is* a situation room, isn't it?"

He shrugged. "I guess it is. But today it's your lip-reading studio. Shall we give it a shot?"

Lynch picked up a touchscreen remote and powered up his system. He pulled out his phone, found the video, and selected it. The gigantic screen flickered, and after a moment the coffeehouse video began. Chloe was sitting alone at her table.

"What do you think?" Lynch asked.

Kendra stepped closer to the screen. "Is there any way you can...sharpen it?"

Lynch tapped his fingers over his remote touchscreen. "How about this?"

The video suddenly became much more clear, with each detail dramatically increasing in definition.

Kendra stepped even closer. "This is great." She pointed at the screen. "This customer just ordered a cinnamon latte."

"You could read her lips?" Lynch asked.

"Yes, no problem. She's closer to the camera than Chloe

and Todd Williams will be, but I think they'll still be close enough." Kendra pointed to the screen again. "The customer now wants to know why they don't have stevia sweetener anymore."

Lynch laughed. "Now you're just showing off."

"Maybe a little. Oh, Williams is coming in now."

They both looked at the screen as Williams walked in and took his seat at the table. Chloe shifted and turned slightly away from the camera to face him.

"Oh, no," Lynch said. "We have a good shot of Williams' lips, but you may have problems reading her from the side."

"You're right. I can probably pick up some of what she's saying, but not everything." Kendra squinted at the screen. "Wait, can you zoom in a bit?"

Lynch pinched the screen of his remote, enlarging Chloe and Williams on the large monitor screen.

Kendra smiled. "Look at the framed print on the wall between them."

Lynch leaned closer. "Chloe's reflection...Can you tell what she's saying?"

"Yes. Almost everything! Rewind to where he first comes in." As Lynch scanned back a few seconds, Kendra activated the recording app on her phone and dictated her reading of the conversation. "Okay, Williams just apologized for being late. He was waiting on a phone call...Chloe says that he scared the hell out of her in their conversation the day before."

"Those exact words?" Lynch said.

Kendra nodded. "He says he's sorry. But they—and her sister—need to be careful right now." Kendra watched closely. On the larger screen, it was easier to see the tension written on their faces. "Okay, she just asked him, how long did he know about...the Dayton Group."

"The Dayton Group? That's the name of the outfit that rented the Baum house."

"Can you go back fifteen seconds?"

Lynch tapped his touchscreen remote again and moved his finger across it. The last few seconds of the video replayed.

Kendra nodded. "The Dayton Group. I'm sure that's what she said. Anyway, Williams says he heard rumors back in the day, but he wanted to tell her and Sloane..."

"Tell them what?"

Kendra didn't respond, instead focusing on Williams' lips. His hand moved in front of his mouth for a moment, but she managed to get most of what he was saying. "He says he wasn't sure if the rumors were true, and if they were, it could be dangerous for the sisters if they started asking around about it."

Chloe leaned forward, and she spoke with such force that it became very easy to read her words. "She's asking him what the plan is. She says she's not stopping now. And Williams says she couldn't stop if she wanted to. That ship has sailed. He needs her to trust him, let him do the asking around. He says he should have done it years ago. He says he has a plan. It's going to be okay. He wants her and Sloane to wait for his call and be ready to go at a moment's notice."

Sloane nodded, and Williams stood and left the shop. She left a few moments later.

Kendra turned toward Lynch. "That's it. Williams was investigating something, and he wanted to protect the sisters."

"It appears he may have planned to hide them someplace."

Lynch thought for a moment. "But it's hard to say if he did that before somebody else got to them first. We need to find him."

Kendra nodded. "And find out what in the hell the Dayton Group is. I suggest that we go to see Breen and tell him about what we saw at the coffee shop. Maybe he can help track down Williams and ask him the questions he wouldn't answer for us. I'm tired of everyone being so careful and tactful with Williams."

"I can see you are," Lynch said. "And if it will keep you from butting heads with Breen or Williams, I'll be glad to take you to visit Breen right now. By all means let's go and see if Breen or Perry will pull a few strings with Williams' cell phone carrier. It might be faster than waiting on my contact."

She made a face. "As long as I don't insist on breaking into Williams' home and scouting around a bit?"

"That goes without saying. I refuse to break you out of jail unless absolutely necessary. And then I get to choose the country to offer you sanctuary. Be content with what you've got, Kendra."

"I'm content...most of the time. That was just a wild thought that occurred to me. I was very frustrated at the time." She grinned. "Besides, you amused me. I couldn't resist."

"A very wild thought. Try to contain them when you're talking to Breen. I haven't noticed that he has a great sense of humor. And perhaps we don't mention the Dayton Group until I've had a chance to make some inquiries of my own."

By the time they got through talking to Breen an hour later Kendra was so exasperated she wanted to kick him. Always before he'd treated her with at least a modicum of courtesy. Today he wasn't even listening to them when they began to talk about Williams and suggest Breen should try to find him.

She was barely able to contain herself as they left the station.

"Did you hear him?" she asked Lynch as she got into the car and slammed the door. "He practically accused me of being an amateur. I'd wager that I've closed more murder cases than he has."

"I'd bet on it."

"He thought I may have misunderstood what Williams was trying to tell me. I expected him to pat me on the head and send me to my room any minute."

"I heard him," Lynch said. "I was waiting for the explosion. I tried to intercede but I couldn't get a word in edgewise. You get very pissed off when someone tries to protect you."

"Don't be ridiculous. I promised you I wouldn't let him irritate me," she said through bared teeth. "And the jackass wasn't attacking your credibility. You were obviously golden as far as he was concerned."

"Should I go back and challenge him to a duel?" Lynch asked. "I'll find a way of punishing him." His voice was lazy but Kendra could detect the subtle underlying menace she had heard many times before. "It would be a pleasure. I promise you."

"No, I'll fight my own battles," Kendra said.

"That's what I thought." Lynch started the car. "You're no fun at all, Kendra."

"Evidently Breen didn't think so, either. I'll have to find a way of convincing him. Or maybe I'll just stick with Perry from now on."

"I'm always at your service," Lynch said. "Are you ready to go back to the condo now?"

"It might be a good idea." She was mentally going over options. "I believe we should do some checking of our own since we've come up with zeros as far as Breen and his cohorts are concerned. I put in a call to Metcalf to see if he has an update for me. Maybe he can help us track Williams down."

"By all means." Lynch was grinning. "Hunt the poor man down. I almost feel sorry for him."

She suddenly stiffened. "Look, I have nothing against Williams. I'd feel sorry for him if he'd just been open and aboveboard with us. But right now I'm only feeling sorry for those two women and I want to know everything I can about why they disappeared. Did I amuse you?"

"Not a bit." He took her hand and gently squeezed it. "There are times when you do terrify me, but there will never be a time when I don't appreciate who and what you are and delight in every moment. I thought you'd realize that by now. I certainly don't make a secret of it."

"You can be difficult."

"So can you. But I wouldn't have it any other way. I'd be bored shitless."

He was staring into her eyes, and she found she couldn't look away. "So would I." She reached for her phone. "I should probably try to call Olivia."

"Coward." His tone was softly jeering. "You almost made it home this time. Next time for certain."

She was already dialing. "Do you have any message for her?"

"Not at the moment," Lynch said. "I'm certain she'll make all her needs known when we arrive. She's never shy about doing that. But I'm even more interested in hearing you talk to Metcalf so that I can observe your technique in getting him to locate Williams for us. I admit I'm looking forward to it. I always enjoy watching how eager he is to please you."

She frowned. "You should enjoy it. He's just a nice, helpful guy trying to do his job."

Lynch grinned again. "And trying desperately to impress you."

"I don't see why you'd find that interesting."

"Maybe I just feel it's my duty to always be on guard when he's around."

"On guard? That doesn't make sense."

"It makes perfect sense to me. But then you've never realized how possessive I can be. Even if I don't see a definite threat, I tend to want to be sure that none exists. I suppose it's the way I was trained in black ops."

She shook her head. "I think you're joking."

"Do you? Maybe I am. Or maybe I'm not." He smiled. "But at any rate, I'm surprised it's taken Metcalf this long to call you back. He usually—" Lynch looked down at her buzzing phone. "Yes, there's your phone ringing. He's calling you back. I'm sure he'll try his very best to give you whatever he can." He leaned back in his chair. "I promise I'll be quiet as a mouse."

"Damn you." She was tempted to throw something at him. But it wasn't fair to keep Metcalf waiting when she'd placed the call to him for information. "Hello, Metcalf. It's wonderful of you to help me out."

"Sure, Kendra. Anytime!"

He did sound eager. She was glad she hadn't put him on speaker. "Did you find out anything about where Williams was supposed to have gone for the weekend? I have a few follow-up questions."

"Like what?"

"Like maybe some more detail on the threads that the Morgan sisters were pulling at."

"It's just that I detect some urgency in your voice. Are you worried about him for some reason?"

Kendra sighed. "Listen, if you weren't able to find anything out, don't worry about it. I didn't think you'd reveal anything to me if the Bureau didn't approve. I know what a straight arrow you are."

Lynch was yawning.

Yes, she definitely wanted to throw something at him.

"No," Metcalf said. "I'll give you what I have." He filled her in on the info he'd gathered. Not that there was very much to it. He'd talked to a helpful neighbor of Williams and been given basically the same information she already had. He was obviously regretful and told her he'd check back in the next day or so. But since there had been no sign of foul play he was fairly confident that Williams was just on a short vacation and they would be able to reach him as soon as he returned. Then he added hesitantly, "Have you checked in with Lynch? It goes without saying that he has some pretty great sources."

"No, I'm afraid he was no help at all," she said curtly,

as she looked at Lynch. "Sometimes he can be difficult. But thanks for your suggestions. You've been very kind."

"My pleasure. I'll be in touch as soon as I hear something."

"Thanks again, Metcalf." She hung up the phone and looked at Lynch. "He told me basically the same thing as that maid. Williams took off in his tan Toyota and he'll be back in a few days."

"Poor Metcalf. I'm sure he's doing everything in his power to impress you, so we could have some results there yet."

---

They arrived at Kendra's condo to find Olivia there, rubbing Harley's belly while *House Hunters* played on the television.

"Hey," Olivia said, "I thought we agreed you were taking Harley everywhere."

"It wasn't possible," Kendra said. "We were at a coffee shop where our four-legged friends weren't welcome. But fear not, Lynch magnificently stepped up in his place."

"Hmm. I'll take your word for that. If I hadn't heard HGTV blaring from your apartment, I never would have known he was here. So where are you in your investigation now?"

Lynch sighed. "Right now, we're trying to find retired detective Todd Williams if we have to search the entire city. He may have some information for us."

"As you can see, Lynch has made himself part of the investigation," Kendra said.

"Good," Olivia said as she stood on the other side of the room. She faced Lynch dead-on. "You and Harley both, right?"

"Yes. He'll be with us from now on. I promise."

"Good," Olivia said. "I trust you. Which is saying a lot after you ended up in that garage and almost got Kendra killed."

"That wasn't his fault," Kendra said quickly. "It was mine."

"Then prove it." Olivia held out Harley's leash to Lynch. "Keep her safe."

"Yes, ma'am." He took the leash. "As you command."

"Damn right," Olivia said. She walked to the front door. "Let me know what's happening, okay?"

"You bet," Lynch said. "I'm already hearing from Kendra's fan club, but there can't be too many." He stepped ahead of her and opened the door. "We'll see you tomorrow, Olivia."

She nodded. "Yes, you will. Count on it."

Kendra frowned thoughtfully as Lynch walked back toward her. "You know, Metcalf was probably right about there not being any real threat to Williams. I guess that's just where my mind is going these days. I've been too worried about the disappearance of those Morgan sisters. But the maid said he appeared to be cheerful, and he paid her before he left that morning."

"Money in your pocket can make you very cheerful indeed," Lynch said. "But that doesn't mean we can't find a way to make sure that you get what we need from him tomorrow when we run him down."

"But was he alone in the car ?" Kendra asked again.

"As far as she could tell," Lynch said. "Like I said, he was cheerful and if you're talking about whether he was being trailed by some creep like the one that murdered that girl in the park the other day, it's extremely doubtful. There was no real sign he was being followed and the Bayside Strangler was probably a freak of nature and possibly a copycat. The maid just thought he was going away for a trip and would return in a few days. Like I said, I'll make sure that we know more details tomorrow. Okay?"

"I don't see why not. Though it seems you're being very helpful for a change. Are you sure you're feeling well?"

"I suppose I have to straighten out my reputation after you falsely maligned me to Metcalf. This is only the first installment." He gave her a light kiss on the cheek. "More tomorrow. I'm going to get a glass of wine. Do you want one?"

She shook her head. "Not right now. Maybe later." She watched him cross to the bar. He was being exceptionally kind; maybe he was trying to erase the tension that she'd been aware of in the car. Or maybe those moments were his way of distracting her. How could she be certain with someone like Lynch? He was an enigma.

Whatever was true, it didn't matter. Not now. She watched him at the bar for an instant and then moved past him toward her bedroom. "I wanted to thank you for trying to take the blame for drawing you down to that garage. We both know whose fault it was."

"Yes, we do, and it won't happen again. But I won't have Olivia blaming you. It was a bad enough day for you." He glanced over his shoulder. "Where are you going?"

"The terrace. I thought I'd get a breath of fresh air."

He shook his head. "Wait for me to go out with you. Give me five minutes so I can have a quick shower, okay?"

"Whatever you say. But it's really not necessary, Lynch."

"Both Harley and his mistress would disagree." He was already heading toward her bathroom. "Five minutes," he repeated.

She watched him disappear around the corner. He was everything she wanted. Why not reach out and take it, she wondered suddenly. Take what she wanted. To hell with it being wise or cautious. It wasn't as if he didn't want her. He'd shown her that the need was as strong as it had been all during their time together. She was the one who had always hesitated and set up boundaries. Lord, she was tired of those boundaries.

Five minutes...

---

She could see Lynch's shadow on the other side of the shower door and instinctively tensed. It had been more than five minutes and he was probably making judgments and trying to decide what she was doing.

"Stop dithering. It should all be fairly clear to you, Lynch," she said with sudden impatience. "The last time you invited me to step into your shower, I told you that I might change my mind about it later. Well, I've changed it. Pauley got in the way the last time. But that wasn't my fault."

"No, it wasn't your fault." He was laughing, and she could see his movements as she tore off her clothes and tossed them aside. "Though there might be a slight disagreement there. But I yield to your vision. And I certainly approve of your actions."

Then the shower door was opening, and she was in his arms.

Lord, he felt good. His muscles taut, his lips against her

throat, his hands on her breasts...She held him close while the warm water sprayed over them. "I missed you," she whispered. "I hated to leave you and I wanted to tell you that but I couldn't do it. It wouldn't have been fair to either of us. It would have interfered...We both have careers and it might get in the way. I knew you wouldn't understand."

"You'd be surprised how much I understand." His mouth was on her breast as he pushed her back against the tiles. She gasped as she felt his tongue. "Ah, that's what I wanted. And one of the things I understand is that sometimes you have lousy timing and it has to be corrected. So will you please shut up and let me do what we both want without arguing?" She was on the floor of the shower, her nails digging into the tiles and she groaned as he dove inside her. "That's better... so good...You're always so good to me. Now let me be good to you, Kendra...Let me go deep and deeper..."

She didn't know how many times she screamed as he held her there. She only knew she was limp and shaking with reaction when he finally released her and carried her from the shower to her bed and gently covered her with her blanket. He carefully started to dry her off.

"Something's wrong..." she managed to say as her hand touched the damp blanket. "Shouldn't be this..."

"Wet? You're absolutely right." He started to laugh. "My fault entirely. I admit to being distracted when you joined me in the shower. So distracted I completely ignored the fact that Harley followed you from the terrace. Somehow he stepped into the shower and sat on the other side without either of us noticing him." He gave her a quick kiss and pointed to Harley, who was lying at the foot of bed sopping wet and staring cheerfully back at them and definitely smelling of wet dog. "Not my best romantic moment," he said ruefully. "Maybe he was trying to protect you. Olivia would definitely approve. But then so do I. Don't move a muscle." He was off the bed and heading for the bathroom. "I'll be right back after I dry him off and clean up this bed."

Kendra watched him for a few moments and then got on her knees and started to help him. "I believe you're wrong. This may be one of your better moments." Then she cuddled closer to him. "And Harley is sure that it is. He recognizes kindness. That's why he's so fond of you." She pressed her lips in the hollow of his shoulder. "And though tonight reminded me of the time we spent in Spain, life can't always be like that. So just hold me and we'll worry about tomorrow, tomorrow. I didn't expect forever when I seduced you. I just wanted to touch and hold you. No strings. Okay?"

"Very much okay." He brushed his lips on her cheek as he drew her closer. "And your seduction was amazing. But we'll discuss strings at some later time when we don't have to worry about wet dogs and Todd Williams hiding out when I promised you I'd find him for you. I'll keep my word, Kendra."

"I know you will. Now hush. You were quite splendid and the only thing you have to do is hold me. That shouldn't be a bother for you."

"Not at all." He cleared his throat. "If you want anything else, feel free to call on me."

"I will." She was drifting off to sleep. "Because I always know I can trust you..."

Rod Wallace wasn't sure why he'd come here to Old Town San Diego. It was never a place that held much fascination for him, though it was popular with tourists and young barhoppers with its western-themed buildings, wooden sidewalks, and numerous bars and restaurants. Maybe it was because he'd missed being here all the years he'd been hiding out in Europe and he'd remembered how exciting and different he'd found those Saturday nights here when the entire town was crowded with people and noise and sometimes provided the blood sport Wallace liked most in the world.

He was driving an ancient Ford pickup truck he'd stolen from a farmer earlier in the day, and as he rolled past the packed bars, he realized that most of these people had no idea who he was and what he'd done. It was as if his mark on the city had entirely faded.

*Don't you realize how important I am?*

*Don't you remember pretty young Greta Waters and how the entire town mourned her?*

Ah, Greta Waters. She put up a good fight.

He parked the truck and walked down the crowded sidewalk.

*Because of me, everyone was so horrified and afraid. They knew then how important I was.*

*It's not right that you all just tossed me aside because I was forced to leave here. But I'm back now. You won't forget me again. I'll make sure that you won't make that mistake...*

His gaze was searching the crowds pouring out of the bars.

*But I should be careful to pick someone who reminds me of Greta and will also show you where your duty lies...*

Ah. He smiled as he caught a glimpse of a tall blond girl

by the door. A little drunk, but that would only make her more compliant.

Because now, Wallace knew exactly why he had come here tonight. That death in the park had only been a dress rehearsal for all the ones still to come. He'd been right to pay no attention to Krebb and his whining. This was what he was meant to do with Kendra and whomever else he chose. One might even call it...destiny.

The excitement was growing as he started striding across the bar toward this delicate-looking blonde who was to be his next adventure...

# CHAPTER 14

Kendra wriggled her toes. "Stop it. That tickles."

She opened her lids and gazed into Harley's blue-brown eyes nuzzling her right foot. The tickling didn't stop. "Stop it, Harley." He rolled over on his back and tossed his legs in the air and started to crawl up the bed toward her. "No, I don't think that's a good idea." It was then that she noticed the note fastened to her ankle. She reached down and unfastened it, opening the message.

It was a short note from Lynch.

*Good morning. As promised I got up early and started to search how to find Todd Williams. I believe I might have an idea or two. You were sleeping so beautifully, I thought I'd let you have a few more hours before I woke you. Though I was having trouble leaving you. You were fantastic...I shouldn't be more than a few hours. I gave Bill a call and you'll find him wandering around the halls, very proud of his fine gun and his duty of watching over you. All the doors are locked and you'll be very secure until I get back. Take care of Harley. Don't let him boss you around.*

*He shouldn't have done this*, she thought as she got out of bed and headed for the shower. It violated what she wanted in the relationship and he probably knew it. But face it, she'd been the one who had jumped in the shower and gone after Lynch. She had no right to complain. And at the moment, she had no desire to complain. Her body felt full, tingling, and he had also been fantastic. So accept it and just do the job and enjoy Lynch for this short time. She could straighten out anything else later. In the meantime she had to push Harley out of the shower and not let him back in until Lynch had returned to the condo.

"He told me not to let you boss me around," she said sternly as she stepped out of the stall. "But you're part of the team now, so it's not really bossing around. Let's just be buddies...Okay?"

---

Lynch didn't show up until almost two hours later, and by that time, Kendra had dressed, located Bill, and whisked him down to Olivia's condo for breakfast. Harley was beginning to get a little impatient.

"She's just fine," Bill said eagerly as soon as he caught sight of Lynch. "No problems, I took good care of her. Just like you said, Lynch. Everything went smooth as silk. Olivia just made us a great breakfast. Do you want me to get you a plate?"

"Not right now. I believe Kendra and I should get on the road. She's probably fairly impatient by now," Lynch said. "No doubt you've noticed that she doesn't like to wait around when there's a job to be done."

"Does anyone?" Kendra asked. "You ran out to do the same thing and left Bill and Olivia to take care of me as if I was a child in arms. Naturally I'm grateful, but I'm also ready to have it over." She tossed Harley's leash to Lynch. "Thanks for everything, Bill. We'll be in touch. You did a fine job." She gave Olivia a quick kiss on the cheek. "I'll let you know if we find out anything."

"Please do." Olivia gestured toward the door. "Can we talk outside for a minute?"

"Sure. Lynch and I were just about to—"

"Just you, okay?"

"Oh. Okay."

Kendra stepped into the hallway with Olivia and closed the door behind her.

"Look," Olivia began, "I know I've been hard on Lynch, and probably on you, too."

"A little. I thought you liked him."

"I *adore* him."

"So what's the deal?"

She paused to put her thoughts into words. "I've known you most of our lives, and there's never been a man better for you than Lynch. He's your perfect match, and I think deep down, you know that, and it scares the hell out of you."

"That's a little strong, don't you think?"

"Is it?"

Kendra didn't reply.

"Anyway," Olivia continued, "it's been keeping you at arm's length from him. He doesn't want to suffocate you, so he reciprocates by trying to give you room. Maybe too much room. Whatever I've said or done in the past few days, it's only been because I wanted you to realize how right you are for each other. Maybe I've been a little ham-fisted in my attempts, but you two can only play it cool for so long before you might just ruin a good thing."

Kendra's eyes stung. "Olivia…We're not going to ruin anything. And Lynch and I both know you have only my best interests at heart."

Olivia nodded. "Good."

Kendra hugged her close then pulled away. "We'd better get back inside. Lynch and Bill are both probably getting antsy with having me out of their sight."

Olivia smiled. "I'm sure of it."

Kendra opened the door to reveal Lynch and Bill staring intently at them. "Everything all right?" Lynch asked.

Kendra squeezed Olivia's arm. "Better than all right."

Lynch turned back to Bill. "I'll call you and we'll have a chat, okay? Thanks for filling in for me."

"I was glad to do it. She's a great woman," Bill said quietly. "There aren't many like her, Lynch. It's no wonder you take such good care of her."

"I do my best. See you later, Bill. Bye, Olivia." He guided Kendra out the door and toward the elevator. "What was that about?" Lynch asked.

"Olivia wanted me to know how wonderful she thinks you are. More specifically, how wonderful we are together. She didn't want me to misunderstand her attitude toward us in the last few days."

"Oh. That's nice."

"Yes, it was. She's a special person."

Lynch pressed the elevator button. "Do me a favor, will

you? Go ahead and phone Bill for me before he leaves here. I have a few instructions for him."

"Instructions?" Her gaze flew to his face and she inhaled sharply as she saw his expression. "Lynch?"

"Just call him while I get on the road. I don't know how much time we have."

"What are you going to tell him?"

"That he's to stay with Olivia and expect one of the FBI agents to pay him a visit to help protect her."

Her eyes widened. "Olivia's in danger?"

"Not as far as I know," Lynch said. "But I'm not taking any chances. She's your best friend. You appear to be particularly attractive to that son of a bitch since you decided to hunt for the sisters, and he might enjoy taking a life in your honor."

"We could go back, and you can tell him all this yourself."

"I don't want to take the time. I just got an interesting text."

"Really?" She moistened her lips. "You've heard something?"

"It's from my source at the SDPD. They believe they've found Todd Williams' car."

"His car?" Kendra said. "But not Williams himself?"

"Unclear," Lynch said.

"What does that mean?"

"It means his Camry is at the bottom of a two-hundred-foot ravine. A hiker spotted it less than an hour ago outside of town, at Palomar Mountain."

"Williams is dead?"

"That's what I'm trying to tell you. They can't reach the

car yet to see if he's inside or not. There's a rescue helicopter en route, but the fire department officers on the scene can't imagine anyone could have survived a crash like that. Metcalf called me and asked if I wanted to let you know so that we could join in the search for Williams. He felt it was the least he could do since you asked him for help." He glanced at her expression. "That's what you wanted, right?"

She shook her head. "There's no way I wanted anything to happen to Williams. I liked him. He just frustrated the hell out of me. I thought he was holding out on us. Just as I told you, the only thing I wanted was for him to give us more information about what happened to the sisters. Now we might never know what happened to them."

"Because we've run into a blank wall?" Lynch asked. He shook his head. "I told you that we'd find out what happened to them. That's why we're on our way to see that wreckage in the ravine. But I'll bet it wasn't just a run-of-the-mill traffic accident. It would be a little too convenient to have an appearance of the Bayside Strangler one week and then another death related to the case the next."

"You think the strangler was after Todd Williams?"

"I don't know. I think there's a possibility. We'll know more when we're able to get a closer look at that car."

"How's that supposed to happen? Even after the rescue copter arrives, it will probably take a crane to get that car out of the ravine."

Lynch shrugged. "Maybe I'll get myself down there first."

She stared at him for a long moment. "You said the fire department couldn't make it down there until the helicopter arrives."

He nodded. "That's what they said."

"So you think you can do what the entire San Diego County Fire Department can't?"

"Possibly. I'll look things over when we get there."

"Dammit, Lynch, you have a death wish."

"Nonsense. I love my life too much. It's just a matter of calculated risk."

"Famous last words."

"Not mine." He smiled. "We'll be there in a few minutes. We'll see what the situation is when we get there."

It took more than fifteen minutes to negotiate the curvy roads ascending Palomar Mountain, a popular spot for nature hikes with spectacular views. Finally, they spotted a cluster of police cars and fire department rigs, accompanied by almost a dozen rescue personnel standing around and doing absolutely nothing.

"This looks like our party," Lynch said. "And I see that Metcalf has already found his way here." He parked, and he, Kendra, and Harley climbed out of the car and walked toward the roadside. A uniformed officer tried to stop them, but Metcalf waved them through.

"Where's the copter?" Lynch said.

"Still aiding in rescue efforts at the Potrero brush fire." Metcalf bent over to rub the scruff of Harley's neck. "It could be an hour or more before they get here."

Kendra peered over the edge of the cliff and saw Williams' Camry resting upright in the ravine hundreds of feet below. She turned back to Metcalf. "Still no sign of Todd Williams?"

"No. The fire department guys have tried to look down from every angle, but they couldn't see inside. They even tried sending down a drone, but there's just too much vegetation to get a good view."

One of the cops motioned for Metcalf to join him at his squad car as he held up his radio microphone. Metcalf stepped away to join him as Lynch studied the cliffside for another long moment. He turned to Kendra. "Stay here with Metcalf and take care of Harley, okay?"

She glared at him. "Where in the hell do you think you're going?"

"Down."

Her eyes widened. "How? Are you wearing a parachute I don't know about?"

"I don't need a parachute. See all those vines growing down the hillside?"

"You do have a death wish."

Lynch turned and walked back to his car, and Kendra and Harley followed. He opened his trunk with his remote key fob. "Trust me. Just last year I climbed the Dawn Wall at El Capitan. Now, that may have constituted a death wish." Lynch pulled out a hardshell jacket and a pair of gloves.

Kendra looked back toward the gathered firemen. "Don't you think you might want to run this by them first?"

"Absolutely not. If Todd Williams is alive and injured down there, there won't be time for a negotiation." Lynch pulled on the gloves and slid into his jacket.

He strode back to the cliff's edge and looked down for another long moment.

Kendra stood next to him and looked again at the two-hundred-foot drop. "Please, Lynch," she whispered. "Don't do this."

"It'll be fine. Just make sure they don't commit me to a mental facility when this is all over."

"No promises. But just so you know, I plan to witness the commitment papers."

"As long as you come to see me on visiting day."

"Again, no promises."

Lynch kissed her, then turned and threw his legs over the cliff's edge. He gripped the vines and moved down the slope, half slipping, half dropping the first thirty feet. It was only then that the firemen and cops on the scene took notice and ran to the stretch of road above.

"Sir, get up here. Now!" the fire chief shouted. "Do you hear me?"

If Lynch heard, he didn't acknowledge the chief or the other firefighters or cops shouting at him from above. He continued to work his way down, occasionally uprooting the vines and shrubs protruding from the ravine's wall.

Metcalf ran toward Kendra. "What the hell is he doing?"

Kendra turned to avoid looking at Lynch dropping down a particularly treacherous section of brush. "He didn't want to wait for the helicopter."

"I don't want to wait, either, but man..."

The chief turned toward Metcalf. "Special Agent, who in the hell is that guy?"

Metcalf sighed. "You mean the one I waved over and allowed to freely cross the police and fire line?"

The chief obviously didn't see the humor in Metcalf's reply. "Yeah, that one."

"His name is Adam Lynch. He's a contract agent who may or may not be working for the DOJ at the moment."

"Care to tell me what he's trying to do down there?"

Several of the gathered officers gasped and one even yelped as Lynch apparently grabbed some loose brush and dropped several yards. Kendra was glad she hadn't been watching.

"He's working a case that involves the owner of that car," Metcalf said. He turned toward Kendra. "Care to fill in any more details?"

"No, not really."

The fire chief cursed under his breath. "Fine. Because I don't give a damn about your investigation. On this mountain, I'm the boss, and the only thing that matters is the safety of the people on it. Understand?"

"Don't tell me. Tell him." Kendra pointed down into the ravine.

"Trust me, I will. If he makes it out of there alive. There might even be a pair of handcuffs waiting here for him."

Kendra wanted to tell the chief not to bother trying to arrest Lynch, since she'd seen how quickly his Washington employers had swooped in and extricated him from any number of sticky situations over the years. "Good luck with that," she whispered to Metcalf.

The firefighters and cops moved away to get a better look at Lynch's progress.

"Halfway down!" one of the uniformed officers shouted.

The crowd buzzed with excitement.

Metcalf gave Kendra a sideways glance. "Ten seconds ago, they wanted to put Lynch in prison. Now they want to throw him a parade?"

Kendra nodded. "Crazy, right? He just has that effect on people."

They moved closer to the ravine's edge to get a better

look. Metcalf must have seen her worried expression, because he suddenly spoke in a comforting tone. "Yeah, you've got to remember all the experience Lynch has with stuff like this. He practically cut his teeth on black ops training. It was even my boss Griffin at the Bureau who suggested we ask Lynch for help if he was available."

"How nice of him," Kendra said. "Then I shouldn't worry at all, right? Because Lynch seems to be always available when there's a problem to solve." She watched Lynch as he climbed farther down the cliffside.

*Don't you dare slip.*

It was more a fierce prayer than anything else. *Do you hear me? Hang on, Lynch...*

Lynch was approaching a section of sheer rock, with no apparent handholds.

"Uh-oh," Metcalf said. "I don't know how he's going to manage that."

"Me neither." Kendra squinted at the ravine wall. "But Lynch wouldn't have gone down there without a plan."

About twenty feet above the sheer rock surface, Lynch stopped and began pulling vines away from the ravine wall. He tugged on them, testing each for strength and casting aside the ones that didn't hold. He bunched the remaining vines together and twisted them together in a long, thick length.

Kendra gasped. "Oh, no."

Metcalf turned toward her. "What?"

"Lynch, you crazy son of a bitch..."

"What? What's he doing?"

Kendra shook her head. "He thinks he's Tarzan."

The realization suddenly hit Metcalf. "You don't think he'd really...?"

"Just watch him."

Lynch moved down the length of braided vines, gripping them in his gloved hands. He held tight as he braced his feet against the ravine wall, then pushed away. He swung back and forth, making an ever-larger arc as he moved toward another cluster of vines and shrubs that would take him lower.

Lynch swung his hips to push himself even closer, but as he did so, the force of his movements caused several of the vines to break off in his hands. He plummeted several feet, eliciting gasps and a few shrieks from the crowd above.

"He can still make it back up here," Metcalf said.

Kendra shook her head. "No way he's giving up."

"Maybe he should."

"This is Lynch, remember?"

He swung farther and higher as even more of the vines broke in his hands. A big clump finally pulled loose entirely. Lynch let go and leaped through the air, grasping at any vine and piece of shrubbery that could conceivably keep him from plummeting the hundred-plus feet to the ravine's rocky floor.

"He made it!" Metcalf shouted.

Lynch had grabbed another vine cluster, slipping only a few feet before securing his new place on the ravine wall.

Several police officers whistled and applauded, but the firefighters were held back by stern glances from their chief.

Kendra pointed to the binoculars hanging around Metcalf's neck. "Lend me those, will you?"

Metcalf handed her the binoculars, and she trained them downward. "Shit."

"What do you see?"

She turned the focus knob. "There's smoke coming from that car. I think I just saw a flame in the engine compartment. But why now, after it's been down there for hours?"

"The car may have been running all this time and leaking fluids." Metcalf took back the binoculars and aimed them toward the car. "There's a fire, all right." Metcalf turned toward the firefighters to tell them, but they'd already seen it. "I wonder if Lynch knows yet."

---

Was that...smoke?

Still gripping the vines, Lynch twisted his body toward the car below him. Flames shot out from the undercarriage, and black smoke coiled upward. Great. Just great.

A moment later, he was engulfed by the smoke. His eyes watered and his nose burned.

Fight through it. Only about seventy-five feet to go.

He moved down the vines, traveling hand under hand as another plume of acrid smoke swirled over him.

Dammit. He closed his eyes and held his breath, hoping against hope that the plume would soon break. It didn't. Shit.

He continued his downward journey, trying to feel his way past a thorny outgrowth of branches.

More smoke, and this plume was even more intense than the last.

It was getting harder, not easier. *Gotta pick up the pace.*

He forced open his watery eyes and half climbed, half slid down the next thirty feet, still holding his breath. Finally, the smoke thinned and moved in a different direction. He looked down. The car was still burning and the fire had spread to some nearby brush. Damn. If Williams was alive in there, his chances were fading fast.

Lynch took advantage of the break in smoke to quickly rappel down the next several feet, then he dropped the last few yards to the ravine floor. He scrambled toward the car and looked through the windows. The broken glass obscured his view from almost every angle, but as he peered through the passenger side window, he spotted a figure slumped on the floor.

Todd Williams.

And he was breathing. Just barely.

Lynch threw open the door and leaned inside. Williams was covered in blood and bruises. Many of his wounds looked as if they came from beatings and instruments of torture rather than an automobile accident.

Flames erupted over the car hood. No time to properly assess Williams' injuries before moving him. Lynch gripped him under each arm and pulled him from the burning car, hoping the man hadn't suffered a spinal cord injury. Williams moaned.

Lynch pulled him another few yards away and knelt beside him. "What happened? Tell me."

Williams coughed up a mouthful of blood.

"I need you to talk to me," Lynch said. "Who did this to you?"

Williams struggled to form words. The only sounds came from the back of his throat. "Don't…know. Wanted Chloe…and Slo…" His voice trailed off.

"Chloe and Sloane?" Lynch asked.

Williams managed a faint nod.

"Whoever did this…thought you knew where to find them?"

Williams became even more glassy-eyed. "Chloe… Sloane…In danger."

"They're alive?"

"Chloe and Sloane…know."

Williams wore a vacant expression. For all Lynch knew, the man could have been reliving a memory from years before.

"What do they know? Tell me."

Williams' eyes fluttered.

"Stay with me." Lynch leaned close. "Is this about the Dayton Group?"

This snapped Williams back into focus. He looked at Lynch with a surprised expression. "You know?"

"Not enough. Help us. What is that?"

A thin line of blood ran from Williams' left nostril. His breath grew labored and raspy. "I tried…to get away. They found me, tried to make me tell…I wouldn't. No way, no how. Lynch…talk to your old boss. Griffin. I think he can tell you more. More than he ever told me…"

Lynch could see that Williams was drifting again, losing focus. He'd seen enough dying men to know the end was near. "We're trying to help Chloe and Sloane. If they're alive, you need to help us find them."

Williams managed a smile. "They're safe. Very safe… They're in Neptune's eye."

"What?"

Williams mumbled something unintelligible.

"Neptune's eye? What is that?" Lynch tried to quash his growing impatience. "Give me more. Please. It's important."

But Williams was gone.

The fire crackled over and around the car behind them, almost completely burned out. Lynch stood. He'd been bracing for an explosion, but as with most car fires he'd seen, it just ended with a whimper, leaving behind a smoldering heap of ash and metal.

He heard a chopping sound up above. A red-and-white fire rescue helicopter roared overhead, and he could see that the crew had already started deploying the harness and tether rig.

At least he wouldn't have to find his own way back.

---

"Neptune's eye?" Kendra was driving back down the mountain with Lynch. After Lynch's helicopter rescue, he spent over thirty minutes practically dictating the fire chief's report for him. The entire team had watched him pull Williams from his car before fire consumed it completely, so there was no longer talk of arrest or handcuffs. Harley was now eagerly licking Lynch's grimy neck from the backseat. The combination of engine smoke and dried perspiration was irresistible to him.

Lynch tried without success to push Harley away. "Neptune's eye is exactly what he said. I'm sure of it. But I don't know how much stock we can put in that, since he was coming in and out of consciousness at the time. It was one of the last things he said to me." Lynch held up his phone and typed with his thumbs. "According to Google, Neptune's Eye is the small dark spot on that planet's atmospheric surface." He scrolled down the search results. "It's also an old song."

"Hmm. Neither of those seem to be a likely hiding place for Chloe and Sloane Morgan."

"Agreed. But I got a strong response from Williams when I mentioned the Dayton Group. He seemed surprised that I knew about it." He added quietly, "And there were signs of torture to the body."

That was worse than she'd thought. "Torture?" she whispered.

He nodded. "I'd say that someone wanted information very badly, but they might not have gotten what they wanted. His clothes were almost torn off his body and there was a bullet in his back as if he'd been shot while he was on the run from his pursuers. They may have been chasing him up this mountain."

"On the run," Kendra repeated. "It could be the same person who caused the Morgan sisters to disappear. Perhaps even the killer the FBI was searching for at the park."

"The Morgan sisters? We don't even know if they're still alive," Lynch said. "The only one who did might have been Todd Williams." His lips tightened. "But we'll find out. We won't let it go on."

"No, we won't," Kendra said. "So much death and cruelty. It seems to go on and on. I want it to stop."

"It will," Lynch said. "I promised you it would. It will just take a little while. In the meantime I want you to stay close to me. There's every chance you could be a target."

"So could you," she said dryly. "I wasn't the one who was shimmying down that cliff just now. He didn't give you any idea what the Dayton Group is?"

"None whatsoever. But his reaction tracks with what we

saw on that coffeehouse security camera video. It was obviously important to him and Chloe."

"So what now?"

"Now…I think I need to speak to Griffin."

"Why?"

"Williams told me to talk to him, for some reason. Griffin was working the case for the Bureau fifteen years ago."

"But he said himself that he didn't get very far with it."

"Yes. Because the killings stopped shortly after the FBI took over the investigation. But I've been researching and talking to people, and something's been bothering me. The killings stopped, but that doesn't explain why more investigating wasn't done into the murders that had already been committed." Lynch thought for a moment. "The San Diego PD did a good job investigating those murders, and the Bureau would have had access to their files and interview transcripts. But when the FBI takes the extraordinary step of taking over a case, they almost always take a fresh look themselves. According to the research I've done, it doesn't look like they did that here."

"That could be why Chloe and Sloane worked so hard to investigate it."

"That could be. I'd like to talk to Griffin about why it happened that way. He was there at the time."

Kendra nodded. "Okay. Shall we go now, or do you want to shower that grime off first?"

"Actually…I think I should go see Griffin by myself."

"What?"

"I should speak to him alone."

She snorted. "Like hell you should."

"It would be for the best."

She shot him an incredulous glare. "How do you figure that?"

"I may be pushing him to discuss some things about the inner workings of the FBI. Things that could be considered extremely confidential."

"So? If he can talk about it to you, he can talk about it to both of us."

"That's the problem. He might censor himself if someone is there without a top-level security clearance."

"Someone like me, you mean."

"I, on the other hand, have a higher security clearance than he'll ever have."

Kendra drove in silence for a moment. Lynch was starting to make sense. Dammit. "But he knows that anything he tells you will go right to me anyway."

"Of course he does. And I'm guessing that would make him happy. But it would be on me, not him. I'm just saying I might be able to get more information this way. Which is what we want, right?"

Kendra sighed. "I don't like it."

"I didn't think you would. But even you have to see the wisdom of this approach."

Kendra cursed. "I want to hear every word he says. Don't leave anything out."

"You have my solemn promise." Lynch checked his watch. "Griffin will be leaving the office right around the time we get there. Drop me off in front. Stay close. I'll call you when I'm finished."

"Skittish, Griffin?"

Special Agent in Charge Michael Griffin stopped in the parking garage and clutched his heart in a pretend-coronary. "Jeez, Lynch. Why couldn't you make an appointment and visit me in my office like a sane person?"

"Time constraints. I knew you'd be out here walking to your car at about seven minutes after five. I figured I'd catch you out here, unless you had a rare late-afternoon meeting, or your wife was out of town. Then you might stay later."

"Seven minutes after five?" Griffin said in disbelief. "I can't be that predictable."

"You are, and you have been for years. I used to work for you, remember?"

"I've tried very hard to forget."

"Aw, come on. We had fun."

"You had fun," Griffin said. "Especially when it was at my expense."

Lynch smiled. "That may have been true, I admit. But I was out of your hair soon enough."

"Surely you didn't come here just to relive old times, Lynch."

"Actually, I did. But your old times, not ours. I just watched Todd Williams die."

"Metcalf told me. I was sorry to hear that."

"One of the last things he said is that he wanted me to talk to you."

Griffin looked totally mystified. "Why?"

"Probably about what happened fifteen years ago, in your first go-round with the Bayside Strangler investigation."

Griffin put down his satchel and crossed his arms in front

of him. "I told you, it was over for us here at the Bureau before we could even really get started."

"Yes, you did tell me that. But what you didn't tell us is... why was it over? The murders stopped, but the killer was still out there. As far as I can tell, the Bureau took the case away from SDPD, then threw in the towel quickly afterward."

"It didn't happen quite that way."

"By all means, enlighten me."

Griffin was clearly annoyed by Lynch's accusatory manner, but he still replied in a calm, reasonable tone. "The strangler never left much usable physical evidence behind, as you and Kendra have no doubt seen in the reports. We just didn't have much to work with. We had no prints, no DNA, and one fairly vague witness description of a vehicle in the vicinity of where the last body was dumped."

"I worked takeover cases with you, Griffin. The first thing you always did was take a fresh look at the evidence, re-interview witnesses, and have your lab run their own tests. That didn't happen here. None of it."

Griffin's expression was very sour. "I always knew you were a boil in my ass, Lynch, but you've never accused me of not doing my job."

"You've never given me reason to. And I have to say, I'm a wee bit repulsed by the disturbing imagery."

"Good. Then it had its intended effect."

Lynch lowered his voice. "Come on, Griffin. On your worst day, you've never been lazy. You never let things just slip through the cracks, especially if it's a case as big and important as this one. It made the papers in London, Tokyo, and Cairo. Don't tell me you weren't getting heat to do everything in your power to catch this maniac."

Griffin looked down. "You know I was."

"So what in the hell was going on?"

Griffin clenched his jaw. Lynch could see he wanted to talk. And he would talk. Almost there...

"This isn't just some cold case, Griffin. Two young women are missing, and it appears that the Bayside Strangler is back and killing again. We need to do everything we can to stop this monster. What am I missing?"

"Lynch...This is a bureaucracy. It's a big reason you left. Things can't always happen the way we want them to."

"Kendra and I don't work in that bureaucracy. I get to make my own rules now. But we need whatever information you can give us. Come on, Griffin. We're risking our lives out there."

Griffin was quiet for a long moment. He glanced around the empty garage deck before speaking. "We have to do this my way. And you can't tell anyone where you got this from."

"Fair enough."

Griffin chose his words carefully. "The decision to take over the Bayside Strangler case was...not one that everyone in this office supported. Obviously, it was a high-profile investigation, and certain ambitious agents were chomping at the bit to be a part of it. But SDPD had already stepped up in a major way, and their task force was covering all the bases. There was no special reason for us to step in and take over."

"So why did you?"

"It came from above. All the way from Washington. They didn't even want to entertain the idea of a joint investigation with SDPD. They wanted us to completely take it over."

"And so you did. But even if you thought it wasn't necessary, why not do everything you could?"

Griffin looked around and spoke even more quietly. "Again, we weren't masters of our own destinies."

Lynch cocked an eyebrow. "Washington again?"

Griffin nodded. "I'm sure, in your adventures for the DOJ, you've encountered stories about Joseph Highcastle, the former attorney general."

Lynch nodded. "I even met him a couple of times. From what I understand, he was at least partially responsible for their bringing me in for my first freelance jobs."

"Well, just days after we took over the investigation, that AG recommended that we not waste manpower on the case. He insisted that the Bayside Strangler would no longer be an issue."

"How did he know?"

"He wouldn't get more specific. But the murders stopped, so he was clearly right. With no new murders being committed, the Bayside Strangler dropped off the headlines and the pressure on us stopped. We didn't know what happened. There was some speculation the killer was a foreign national who was caught and deported by the CIA."

"Deported...or worse," Lynch said.

"I'm guessing you may have been part of such operations."

"Which I can neither confirm nor deny. But we both know that those classified operations happen all the time."

"Of course."

"It's one way of getting around the problem of diplomatic immunity. Either we let our international partners take care of their own black sheep, or we take care of it ourselves without creating an international incident." Lynch thought about this. "Whatever was going on, the higher-ups didn't want the truth to come out."

Griffin nodded. "But we still have a lot of law-enforcement officers and victims' family members who want answers."

"Tell me this," Lynch said. "Have you ever heard of something called the Dayton Group?"

Griffin thought about it. "No. Should I have?"

"Chloe Morgan discussed it with Todd Williams a few days before she disappeared. And I discussed it with Williams a minute or so before he died today. He was surprised when I asked him about it. He acted as if it was important."

"And yet you didn't think it was important enough to tell Metcalf when you were still on the scene?"

"I wanted to discuss it with you first."

"The Dayton Group...I've never heard of it." Griffin pulled out his tiny Moleskine notebook and jotted down the name. "I'll see what I can find out."

"I'll do the same. While you're writing things in the world's smallest notebook, I got another one for you. Neptune's Eye."

Griffin stared at him in disbelief. "Really?"

"That's what Williams said. It may have something to do with Chloe and Sloane's location."

"Hopefully it doesn't mean they're somewhere in the far reaches of the solar system."

"Kendra and I would go there, if that's what it took."

"I know you would. I hope they're alive." Griffin picked up his satchel and pulled his car keys from his pocket. "I don't suppose Williams told you anything else."

"Actually, he did, though he didn't realize it. His phone

was somewhere in his car. Before it burned up, my phone tapped into it and copied its contents."

"All by itself," Griffin said.

"Well, it was an app I helped design. I activated it before I went down there. I now have all his emails, texts, everything. I'll gladly share them with you. I would have already downloaded them to your phone, but..." Lynch raised his own phone and glanced at the screen. "You're two point two gigabytes short of the memory you'd need to hold it all."

"Dammit, Lynch. I could arrest you right now for hacking into my phone."

"You could, but you won't. Instead, you'll click on the link I placed on your home screen, which will enable you to forward the contents of Williams' phone to your IT techs. I'll accept your thanks later."

Lynch turned and walked toward the stairwell.

---

Kendra pulled up in front of the FBI building. Lynch jumped into the passenger seat and pulled the door closed.

"Was it worth it?" Kendra said.

"It was interesting."

"Interesting how?"

Lynch filled her in on Griffin's explanations, and when he was finished, she drove in silence for a moment. "Okay, maybe it was best that you talked to him alone. If someone wanted the case derailed so bad that they leaned on the FBI to shut it down, what might they do if Chloe and Sloane looked like they were getting close to uncovering the truth?"

"Not to mention Detectives Chase and Williams. We may be too late to help those detectives, but maybe we can still find the sisters. Williams gave me the impression that they were still alive, but in danger. In that coffeehouse security camera video, he told Chloe he had a safe place for her."

"But where?"

"To be determined." Lynch gently pushed Harley away again. "Right now, I'd love nothing more than a hot shower. Care to join me?"

"We'll see. First, you'll have to get a lot cleaner than you are now. Sorry to tell you this, but between that burning car, dirt, and vines, you kind of stink, Lynch."

---

After a hot shower for two and take-out dinner from Kendra's favorite Chinese restaurant, Lynch stared at his phone for a long moment.

"What is it?"

"It's a text from Griffin."

"Did he forget to tell you something?"

"No. The message is really for you, but he's giving me the option of passing it along to you or not."

Kendra wrinkled her brow. "Why would he do that? You're not my gatekeeper."

"I think he's actually being considerate for a change. After that maniac tried to kill you in your garage, I guess he isn't sure if you're up for more serial killer mayhem."

Kendra rolled her eyes. "When has that stopped me before?"

"Well, never. But maybe it should sometimes."

"In any case, it should be my decision."

"Agreed. Hence, my decision to tell you about it."

"Well, you haven't yet. So what's the mayhem?"

He paused a long moment before speaking. "It looks like the Bayside Strangler has struck again."

Kendra had been bracing herself, but the news still took her breath away. "Where?"

"Old Town. The victim worked at a bar there and went missing last night. She was a junior at San Diego State. Her body was just found in the back of a pickup truck."

Kendra nodded. "You know I'm going, right?"

"Of course."

---

Kendra had never been to Old Town at any time when it wasn't absolutely packed, so it was chilling to roll through the deserted streets as she and Lynch drove to the location of the Bayside Strangler's latest victim. Young Tessa Davies had been found in the bed of a stolen pickup truck almost twenty-four hours to the minute after she'd been reported missing.

Work lights and police flashers signaled the exact location of the body. Lynch pulled over, and he and Kendra climbed out of his car and walked past the dozen or so onlookers.

Perry was working the scene with Metcalf, the medical examiner, and the SDPD forensics techs.

"Look at this," Kendra said. "The FBI and the SDPD working together like one big happy family."

"Well, maybe a slightly dysfunctional family," Metcalf said.

Perry nodded in agreement. "Slightly. But nothing a little family therapy can't fix."

Kendra looked at the 1970s-era pickup truck parked on Calhoun Street, one of the community's main thoroughfares.

She turned back to the investigators. "The victim was found in the back of the truck...Was she covered up?"

Perry shook his head. "No, not at all. She would have been plainly visible to anyone walking by on the sidewalk."

Kendra shook her head. "How long was she out here?"

"Somewhere between two and three hours," Metcalf said. "There are a lot of bars in the area, so people walking by probably thought she crawled in there and passed out. That's what a pair of local cops thought until they saw the bruising on her neck. They're the ones who recognized her as a missing person."

Kendra walked around the pickup truck, which was in amazingly good condition for a vehicle that was fifty years old. "What about this truck? Who owns it?"

"It was stolen from a farm about seventy miles east of here," Perry said. "From what we can gather, it was driven into town and parked here just after dark with the corpse already in the back. The driver walked away without anyone spotting him, best as we can tell."

"Ready to take a look?" Lynch said to her.

She took a deep breath. "Ready as I'll ever be."

Perry grabbed the edge of a black tarp that had been spread over the truck bed. "We should make this as quick as possible. A little while ago, some sickos were flying their drone cameras overhead to try to get some shots of the body."

"Don't worry," Kendra said. "I won't want to linger over this."

Perry lifted the tarp, revealing Tessa Davies. She was a pretty young woman, dressed to the nines for a fun evening out. Tessa was bound by the strangler's restraints of choice, but her body was angled so that they could not be easily seen by passersby.

Damn.

As usual, Kendra's first emotion was overwhelming sadness, followed by anger. How in the hell could anyone do such a horrible thing to her…or anyone?

Time to focus. Kendra closed her eyes, took a deep breath, and caught a whiff of Dolce & Gabbana Light Blue perfume. But there was something else…It was that trace of ammonia again.

"She was staged in the same old walk-in cooler, wherever it is," Kendra said. "Just like the last victim. And it looks like she might have gotten some good scratches on her attacker. She's missing two of her fake nails. And, I'm not sure about this, but it looks like her attacker may have washed her hair after she was killed."

"Really?" Metcalf said.

"Look at her scalp. It didn't absorb the conditioner the same as it would've if she'd been alive. I don't think he's done this before, but he has beautified his victims before displaying them. In the past, it's just been things like brushing the hair and tweezing eyebrows for the best presentation. I don't know. Maybe he's learned some new tricks."

# CHAPTER 15

Early the next morning, Kendra and Lynch were awakened by the sound of Kendra's phone buzzing. She looked at the caller ID. Griffin.

She showed the phone to Lynch. "It's your buddy."

Lynch tried to focus on the screen. "Are you going to answer it?"

"Still deciding." Kendra finally pressed the TALK button. "Good morning, Griffin. We had a late night in Old Town, and it wasn't exactly fun. So unless you have something incredibly interesting to say, I'm not positive I'll be able to stay awake through this call."

"How about this: Your recent set of deductions have turned out to be incredibly useful."

Kendra sat upright in bed and put the phone on speaker. "Ooh. Okay, that did it. What are we talking about here?"

"The Bayside Strangler's first new victim, Anna Mae Robinson, and your thoughts about her being stored in an old leaky walk-in freezer near the waterfront. SDPD took you seriously, and they've been combing the bayfront buildings ever since. They found something."

Lynch sat up and leaned toward the phone in Kendra's hand.

"Are you going to tell me?" Kendra said. "Or do I have to guess?"

"It was a body in the cooler, another young woman. Looks like yet another one of the strangler's victims, but this time he didn't get a chance to display it."

"Damn. Have they ID'd her?"

"Yeah. I don't have her name in front of me, but she went missing near Balboa Park a couple of days ago."

Kendra felt awful for the relief she experienced upon hearing it wasn't one of the Morgan sisters.

"Kendra?"

"Yes."

"If you're up for it, you might want to get down there. The FBI and SDPD are still working this together. It's gonna be a party."

---

Kendra and Lynch loaded Harley into the Lamborghini and drove to Barrio Logan, an industrial waterfront neighborhood just south of downtown. It was a community with a heavy Mexican influence, and in recent years much of the area had become a vibrant arts and cultural scene. That renewal, however, had not reached the address Griffin had given her, a street populated with several abandoned industrial buildings.

The normally quiet street was now teeming with activity, with police cars, forensics units, and FBI evidence collection vans taking most of the nearby parking. Kendra and Lynch found a shady spot down the block, cracked a window open for Harley, and walked to the two-story building.

"Look what you did," Detective Perry said to Kendra as they approached the main entrance. He smiled and waved his arms around at all the activity. "This is all your fault."

"Don't put this on me, Perry. I just noticed what was in front of my face."

"It was in front of all of our faces, but you were the only one to put it together. Good work."

"So what's the story?"

"Your observations about Anna Robinson's murder scene made a lot of sense to us, especially the idea that her body had been refrigerated in an ancient industrial cooler near the waterfront. We started combing all the bayfront neighborhoods and checking out the old buildings. We've probably been to every former fish processing plant in the city. Somebody eventually found this place."

Lynch stepped back to look at the faded sign. "What was it?"

"Small-scale meat processing. A wholesale butcher that used to serve a lot of the downtown restaurants. They have a working built-in freezer, and one of our detectives noticed that the refrigeration exhaust system was engaged, even though the building had been abandoned for a while. We got permission from the owner to conduct a search, and we found the victim inside. Everything tracks with the Bayside Strangler's victims. The ligature marks on her throat, hand and feet bindings, everything. Want to see her?"

*Hell no*, Kendra wanted to say. Even though it was the entire reason she had come. But she knew she had to go inside, for Chloe, Sloane, and whomever else this monster might victimize.

"Yes," she finally replied. "Let's do this."

They entered the building, and there was little immediate evidence of the structure's former use. There were no fixtures, shelves, or counters, and the entire first floor was basically one large concrete slab. Large windows ran the length of the building, mostly painted black except for a foot or so on top of each pane.

Perry motioned for Kendra and Lynch to follow him down a short hallway on the right, which was crowded with a dozen law-enforcement personnel. They entered the large walk-in cooler, which measured perhaps ten by fourteen feet. Inside, it was difficult to hear anything but the roar of the refrigeration unit and fans. It was frigid in there, of course, even with the door propped open by an empty plastic crate. The unit was empty except for a few rusty metal racks.

And, of course, the body of a beautiful young woman.

"Who is she?" Kendra asked, trying to keep her composure.

Perry checked his phone's notes app. "Her name's Lanie Campbell. She went missing two days ago while running in the Golden Hill neighborhood near Balboa Park. She was twenty-six years old. She leaves behind a husband and a baby girl."

Kendra wanted to turn away, but she couldn't take her eyes off Lanie Campbell, with her long blond hair and beautifully sculpted cheekbones. She wore formfitting athletic clothes and running shoes. Her throat displayed the same patterned bruising as victims going back fifteen years, and as Griffin had said, the corpse was bound by the distinctive restraints that had become the killer's trademark.

Kendra stepped closer. There was a gold locket around the corpse's neck, and she wondered if it held a picture of her infant daughter or her husband. Maybe both, Kendra thought, as the sick feeling rose in her stomach.

She turned away. "I've seen enough."

Lynch grabbed her arm and steered her through the group of FBI forensics techs who were just entering the cooler. Once they had cleared the crush of investigators in the hallway outside, Kendra leaned back against the wall.

"Tough one," Lynch said.

"They're all tough, but...yeah."

Perry finally made his way through the crowd and stood next to Kendra. After a long moment of silence, he leaned against the wall next to her. "When I started out in this job, I hated having to pretend like it didn't bother me to see things like that. But I have to tell you...what I hated even more is when I realized I wasn't so bothered by it anymore. Hang on to that feeling, Dr. Michaels."

She managed a smile. "I don't think I have much choice."

"Good. Listen, we have the building owner outside. He met the guy who rented this place. Wanna go talk to him with me?"

"Sure."

Lynch's phone vibrated in his pocket, and he pulled it out and glanced at the screen. "You two go ahead. I've been waiting for this text."

Kendra and Perry stepped out onto the front sidewalk, where a uniformed officer was standing with a rotund man in a floral-print shirt. Perry thanked the officer and turned to the man. "You're Frank Gorham?"

"That's me!"

Kendra was surprised. Gorham seemed far too chipper for someone who'd just had a corpse found on his property.

"I understand you just rented this place out last month. Can you tell us how that happened?" Perry asked.

Gorham shrugged. "How it always happens, I guess. Someone gives me money, and they move in. This place belonged to my grandfather. It was a wholesale butcher shop for, like, thirty years. After he closed it, he didn't have any luck renting this building out, and neither have I. I don't want to sell right now, because this neighborhood is changing. I figure if I wait a few years, I might be able to get a lot more. Anyway, someone saw the FOR LEASE sign and called me. We met the next day."

"What did he say he wanted it for?" Kendra said.

"He planned to start a delivery kitchen, and he thought this place might be good for that. He said he'd pay five thousand dollars a month until he got it up and running, then it would go up from there."

"What did he look like?" Kendra asked.

"Longish dark hair, beard, horn-rimmed glasses. He seemed like a cool guy."

Right, Kendra thought, remembering the dead young mother she'd just seen inside. A real cool guy.

She pulled out her phone and displayed one of the sketches Bill Dillingham had drawn of her and Pauley's attacker. "Did he look like this?"

"Mmm, sort of. But not really."

She flipped through the alternative sketches he'd done,

and Gorham had similar responses to each. She made a mental note to have Bill draw one with a wig and a fake beard and show it to this guy later.

"You had a rental contract with him, right?" Perry said. "Did you have it witnessed by a notary, or happen to get a copy of his driver's license or maybe even a thumbprint?"

Gorham tugged on his shirt, which was a size too small for his ample frame. "Uh, no. None of those things. Sorry. I just downloaded a property rental agreement from the Web."

Back inside the building, there were raised voices that were unmistakably urgent and excited. Perry turned. "What's going on in there?"

After a moment, one of the forensics techs stuck her head out the door. "Detective, you should come see this." She turned to Kendra. "You too, ma'am."

Kendra was surprised to be summoned alongside Perry, but she followed him back into the walk-in cooler, where the forensics techs and photographer had cleared a path for them. The corpse's gold locket was now open on her chest, probably after being examined and photographed by the crime scene investigators.

"Oh, my God," Perry whispered. He stood in front of it for a long moment.

"Are you going to let me see?" Kendra said.

"I really don't know."

"What are you talking about, Perry?"

He looked dazed as he finally stepped aside to allow Kendra to see what was causing all the fuss. She bent over to look at the locket.

There, Kendra saw a picture of herself.

Her breath left her as she straightened and backed away. "What in the hell—?"

"He knew you'd see it," Lynch said.

She turned. Lynch was now standing behind her.

Perry nodded. "He's toying with you. He knew we'd have you out to take a look, wherever he decided to drop her off."

Kendra looked at the photo again. "This is my head shot, the one I use for academic conferences. He could have gotten it anywhere." She shook her head. "As if I didn't think he was a sick bastard already."

Lynch rubbed her arms. "Come on, let's get out of here."

They turned and left the building.

---

They walked in silence most of the way back to the car before Lynch spoke. "How are you doing? Okay?"

"Yes. I mean, it's disturbing, but it's not as bad as a maniac trying to kill me in my garage."

"An interesting perspective."

"Some days, you just gotta see the glass as half full."

---

As they drove away from the factory, Kendra looked back at the crush of squad cars, forensic vans, and television news trucks. "Did it occur to anyone that maybe they should keep things quiet and just watch and wait from one of these buildings across the street? The Bayside Strangler was definitely going to come back here to get his victim and take her to display somewhere. It was his MO."

"You're right," Lynch said. "But you don't realize how

incredibly difficult it is to keep a secret like this in a big-city law-enforcement agency. Especially in this age of social media and so-called citizen journalists. It will be interesting to see how long they can keep your locket photograph a secret."

"I understand, but they may as well put up a neon sign that says BAYSIDE STRANGLER, STAY AWAY! I'm kind of sorry I told them where to look. You and I could have found it and set up our own stakeout."

"True, but there's no guarantee he would lead us to the Morgan sisters. I'm rather hoping he can't."

She nodded. "You and me both."

At that moment, a black Lincoln town car swerved in front of them and abruptly stopped. Lynch had to jam on his brakes to keep from hitting it. "Shit!"

The town car's back door opened, and an elderly man in a turtleneck and a blazer stepped out. He looked up and down the deserted side street, then waved to them.

"What's he doing?" Kendra said.

"Saying hello." Lynch gave a slight nod back. "I know him."

"From where?"

"From work. That's Joseph Highcastle, former attorney general of the United States."

The man walked toward them with a stiff gait and stepped around to the driver's side window. "Mr. Lynch, Dr. Michaels...I would very much like to speak to you. If you would like to join me in my car, I promise to take only a few minutes of your time."

Lynch nodded. "Sure. But not in your car."

"I assure you that—"

"Downey Square is a couple of blocks down on the right. We can talk there."

Highcastle shrugged and walked back to his car.

"You don't trust him?" Kendra asked.

"I trust very few people in this world. It doesn't hurt to be cautious."

They followed Highcastle's car to a corner plaza adjacent to one of the city's largest office buildings. They parked on the street and climbed out of their cars. Highcastle motioned toward a bench across from a low fountain, and Lynch nodded. They joined him on the bench.

Highcastle leaned toward Kendra. "Pleased to meet you, Dr. Michaels. I assume you've been told who I am?"

She nodded. "Yes, Mr. Highcastle. I've just been filled in."

Highcastle turned toward Lynch. "And it's very good to see you again, Mr. Lynch."

"It's been a few years. I thought you were retired."

"I am. I've been enjoying it thoroughly. But I occasionally help out where I can."

"Is that why you're here? Helping out?"

He nodded. "You two have been creating quite a stir."

"Only in the best possible way," Lynch said. "We're just trying to find Chloe and Sloane Morgan."

"Or were they creating a stir, too?" Kendra blurted out.

Highcastle smiled. "They were, actually. But I have nothing but admiration for those two young ladies. They've been incredibly persistent in investigating their mother's murder. I think their efforts have been so inspiring that a former government employee recently revealed some extremely sensitive information to them."

"Information like the Dayton Group?" Kendra asked.

"Among other things. The man's name was Justin Setzer. I'm sure his heart was in the right place, but it immediately placed the Morgan sisters' lives in great danger. And his own. He was murdered shortly before those women disappeared. And it might just place your lives in danger."

"How?" Lynch said. "Tell us about the Dayton Group. What are we up against here?"

"I don't suppose you'll just accept my warning and let it go at that."

"Not on your life," Kendra said.

Highcastle chuckled. "I wouldn't have flown in from Maryland if I thought I could have gotten away with that."

"Then tell us," Lynch said.

Highcastle let out a long sigh, then went into it. "There was a government intelligence group based here in San Diego. It was headed by an officer named Victor Krebb. He was a good man. They were extremely effective at hunting down spies, saboteurs, and other enemies of the United States, and their methods could be brutal when the situation demanded it. When there were concerns about possible foreign surveillance of the government building where they were based, they eventually moved some of their most sensitive operations to a house they rented in Coronado."

"The Baum house," Kendra said.

"Yes. That's when they adopted the name the Dayton Group."

"The Dayton Group..." Kendra said. "That's the name they used to rent the house."

Highcastle nodded. "Yes. Certain purchases and travel arrangements were made and expensed under that name. I still haven't gotten a straight answer as to why they called themselves that, but creating corporate fronts for covert operations isn't all that unusual. Anyway, it was around that time that a young man named Rod Wallace joined the team. He was an army vet, and his psych profiles were right on the edge of acceptability. But he was extremely good at what he did. He could be counted on to do what needed to be done, no matter how distasteful it may have been to other members of the team."

"Charming," Kendra said.

"Well, that wasn't even the worst of it. Apparently, his work for the Dayton Group wasn't enough to satisfy his appetites. Soon Krebb and his team discovered he was none other than the Bayside Strangler."

Kendra slowly shook her head, sickened at what she was hearing. "So what happened?"

"He was arrested, of course, but no one quite knew what to do with him. There couldn't be a public trial, because that would have meant revealing the activities of the Dayton Group. Eventually, it was decided that he would be held in one of our 'partner prisons' overseas."

"Like the ones where we hold international terrorists for interrogation?" Kendra asked.

Highcastle nodded. "Those facilities serve an important and necessary purpose."

"If you say so. Why isn't he there now?"

Highcastle took a deep breath. "He never made it there. He escaped during the transfer process. He was familiar with our protocols, so it was probably too easy for him. The Dayton Group and their team leader, Krebb, immediately swung into action to track him down. Within two weeks, Krebb reported that Rod Wallace had been killed in a boat explosion. He even testified to it in a classified oversight hearing. What went unsaid is that the Dayton Group may have been responsible for his death, but no one was too upset about that."

"Of course not," Lynch said. "His death would solve a problem for everyone."

"That's what we thought. The Bayside Strangler murders stopped, and everyone went on with their lives. What we didn't know is that Rod Wallace was alive and well, traveling through western and central Europe and continuing to do lethal jobs for Victor Krebb. We can't prove it yet, but it appears that Krebb may have helped him escape and fake his death so that he could be Krebb's own personal secret weapon. The Dayton Group was eventually disbanded, but our intelligence suggests that Krebb may now be in charge of his own team of mercenaries doing jobs for the highest bidder. No one seems keen to pursue charges against him, since he has knowledge of actions that would be embarrassing to many powerful people."

"What happened to the Morgan sisters?" Kendra asked.

"Frankly, we don't know. They may not even be alive."

"I think they are," Lynch said. "I spoke to Todd Williams just before he died yesterday. He wasn't extremely coherent, but it seemed like whoever killed him was still looking for Chloe and Sloane."

"Well, obviously we suspect it's Krebb and his team who have been trying to hunt them down and seize the information they've gathered that exposes the involvement of the Bayside Strangler with the Dayton Group."

Lynch nodded. "And you suspect that Krebb brought

Wallace, the Bayside Strangler himself, back here to help in the search?"

"Surely it's more than a coincidence that his killings have suddenly resumed after all this time. Our profilers think that being back in San Diego may have triggered a compulsion for Wallace to resume his most famous string of crimes."

Lynch looked at Kendra for a long moment before turning back to Highcastle. "You've gone to a great deal of trouble to tell us all this. Why?"

Highcastle shrugged. "Much of this went on under my DOJ, and I bear some responsibility. I've been brought in to consult on this case in the past week or so, and I understand what the two of you have been going through. You've been feeling your way in the dark, and in doing so, you risk exposing more than anyone in government wishes. Of course, the Department of Justice also values your relationship with them, Mr. Lynch. Naturally all our gratitude is very deep and sincere."

Lynch was smiling but there was the faintest thread of sarcasm in his tone. "Thank you. I'm honored by your trust."

"What now?" Kendra asked.

Highcastle stood. "That's entirely up to you. I think you're doing a noble thing by trying to find those women. We've been operating under the assumption that they're probably dead, but your conversation with Todd Williams gives us alternatives to consider. If they are alive, it's only a matter of time before Krebb, Wallace, and those mercenaries track them down."

"That's why it's important that we find them first," Kendra said.

Highcastle smiled. "Like I said, very noble of you. We

know who the Bayside Strangler is, but until we catch him, there's every possibility he'll disappear again. He's good at that, and who knows when he would ever reappear?" Highcastle straightened his jacket. "I trust you'll appreciate the sensitivity of this information and not spread it unnecessarily. Nice to see you both."

Highcastle walked back to his town car and climbed into the backseat. The car pulled away from the curb, leaving Kendra and Lynch still staring stunned on the plaza bench.

"We have to find Chloe and Sloane," Kendra said. "Fast."

"I may have found something that will help us."

Kendra stared at him. "When?"

"When we were in that factory. I told you I was able to get the contents of Williams' phone, but his email was encrypted. I turned it over to a miraculous friend of mine based in Romania. She cracked it and sent the unencrypted email files back to me. That's what I was looking at when you and Perry were talking to the building owner."

"What did you see?"

Lynch pulled out his phone and showed her the email. "A booking confirmation for a charter boat trip leaving Catalina Island. The charter is for Williams and two other passengers, the day after Chloe and Sloane went missing."

Kendra took the phone and looked at it. "Does it say where he was planning to go?"

"Afraid not. But it looks like they went to Catalina and hired a charter. We'll have to contact the charter boat company and see if they know."

Kendra smiled. "He took them there."

"We don't know that for sure."

"But don't you think it's likely? He tells Chloe he has

someplace safe for her, and within forty-eight hours he's booked a boat charter that departs from Catalina, and she and her sister are gone."

Lynch nodded. "I think it's very likely. I'm just saying that it's not enough to go to Griffin with."

"Of course not. I'm just saying...We have to go to Catalina."

"Even if Chloe and Sloane were with him, they may not be there any longer."

"I know that. The fact that he booked a charter there makes it a strong possibility he may have taken them somewhere else from there. We need to find that charter service and find out where they went."

"I agree." Lynch punched a phone number. "And I have just the way to get there."

"You know we have to bring Harley, right?"

Lynch looked back at his car, where Harley had pushed his snout out the slightly open back window. He sighed. "Yes, but I'm not sure that island will ever be the same."

# CHAPTER 16

Kendra and Lynch valet parked at the Hilton Bayfront and walked around the hotel plaza to a line of yachts lining the harbor. Lynch motioned toward a sleek blue craft that was almost stunning in its appearance. "There's our ride."

"Sure it is," she replied. "Come on, how are we going to get there?"

"I'm serious. The *Starshadow* will be our home for as long as we need it. It belongs to a friend of mine. He's in Brazil for the season."

"Another one of your insanely wealthy and well-connected friends?"

"What can I say? I move in interesting circles."

"Obviously."

"Another friend down here has a yacht with a helicopter pad on the top deck, but I'd need a full crew to help me with that one."

"You know, with a coupon, I think the Catalina ferry tickets are only forty-nine dollars."

"I'm guessing that's what Williams and the Morgan sisters took to get there, and their charter boat took them someplace else. But this cruiser will fit the bill nicely for us."

"I'm not arguing. The cruiser it is."

Kendra and Harley stepped up the ramp while Lynch moved to ready the boat.

It took slightly more than an hour to reach Catalina Island's Avalon Bay, which formed a breathtaking entranceway to the small resort town of Avalon, with its waterfront hotels, restaurants, and landmark art deco casino. At any given time, there were hundreds of boats anchored in the bay, each a short water taxi ride away from the community's main pier.

The owner of *Starshadow* had secured one of the rare harbor berths on the south end of the waterfront pedestrian walkway, and it was here that Lynch moored the cruiser and tied it off. They checked in at the Hotel Atwater, where, to Kendra's surprise, Lynch had already arranged delivery of two changes of clothes from one of the local boutiques.

She held up a Valentino Garavini blouse. "When did you do this?"

"I emailed the shop from our boat. If they're not to your taste, we can exchange them. The boutique is just around the corner."

"I'm sure they'll be fine." She laughed. "Thank you."

"Why don't you freshen up and change, and I'll walk Harley and find out about this charter service that Williams took from here. Then we can walk over together and get whatever information we can."

"Sounds good. Then all I'll have to do is decide between the Christian Louboutin pumps and the Ferragamo loafers."

Lynch returned in less than thirty minutes, and he, Kendra, and Harley strolled along the pedestrian walkway to the north end of the bay.

"I could get used to this place," Kendra said as she strolled past the iconic casino building. "Good wine, beautiful sea breeze, and I love the seals."

"So does Harley," Lynch said dryly. "He thinks they're his playmates. I could barely keep him from trying to set up a commune with them when I was walking him. He was so intrigued that I almost didn't get him back to the hotel. He became quite distracted."

"He appears fairly calm right now," Kendra said. She reached down and patted Harley's floppy ears. "Why was he distracted?"

"Sometimes it happens. I managed to take care of it."

"Like you take care of everything? If I remember correctly, Harley is very well trained. You did some of the training yourself. That's why he's so blasted fond of you."

"Come on, he's fond of everybody."

"Maybe. So what did you find out about the charter boat?"

"Evidently the owner of the boat, Darlene Gatwick, is something of a character. I called her, and she refused to talk to me. She said all of her clients had a right to their privacy. And she assured me that was what was wrong with the world these days. Everyone was nosing around in everyone else's business. Her boat is moored a few hundred yards north of the casino, just outside the bay area."

"Good," Kendra said. "Let's not take no for an answer.

Let's find out everything she knows about Williams and the guests he might have taken on a chartered trip from here."

He smiled. "I thought that would be your reaction. By all means, let's go see what the lady knows. But even if he was here with them, there's no guarantee they're still alive."

"I know that, Lynch. Whatever we find out here, you've been extraordinary. No one could do more than—"

"Shit!" Lynch jerked the dog's leash away from Kendra as the dog took off at a dead run, jerking her down an alley off St. Catherine Way.

"What on earth!" Kendra followed at a dead run. "Is this what you meant when you said Harley was chasing those seals? I believe you now."

"No!" Lynch was holding out his hand to stop her. "Stay, dammit."

"Stay?" She was laughing. "Not the right word for me, Lynch. I'm not Harley."

"Stay! Don't move!" Lynch was running down a side street. "I don't think it was the seals..."

Kendra stopped short at the curtness of his voice. No laughter there. Then she started to rush toward the direction of his voice. "Lynch!"

Then she saw him standing at the end of the alley holding Harley's leash. "You've got him?"

"I've got him." He grabbed her arm and pulled her back toward the harbor. "He wasn't running from me. I think he was on the attack."

"Nonsense. No dog is gentler than Harley."

"Except when his protective training kicks in. We've both seen him pretty fierce then. Let's go back to the cruiser."

"Why?"

"I want to check things out."

They reached their cruiser in a few minutes, and Lynch jumped aboard. He lifted her and Harley from the pier to the deck. "I'm going to look over the boat. Stay here with Harley."

"Any particular reason for all this?"

"I want to make sure we're not going to have any passengers hitching a ride."

She stiffened. "You saw something in that alley?"

"No, but I'd swear Harley saw something or someone he didn't like before I caught up with him. I thought I caught a glimpse of someone following us when I was walking him earlier. This time I was keeping an eye on Harley to make sure it wasn't those seals that he wanted to go after and adopt."

"You're sure that it wasn't?"

He shrugged. "Not positive. But whoever it was disappeared before I could get over to the next alley to check them out."

"Could you recognize them again?"

"No, I only caught a flash of a white shirt and navy cap."

"Nothing else?"

"Sorry, I was too busy corralling Harley to pay attention to high fashion."

"I suppose it might have been a tourist?"

"It could be. But you know how suspicious I am. Will you stay here with Harley?"

She shook her head. "I'm not playing that game any longer. I'll go with you."

"I thought that was the way it would work. Do you also still want to go with me to interview our Darlene Gatwick? We could skip it."

"No, we can't. You'd end up by stashing me someplace 'safe' and going off and doing it alone. Where do we search first?"

"The galley." He gestured that way. "If it pleases you."

She pulled her handgun from her jacket pocket. "It pleases me."

He grinned. "And that pleases me. So we'll both be happy. I hope you keep that toy with you all the time we're on the island."

"It's not a toy. I'm still a very good shot." She met his eyes. "And I'll never leave it behind again when there's a chance you may need me. I'll always remember crawling around on that blasted garage floor when I knew it was my fault you were there." She started toward the galley. "May I go first this time?"

"Hell, no."

She smiled. "You're so predictable. By all means, show off for Harley and me. We both appreciate your amusement value."

"You're maligning me again. However, I'll forgive you because you've promised to protect me."

Lynch stopped and pulled a card-shaped object from his wallet. He propped it against a vase in the main cabin.

Kendra bent over to look at it. "What's that?"

"It's a Bluetooth-connected motion sensor. It'll send a signal to my phone if this boat gets any unwelcome visitors. I didn't think it was necessary before, but better safe than sorry."

"Cool gadget." She straightened up. "Boys and their toys."

After they left the cruiser, Lynch, Kendra, and Harley

walked up Crescent Avenue to the spot where Darlene Gatwick moored her boat between charters.

"Ahoy there, Captain Gatwick," Lynch called as they approached the boat. "Sorry to disturb you, but I decided that it was necessary that we have a little talk. I promise I won't bother you or your guests again after I get the info I need. I'd be happy to reimburse you generously for your time."

Darlene Gatwick was peering at him from the other side of her boat. "You're damn pushy, Lynch," she called out. "I told you that my clients like their privacy. Yet you come out here in that fancy cruiser and think that I'll be impressed? Screw you."

"I'm the one who is impressed," Lynch said. "There aren't many captains who have your sense of honor. I'm sure that's why Williams chose you. He was desperate to keep his privacy intact from people who might want to damage or destroy his mission."

"Mission? Williams told me he was no longer working with either the military or the police. He said he just wanted to have a peaceful vacation and catch a few fish."

"Tell her, Lynch," Kendra said quietly as she took a step forward to lean over the rail. "She might know something."

"I believe you aren't going to wait for me to get around to it," he said ruefully. He waved his hand at Kendra. "May I present an employee and old friend of Todd Williams, Captain Gatwick? This is Kendra Michaels, who is very concerned about Williams and his family."

"That's true," Kendra said. "And I admire the fact that you're trying to protect him." She hesitated and then said, "But I'm afraid it's too late to do that now. Todd Williams is dead."

Darlene was obviously trying to maintain a callous expression, but this seemed to hit her hard.

"He was killed in San Diego. Now all we can do is try to find the two women who trusted him with their lives. You're one of the last people he contacted. Do you have any information about where we can find these two women?"

"Women?" Darlene repeated blankly. "His charter reservation was for three people, but I never actually saw the others. He came up here by himself. When he got here, he didn't want the charter he'd booked with me. Instead, he wanted to rent my boat for two days. That's not what I do, so I turned him down cold." She was silent for a moment. "Williams is really dead? Shit. I liked him. He was a good guy. How did it happen?"

"An accident in the hills," Lynch said. "Do you have any idea where he was going from here?"

"When I couldn't set him up for a rental, I gave him the number of another captain who works out of Mexico and is pretty reliable. Marcus Delgado. He's due back here tomorrow to drop off clients. He's fairly money-hungry and I think he probably would have taken the deal if Williams offered it to him." She scrawled a name and number on a scrap of paper and handed it to Kendra. "I hope you find those women."

"Me too," Kendra said. "Thank you for your help, Darlene. We appreciate it."

"He should have told you to ask me in the beginning," Darlene said tartly. "You can't trust those pretty boys. I know he looks like some kind of movie star, but we women have to stick together."

"I'll remember that." Kendra was trying not to smile. "Most of the time he's okay."

"Yeah, sure." Darlene made a sound that might have been a distinct harrumph and stomped toward the steps. "Aren't they all?"

"Pretty boy?" Lynch murmured.

"Definitely," Kendra said. "She obviously calls them as she sees them."

"In any case, I suggest we make our way back to the hotel so that I can call Delgado."

She gazed at him curiously. "What are you going to ask him?"

"Many things. First I want to make sure that Delgado actually rented his boat to Williams when Captain Gatwick turned him down. Next, I want to know where he took Williams and the girls once he was hired. Preferably the entire route."

"So do I," Kendra said fervently. "It's really our best hope of tracking them down, isn't it?"

"Yes." He reached out and took her hand. "Even if I can't get hold of him now, we know he'll be in port tomorrow. Once I contact him, we'll be that much closer."

She smiled. "Maybe you're not just a pretty face after all."

He flinched. "You really know how to hurt a guy."

"Nonsense. I'm just following Darlene's advice. She's older and wiser than I am."

"Then heaven help us..."

Lynch didn't reach Delgado by phone, so instead they dined outdoors by the bay at Bluewater Avalon, which Kendra decided had some of the best seafood she'd eaten on the West Coast. Lynch, however, looked uneasy.

"What is it?" Kendra said. "Have you seen our friend in the cap?"

"No, and I've been looking. It's just...I hate waiting around when we should be *doing* something."

"I know. I feel the same way. If I thought we could find this Delgado guy right now, I'd set out on our cruiser and track him down."

Lynch waved his hand toward the ocean. "A needle in a haystack. I'll keep trying to text and call. Maybe he'll answer sometime during the night."

After the meal, they retreated to their oceanfront room, where Kendra expected to toss and turn all night. She didn't. The soft bed and the sounds of the ocean outside provided her with the best sleep she'd had in days.

She woke in the morning to find Lynch fully dressed and staring at his phone.

"Anything?" she asked.

"I just got a text from Captain Delgado. He said he'd meet us at the dock at noon and he'd discuss renting me his boat for a few days. Though his fee is fairly outrageous."

"Too bad," Kendra said. "Tell him to go jump in the harbor. We'll find out what he knows and hire another captain and boat. Or we'll take our cruiser and get there ourselves."

"I want this one," Lynch said. "Delgado's. I'll try to negotiate. It may not be that difficult. Anyway, want to go to brunch? I hear good things about the Avalon Grille."

"Sure. Let me take a quick shower." She felt guilty as she headed for the bathroom since she knew Lynch had probably been in protective mode and awake much of the night.

After a wonderful brunch, they walked Harley along

Front Street and finally made their way to the berth where Delgado was scheduled to arrive.

Delgado was a small mustached man, and he stood proudly on the elevated express bridge of his forty-foot white boat as it pulled up to its berth. After bidding goodbye to his guests, he turned to Kendra and Lynch.

"So," he said with a Spanish accent, "you want to rent my boat?"

"I do," Lynch said, "but I find your terms a bit unreasonable."

Delgado shrugged. "There are many other boats for rent here. Hundreds, probably. Take one of those."

"I could, and I might. But I've heard wonderful things about *Excalibur.* Can we discuss this?"

Lynch and Delgado haggled for another fifteen minutes, and by the end of it, Delgado was laughing and hugging Lynch like an old friend.

Lynch turned to her and held out his hand. "This is Captain Delgado, Kendra. He was very cooperative once he understood my problem. Kendra Michaels is going to accompany me on my trip aboard your fine boat. She was a good friend of Todd Williams."

"Delighted," Delgado said as he shook her hand. "My sympathy for your loss." He turned back to Lynch. "But the terms are still the same."

"He strikes a hard bargain, Kendra. But we've come to an agreement. He's going to let me rent his fine boat for the next few days for an exceedingly expensive amount. Isn't that kind?"

"If you say so," Delgado said sourly. "Four days and I get my boat back. Not one more day."

"Didn't I promise?" Lynch asked. "Get in the boat, Kendra. Señor Delgado needs to leave for his luncheon appointment." He helped her on the boat. "Thank you for your services, Señor. You're a true gentleman." He handed Delgado a huge wad of cash. "Four days."

Kendra's eyes widened as she saw the denominations of the bills. "I believe I gave you a suggestion about that payment. Are you sure that—"

But Delgado was reluctantly stepping off the boat and Lynch was now speeding off across the water away from the docks.

Kendra was looking back at him. "That was a huge amount of money."

"I had to work fast," Lynch said softly. "Delgado was tempted to back out if I hadn't made it irresistible. Stop complaining. We'll be safely away from here in another fifteen minutes and I'll explain everything."

She made a face. "I detest being held up like that."

"You've made that clear and I'm grateful for your concern. But it's my money, Kendra. You don't have to stand guard over me."

"Someone should." She glanced at Harley curled up happily by Lynch's feet. "Where were you when he needed you? Don't you recognize sheer robbery when you see it?"

Lynch was shaking his head with amusement. "I believe it's time to change the subject when you're attacking Harley. Suppose I tell you what I learned from Delgado before we made our deal? His response was basically the same as Darlene Gatwick's. He said that Williams didn't mention having any other passengers aboard his rental boat. As far as he knew, the Williams job was going to be a solo fishing trip."

"That's a disappointment."

"If it was the truth. He appears to like cash. Williams could have bribed him to say anything he wanted."

"At least you realize how Delgado is trying to play you."

"It did occur to me, you know."

"Then why were you determined to hire this particular boat?"

"Perhaps I had a reason." He tilted his head. "What do you think?"

She was gazing at him with narrowed eyes. "I think you'd better explain in detail before I get very annoyed." She suddenly snapped her fingers as it came to her. "The navigation system."

"You got it."

She slapped her forehead. "I can't believe I didn't think of it until now. There's a GPS record of all this boat's trips in there."

He nodded. "As soon as I'm sure we're totally out of sight, I'll examine the navigation console and cycle it back through several trips."

She gazed eagerly at the map. "And you'll see where the boat has gone and trace Todd Williams' journey."

He nodded. "That's the idea. Does it meet with your approval?"

"You bet it does." She gave him a quick hug. "Brilliant. Let's get started. And I'll definitely have to tell Darlene that you're not just a pretty face!"

"What a relief," he drawled. "I can't tell you how worried I was about that."

---

Wallace smiled as he focused his binoculars more closely on the boat that was now almost flying across the water. It was all going exactly the way he had planned, he thought. He had been right to be patient when he hadn't been able to take down Kendra as quickly as he had hoped after Lynch began interfering. But her death would be all the more satisfying now that his plans were coming together. It would be the ultimate pleasure to see the light fading from her eyes.

He switched his focus so that he could enjoy gazing at the bitch where she was sitting on the boat. She looked wonderfully happy today and quite beautiful. She was wearing white shorts and a red-and-white sweater and the sun was shining on her hair and making her seem to glow. Or maybe it was that bastard, Lynch, who was making her this happy. He must be screwing her or he wouldn't be willing to risk his neck as he'd done lately. *Go ahead, get it while you can. Make her glow so that those final moments will be that much more satisfying for me when she knows what I'm taking away from her.* He enjoyed that particular part of his work most of all, and he was looking forward to all the agony and sadness he'd be able to inflict on this woman who had the nerve to hurt and defy him. No one was allowed to do that. He was the one who had to be in control.

But his phone was ringing now. Victor Krebb. This should make the son of a bitch happy. He reluctantly shifted his glance away from Kendra to answer it. "Hello, Victor. I was just about to call you."

"But you didn't," Krebb said curtly. "Look, Wallace, you can't keep ignoring me to go your own way. Remember, I'm the one who saved your life when you managed to annoy everyone, even the president. I've been giving you profitable work that will benefit us both. But you have to cooperate with me."

He didn't have to do anything he didn't want to do, Wallace thought. Krebb had never learned that in all these years. "Why, I am cooperating, Victor. I was just going to call you and tell you that Kendra Michaels and Lynch have rented Delgado's boat and are skimming toward you and your men even as we speak. I told you what I thought they'd be planning. Soon all we have to do is set up a trap and then gather them in."

"You mean *I* will," Krebb said sourly. "I haven't seen you helping me lately."

"I've been doing your dirty work for you all over Europe for the past fifteen years. I'd still be there now if you didn't need me to come back and help clean up the mess you made for yourself here."

"Your mess," Krebb said. "It was only fair that you come back and help perform cleanup duty after Setzer opened his mouth to those sisters."

"I took care of Setzer with my usual efficiency," Krebb said. "Your men were supposed to take care of the rest."

"Plans change. You know that, Wallace. We needed your help to track down every person privy to our little secret and every piece of evidence that might give us away. Again, your fault."

"We both have our places in the scheme of things," Wallace said. "You have a lethal group of men to order about and keep our enterprises afloat. I have superior brains and a fine intellect, which you lack."

"Bullshit," Krebb said. "I'm getting sick and tired of you trying to tell me what to do. You're not moving fast enough. You've gotten distracted from the real mission here. This isn't one of your sick games, Wallace. If you don't start giving me what I need, you might find me going on the attack by myself."

"Really? I wouldn't suggest you do that," Wallace said softly. Krebb was doing it again, he recognized with annoyance. Perhaps it was time to make certain it never happened again. "I know what needs to be done."

Krebb didn't answer immediately. He might have sensed how dangerous it could be. Wallace found himself disappointed. He'd already begun to wonder whether he needed to use a dagger or a gun to teach Krebb his lesson and exactly where to land the first blow.

Krebb finally spoke in a subdued tone. "I just need you to respect me and to move a hell of a lot faster."

"Then consider it done," Wallace said. "Whatever you want, Krebb."

"Yeah, sure. I'll keep an eye on that boat and call you if they seem to have an agenda or destination you might be interested in."

"Great idea. Naturally I'll do the same. Have a good day, Victor." He hung up the phone and picked up his binoculars and once more trained them where Kendra was sitting on the deck. He much preferred watching her to baiting Victor Krebb. Though Krebb might be future amusement. What he was going to do with that smart, glowing bitch was the stuff his dreams were made of...

# CHAPTER 17

It was just before sunset and the waters were choppy as Lynch piloted the boat toward a mountainous, green-sloped island.

"What's this?" Kendra said.

"Another one of the Channel Islands." Lynch looked at the navigation screen. "San Clemente."

"I've never been to that one."

"Most people haven't. It's administered by the navy. They took control of all of these islands during World War Two. They used some for bombing practice ranges, and others as outposts to monitor possible foreign invasions. Most have been turned over to the park service in the last few years."

"What's this one used for?"

"I honestly don't know. Probably training, but from this map, it looks like the few structures are clustered on the island's north side."

"Is that where we're headed?"

"No. It looks like we're going to a cove on the south side. Williams steered this boat there, then went back to Catalina about ninety minutes later. We'll go there and take a look around."

"What if the navy objects?"

"It's a fairly big island, and it looks like Williams was almost twenty miles away from the only active installation. We should be okay, but I'll steer clear until after dark."

Forty-five minutes later, Lynch steered the boat toward the isolated cove, which was home to four dilapidated buildings made of corrugated tin, a loading dock, and the remnants of an antenna that once towered over the complex. Vines now covered much of the area.

Lynch pointed toward the antenna. "This looks like one of those old monitoring stations I told you about."

"Well, it kept the homeland safe during World War Two. But I'm not sure why Williams would bring the Morgan sisters to a place like this."

"To seal them off from the world. Or, more importantly, to seal the world off from them. I can't think of a better place. I actually feel good about having you here right now."

"If you're having thoughts about leaving me here, forget it."

"I wouldn't dare."

Lynch eased the boat up to the loading dock and cut the engines. Kendra tied the landing ropes to the cleats. Only when Lynch turned off the deck lights did she realize how incredibly dark it was out there. There were no lights and no power at this long-abandoned installation, and the only sounds were of water lapping against the nearby rocks.

Lynch handed her a flashlight. "I think you'll need this."

Kendra, Lynch, and Harley left the boat and walked across the boarding dock, which creaked and splintered beneath them. Kendra could feel herself wincing with each step. Was this thing going to hold?

They finally made it.

Lynch aimed his flashlight beam toward the right, at a building that appeared to be living quarters. "Let's start there, and we'll work our way to the left."

"No."

"No?"

"It makes more sense for us to separate and start on each end. We'll work our way to the middle, so we won't miss them if we send them scurrying. I'm sure it's what you would have done if you were here with anyone else."

"I don't like it."

"I'll have Harley, plus..." She flipped up her shirt to show the holstered automatic she was carrying. "I'll be okay, Lynch."

"I still don't like it, but you're right. It is what I would do with anyone else."

Kendra nodded. "I hope we do find some sign of Chloe and Sloane and that it's not going to be just another tragic ending." She closed her eyes for an instant. "We've had too many of those lately. I don't want another one."

"Neither do I." His arms were suddenly around her, holding her. God, he felt wonderful. He reached into his knapsack and pulled out a walkie-talkie. "Reach out if you get into trouble."

Kendra held the device as if she'd been presented with something from another world. "A walkie-talkie? I haven't seen one of these in a while."

"Still very useful in places where there's no cell reception. That one you're holding has saved my life twice."

If it was anyone else, she might have thought he was exaggerating. But she had no doubt Lynch was telling her the truth. She clipped the walkie-talkie to her belt. "Got it."

"After I check out the buildings, I'll walk up to higher ground and see if I can spot any other boats on our tail. It'll be difficult in the dark, but I'll give it a shot."

Just then, they heard the barking of seals in the distance. Harley returned the barks and ran ahead of Lynch.

"So much for my protector," Kendra said. "Seals again. I'm beginning to think bringing Harley was a mistake."

"He'll be fine. I'll meet you back here in twenty minutes." He kissed her. "Twenty minutes. If you're late, I'll sick the dog or the seals on you."

She smiled and waved until she couldn't see him any longer. It seemed strange to not be with him any longer after all this time together.

Good heavens. Exactly what she'd been trying to avoid since she first met him. Where was her independence?

She turned and started down the broken concrete path that led to the radio shack. A faded statue was positioned just before the front entrance. It was Neptune, the Roman God of water and the seas. This figure was gazing out at the ocean, keeping a watchful eye.

"The eye of Neptune," she said aloud. It's what Williams was trying to tell Lynch in his last moments.

They had come to the right place.

The structure's front door was chain-locked, but there was ample room to enter through the other side, past the broken hinges. Kendra slid through and trained her flashlight around the installation. It had clearly been a radio room, although there was no longer equipment on the well-worn wooden tables. There were faded maps and posters on the wall, showing hundreds of call signs and radio relay stations. The place clearly hadn't been used since the mid-1940s.

Kendra moved through the room and down a narrow hallway. It didn't look like there was much more to this building, except a bathroom and maybe a—

BAM!

A figure jumped from the shadows and hit Kendra with a flying tackle! Before she could react, she was on the floor and two hands closed around her throat.

"Can't…breathe…"

The figure leaned close, squeezing even tighter. "Who are you?" her attacker whispered.

Kendra thrashed from side to side, trying to break free.

Just then, someone grabbed her assailant and pulled her away.

Lynch?

No, she realized. It was a woman. They both were women.

"Back off!" the second woman ordered. "Don't you know who this is?"

"Who?"

"It's Kendra Michaels." She knelt beside Kendra and helped her sit up. "Are you okay?"

Kendra squinted to see in the darkness. "Chloe?"

Chloe Morgan smiled. "Pleasure to meet you."

Kendra turned to the other woman. "And you're Sloane. Hello."

Sloane rolled her eyes. "Oh, shit. It is her."

"You know who I am?"

Chloe nodded. "Of course. We've spent most of our lives trying to catch a serial killer. And you've helped catch quite a few of them in our hometown."

"I was brought into this case by an acquaintance of yours. A retired detective, Paula Chase."

Sloane gasped excitedly. "She's here?"

Kendra decided to wait to break the bad news. "No. I'm here with a friend. When you meet him, I don't recommend lunging for his throat."

"Sorry about that."

Chloe grinned. "My sister is paranoid about drop-in visitors."

"I've been learning a lot about both of you." Kendra was rubbing her throat. "From Paula, Detective Todd Williams, and a certain auto mechanic named Charles Davenport."

Chloe grimaced. "Oh, God."

"Yes," Kendra said. "I must say, I dislike your taste in men enormously."

"So do I," Sloane said with a frown. "I made a lot of mistakes when I was younger. I've been trying to make up for them lately."

Kendra was still rubbing her throat. "Any reason why you started to strangle me just now?"

She shrugged. "You were a stranger. I couldn't trust you. But I didn't finish it."

"Thanks to your sister."

"I was protecting her, too."

"She's not as bad as you think," Chloe said quietly. "Apologize, Sloane."

Sloane nodded. "I'm sorry if I hurt you. But I've been

training for a long time and I could have really damaged you if I'd tried."

"So that was practice."

She nodded. "Sort of."

"Then I should tell you that I also practice a good deal." She looked at Chloe. "I work just as hard as you do and I'm very dedicated." She patted the gun on her hip holster. "Another few seconds, and I would have gone for this."

Sloane's eyes widened. "How good are you?"

"Good enough. But that's not why I'm here. We should talk about it later."

"Why are you here?" Chloe asked. "Did Detective Williams think we might need more supplies? Heaven knows he gave us more than we could possibly use. But then he was always like that. Always taking care of us."

"Yes, he cared for you both very much."

Oh, shit. Sloane was sitting straight up, her gaze on Kendra. "Be quiet a minute, Chloe. She's trying to tell us something and it's not easy for her. Isn't that right, Kendra?"

"Kendra?" Chloe whispered.

Kendra drew a deep breath. "She's right. It's not easy and it's never going to be any easier. But you have to hear it, because it would be what I would want. Because you have to know he risked his life for you both."

"He's...gone." Chloe said. "He didn't just...send...you?"

Kendra shook her head. "In a way he did. It's why you need to hear this."

"Go ahead," Sloane said as she went to sit beside her sister. "We talked about it. We knew he was putting himself in danger for us."

The two sisters had gone through so much heartbreak

over the years, Kendra thought. She hated to be the one to bring this new threat to the forefront. And it wasn't over; new agony loomed on the horizon.

Get it over with. They could take it.

"Well, then I guess I should begin where it started for me when Paula asked me to help with the case she and Williams had worked together when you were children. At first I didn't want to take it. I didn't know enough..."

She had expected questions but both girls were silent as she told them about Paula Chase's murder, Williams' story, and later the rest of the events that had brought her here. Toward the end there were tears but she found she was also crying as she tried to comfort them. But there was no real comfort to be had at this time.

After she finished, she found that one of the girls had brought her a cup of tea. She didn't even remember which one but was grateful for the kindness.

She finished the tea and set down the cup. "Enough?"

"Too much," Sloane said. "You knew it would be, didn't you?"

She nodded. "But we couldn't even begin to try to solve it until you knew everything. It's not over, you know." She smiled. "As startled as I was by Sloane's tackle, I totally understand it. And I appreciate that you've been on high alert out here. Williams obviously brought you both here because he thought it was one place you could stay safe. But what brought him—and you—to this point?"

Chloe let out a long breath. "It was my fault. I was the one who reached out to him."

"You two were reaching out to everyone connected with the case, weren't you?" Kendra asked.

"It was different with Detective Williams."

"You should probably go back and tell her about Setzer," Sloane said.

Chloe nodded. "After we started re-interviewing people, I was approached by someone named Justin Setzer. It was no one I'd ever heard of. He said he had some information for us, but he was limited in what he could say. We had to do the follow-up work ourselves, but he said he could guide us and push us in the right direction if he thought we needed it."

"What did he tell you?"

"He told us to look into the Dayton Group and what they were doing at the Baum house around the time that our mother was killed. We started asking around, but we didn't get far at first. So Setzer started telling us more and more."

Kendra nodded. "We know about the Dayton Group."

"Well, we didn't have any idea until Setzer told us. He eventually admitted that he was a member of the group. He revealed how the Dayton Group enabled and covered for the Bayside Strangler, whose name was Rod Wallace. Setzer told us he even helped fake Wallace's death."

"Really?" Kendra thought for a moment. Although Highcastle suspected the man's death had been faked, this confirmed it.

Chloe nodded. "I think he felt guilty that they had enabled this psychopath for as long as they did. Setzer left the Dayton Group not long afterward and started his own private security company. Anyway, we told Detective Williams all of this, and we probably would have gotten in touch with Detective Chase if we'd had the chance. Williams had just started reaching out to his law-enforcement and intelligence sources to confirm and investigate the story when Setzer was murdered. That's when Detective Williams decided it was too dangerous for me and Sloane to stick around. He figured that Setzer's old Dayton Group teammates found out that he was being too forthcoming with information about their activities, and they silenced him. Williams wanted to get us the hell out of Dodge as soon as we could."

"Leaving behind your phones, purses, credit cards, everything?" Kendra said.

"He didn't want us bringing anything that could possibly be tracked. Phones, of course, were out. But driver's licenses and credit and ATM cards have RFID chips that can flag sensors all over the place. When Williams realized what we may be up against, he didn't want to take any chances. He said that these people have resources we can't imagine. He even made us take off our Apple Watches and fitness trackers. I took his file and the file we had started for Setzer and left everything else behind."

"The bad guys were aware you knew about all of this," Kendra said, putting it together in her own mind. "And they figured you most likely had some written evidence in those files of yours. That's why they wanted your files so badly."

"We gave those particular folders to Detective Williams," Chloe said.

"I wish he had stayed here, too," Kendra said.

"We asked him to stay, but he wanted to get back and get to the bottom of things," Sloane said. "I guess that's what he was working on when he was killed."

"He was probably reaching out to his old law-enforcement contacts," Kendra said. "I wish he had confided in Lynch and me sooner. But he didn't really know us, and I think he was a little suspicious of Lynch because of his government work."

Sloane shrugged. "Well, when Detective Williams left us alone on this island with food, blankets, and his old service revolver, we couldn't be sure of surviving. We knew he would try to help us but he obviously didn't want us to have any contact with the outside world until he could make it safe for us." Her lips twisted. "But evidently that wasn't going to happen. We decided that we were going to have to take care of ourselves. So we set out to do it. We did everything from setting up sentry posts to watching for any bad guys who might be coming after us over the horizon."

"Speak for yourself," Chloe said. "Don't let her bullshit you, Kendra. She's the one who set up all those defensive moves because she liked the idea of training herself to be Rambo." She was grinning affectionately. "But I have to admit she did a good job of it. I just did what she told me."

"Except for the cooking," Sloane added.

"It kept me busy," Chloe said. "Paradise can be extremely boring with nothing to do."

"I imagine it could," Kendra said. "I've never had to worry about that." The sisters were obviously completely different and yet she could see the affection. She rubbed her throat again. The flesh was still sore, and she was glad she hadn't had to deal with Lynch when she—

Lynch!

Dammit! She didn't have to check her watch to know that she'd been more than twenty minutes. She headed for the door. "I'll be right back. I forgot that I promised to meet Lynch."

"Ah, the mysterious Lynch you told us about," Sloane said with a smile. "I can hardly wait. Do you need us to run interference?"

"That's the last thing I want. You might make him a sandwich if you like. Since he's been trotting all over this island while I've been tucked in here with both of you for the past half hour." She didn't wait for them to answer. She was out the door in three minutes but she ran into Lynch just outside the radio shack. He didn't look pleased.

"I know, I'm late." She held out her hand to ward him off. "But good news: I located Sloane and Chloe, and they're both alive and well."

He nodded. "Well, that's a relief."

"They appear to be very familiar with the island. Did you see any sign of boat or helicopter activity while you were searching? Sloane said she's been keeping an eye out and she'll be glad to show us around."

"How kind," Lynch said caustically. "But I believe I'm up to date at the moment on Wallace and his ugly crew. Perhaps later." He took a step closer to her. "What I'm really interested in knowing is how you managed to get that ugly bruise on your throat? I know you didn't have it when you left me." His fingers touched the bruise. "How?"

"An accident." She moistened her lips. "A misunderstanding with Sloane. Now drop it, Lynch."

"I will. I'm going to let you take me inside and I'll be very charming. I just want you to introduce me and let me set the rules. Then it will be over."

"I set the rules," she said firmly. "They've lost people they care about."

He nodded. "And I have no intention of losing anyone I care about. Don't worry. I won't be ugly." He opened the door of the radio shack with a flourish. "So introduce me, Kendra."

"I have to admit, he's very interesting." Chloe was watching Lynch move around the kitchen half an hour later. "And he's getting along with Sloane very well, which is a relief. I was afraid that she'd be antagonistic toward him when he started telling her all the places on the island he was going to ask her to take him after dinner."

"She offered to do it. I heard her." Kendra shrugged. "Why were you surprised?"

"Because she regards this island as her own special place these days...and he's a very dominant personality. Of course, he probably won her over when he ran out and got Harley and brought him back here. He's a very appealing pooch."

"Yes, he is," Kendra agreed. "Though he's capable of getting in a great deal of trouble. That's why we try to keep him away from the seals. But everyone does love him." She looked Chloe in the eyes. "Even Todd Williams liked him."

"I'm sure." Chloe smiled. "One blue eye and one brown. Detective Williams had a big heart. He could never resist an animal that unusual."

"Lynch told you what happened when I took Harley to see Williams?"

"A few things," Chloe said. "We were asking a lot of questions and Lynch was kind enough to answer them." She was silent a moment. "And then he went on and told us how Todd Williams died and his last words to and about us." She was blinking tears away rapidly. "And then we realized how kind a man your friend Lynch really could be."

"Yes," Kendra said quietly. "You should have seen Lynch

after Williams' car was found. He risked his life to get to him, and I believe Williams knew it. I think he knew we'd never stop looking for you. Because he trusted us."

"So do we," Chloe said. She smiled. "And you found us."

"We located you," Kendra corrected. "But we haven't really found you until we bring you home. That comes next." Her smile faded. "And it's difficult waiting right now. I want it over. I want all the deaths to stop."

"Me too," Chloe said.

Kendra lowered her voice. "One question, Chloe...Why did you have a garrote under the floor of your bedroom? It looked like the same contraption the killer might have used."

Chloe looked stunned. "You found that?"

Kendra nodded.

This obviously flustered Chloe. "I can't believe it," she whispered.

"Where did you get that?"

She looked down, unable to meet Kendra's gaze. "I made it."

"Why? Chloe, what was it for? Were you planning to use it?"

"Yes. But not in the way you probably think."

"Then in what way?"

Chloe still didn't look up at her. "When I was a freshman in college, I thought I'd found my mom's killer. All the evidence I'd gathered seemed to line up with him. I presented it all to the police, and no one took me seriously. I decided if they weren't going to do anything about it, I'd take things into my own hands. I made that garrote out of an electrical cord, the exact same type and gauge that the

Bayside Strangler used. I was going to plant it in his place to help make my case. For a time, I thought I might even kill him and call it self-defense. But later, I decided it would be enough to plant the evidence I needed to have him locked up for good. Eventually, I lost my nerve and didn't do anything. Good thing, because he wasn't the strangler after all. He was just some creep who was fascinated by the case, and all serial killer cases."

Kendra smiled. "I know a guy like that. They're not all creeps."

Chloe finally looked up. "I was going to burn my garrote, but something made me want to hold on to it. Maybe I thought I still might use it someday, I don't know. But I tried to put it someplace where no one would ever find it."

"It almost worked. So, that was your blood on it?"

"I thought I'd wiped it all off. I tried it out on myself to make sure it left a mark identical to the strangler's garrote." She managed a smile. "Kind of ridiculous, huh?"

Kendra put her hand on Chloe's. "We all work through these things in our own way."

"I still dream about the day my mother died. I don't think it will ever be over."

"Soon," Kendra said. "I promise you." She squeezed Chloe's hand. "You won't lose the memories, but someday the nightmares will end." She shook her head to clear it. "What else do we have to do to finish dinner? Your sister and Lynch have done all the work."

"I'm not worried," Chloe said. "I could tell Lynch knew what he was doing when he offered to help cook this meal. What kind of training does he have? He appears to be ultra-competent."

"You wouldn't believe me if I told you. I suppose we could start at Hell's Kitchen and go from there..."

---

The foursome talked more over dinner, and Kendra was interested to discover how different the Morgan sisters were from the impressions she'd formed during her investigation; although much of their lives had been defined by their mother's horrible death, there was little evidence of the serious, somewhat grim young women she'd expected to find. Chloe and Sloane were engaging and witty, and they seemed determined to enjoy life despite their shared tragedy.

Lynch was his usual charming self, but as the meal went on, he seemed anxious and distracted. Finally he stood. "I'll be right back."

After he'd left the shack, Chloe and Sloan immediately turned to Kendra. "Is everything okay?"

Kendra nodded. "Lynch is hypervigilant. If I know him the way I think I do, after we go to sleep he's going to spend the entire night on that hill behind the sheds, keeping watch with his binoculars."

Sloane looked away. "And tomorrow you'll take us back to San Diego?"

"That's the plan."

"I don't know if I'm ready for that," Sloane said. "I've felt so safe here."

"Lynch knows people. He'll make sure you're okay."

Chloe was about to say something when Lynch burst back into the room.

"Turn off the lights! All of them!"

Kendra jumped to her feet. "What is it?"

"We have company. One small boat has dropped anchor about half a mile off shore, and a slightly larger one is now headed this way."

"Is it a navy patrol?" Chloe asked as she turned off the solar-powered battery lantern. "Detective Williams told us they might sometimes circle the island, but he says they almost never come down this way."

Lynch shook his head. "It wasn't a navy craft. It was an electric speedboat, very stealth. I might have missed it were it not for the running lights. I counted at least six people on deck."

"Shit," Sloane said. "I can probably only handle three of them. Four, tops."

"Stop it, Sloane," Chloe said. "This is serious."

"Whatever. Do you think I'm not? I'm not going down without a fight."

Lynch pulled out his automatic and popped in the ammo cartridge. "We're not going down at all. But we need to get away from these buildings. They'll be the first things targeted. Is there a back door here?"

Chloe nodded. "At the end of the hallway."

"Let's use it. I want to be at the top of the hill by the time that boat gets to shore."

They ran from the building and scrambled up the hillside, a task made more difficult by the darkness. They finally reached the top and turned to face the water.

"I don't see it," Chloe whispered.

"It's out there," Lynch said. "They've just cut the running lights." He raised his binoculars and scanned the area. "Straight ahead. They're about to reach shore. They've seen our boat."

Sloane stepped forward, watching as the boat tied to the landing and the half-dozen men jumped off. "He's one of them, isn't he? The man who killed our mother..."

"We don't know that," Kendra said. "We can't be sure yet."

"And we can't lose focus," Lynch said. "Our goal right now is to get you off this island alive."

But they could tell the sisters weren't listening. They were staring straight ahead, jaws clenched and eyes narrowed, passing their own binoculars back and forth as they watched the men gathering.

One of the men switched on a battery lantern, and the others took their places around him.

Kendra turned to Lynch. "Do you recognize any of them?"

"I see Krebb. He's the one with the white hair. He doesn't usually go into the field. He prefers that others do his dirty work. We must be scaring the hell out of him."

"Good," Sloane said.

"And I see our friend with the blue hat from Catalina," Lynch said. "He's still wearing that hat. We *were* being watched there."

"Give me those," Kendra said to Lynch as she grabbed his binoculars. She trained the glasses on one man at a time. "Okay, I think we might also have the guy who attacked me in Sloane's condo."

Sloane turned toward her. "Wait. You were in my condo, and some guy attacked you in it?"

Kendra kept the binoculars trained on the men. "Yes. I was going to tell you about that."

"When?"

"Soon. We've been keeping fairly busy since we arrived on this island." She focused more precisely. "The guy standing next to Krebb is missing his right front tooth. The same one I knocked out."

"Nice work," Chloe murmured.

"Thanks. We recovered it near Sloane's dining room table." Kendra gasped as a chill ran through her.

"What is it?" Lynch said.

Something kept Kendra from wanting to immediately say the words out loud. How did you tell these young women who had been searching most of their lives for their mother's murderer that he was standing here before them? "Rod Wallace. We told you that he'd made another appearance in San Diego lately." She turned to Chloe and Sloane. "The Bayside Strangler is here."

"Which one is he?" Chloe asked as her fists clenched. Even in the darkness, Kendra could see her face flush with rage. "We haven't even seen a picture of him. Point him out to me."

"The one with his arms crossed, standing directly across from Krebb. Lynch and I encountered him in my building garage a few days ago. He bragged about who he was and… what he'd done."

"Are you sure it's him?" Lynch said.

"Positive. Bill Dillingham captured him perfectly in one of his alternative sketches. The guy was wearing a fake nose and maybe some fake bushy eyebrows, but Bill gave us a possibility that was right on the money. Pauley also deserves credit for remembering that face as well as he did."

"So did you," Lynch said quietly. "For picking up the odor of that prosthetic glue."

Kendra gestured impatiently. "No big deal." She turned back to the sisters. "Are you okay?"

"I can't believe it," Sloane said slowly. "After all these years…"

Chloe's lips tightened. "We can't leave this island until we bring him down."

Kendra and Lynch exchanged a look.

"We'll get him one way or another," Lynch said quickly. "It doesn't have to be here and now. We can wait until the odds are more squarely in our favor."

"We can't let him get away," Chloe said. "How can you say that? He's been getting away with our mom's murder for fifteen years. We can't ever forget the way she died."

Kendra put a hand on her arm. "We know that. But I also know that your mother wouldn't want you to do anything to hurt yourself. Would she?"

Sloane looked down and then away. "So what are we supposed to do?"

"Well, there's no way we're going to ignore those sons of bitches," Kendra said flatly. "First of all, I'm going to tell you exactly what those guys are planning."

Chloe gave her an incredulous look. "How do you think you're going to do that?"

Lynch smiled at Kendra. "Can you do it?"

She smiled back at him. "As long as no one turns their back to me."

Sloane looked between the two of them. "What's happening…?"

Kendra raised the binoculars just in time to see Krebb start to brief his men. As luck would have it, light from the lantern illuminated Krebb's lips. "Okay," Kendra began, "they know there's four of us here and don't expect any backup. Adam Lynch is the only one they regard as a serious threat. With that in mind, their orders are...to kill him on sight."

Lynch cocked his head. "Harsh."

"If even one of us gets away...He's reminding them they could all spend the rest of their lives in prison, or maybe even facing the death penalty. But the three of us women need to be kept alive long enough for in-depth interrogation."

Lynch shrugged. "Huh. My shoot-on-sight thing doesn't seem so bad now."

Kendra squinted to see as the movement of the lantern cast a momentary shadow across Krebb's face. "He's telling them that it's just as important to secure any written or digital evidence. Any computers, tablets, phones, or written material are to be seized...along with anything we brought with us here. Oh, and they'll be towing our boat out to sea and sinking it before sunrise."

Lynch clicked his tongue. "Poor Delgado. My new friend will not be happy."

"The two men on the right are being sent around and up the hill. They'll move toward the installation buildings from the rear, then signal via walkie-talkies when they're in position."

"They won't make it," Lynch said. "I'll make sure of that."

"Two of the men will approach from the front, one at each side, then move to the center simultaneously."

Lynch nodded. "A squeeze play."

Kendra studied Krebb's mouth as he finished his briefing. "Krebb and Wallace are going to hang back and watch for any attacks from the installation's front flank." She turned to Lynch. "Krebb is keeping Wallace close."

"Wallace has probably killed more people than the rest of them combined. Krebb might think he offers a certain level of personal protection. Or he may think Wallace is a wild card and want to keep him on a tight leash."

"Both are possible," Sloane said. "And knowing their intentions, we're perfectly within our rights to kill any of them the second they make a move toward us. Right?"

"Of course," Kendra said. "But our main objective is to get the hell away."

Neither sister responded. They clearly had their own objective, and deep down, Kendra couldn't blame them. She would probably feel the same way if it was her mother who had been so brutally murdered.

Lynch motioned toward the rented boat. "We're lucky enough to have a boat that's faster than theirs. If we can get back to it, we'll have no problem getting away."

"That's a pretty big if," Chloe said.

"Not if we have a plan and stick to it," Lynch said.

"And what, exactly, is that plan?"

Lynch turned to Kendra. "Are they finished down there?"

"They're done talking. Right now, they're just loading ammo clips into their automatic rifles."

"Comforting. Okay, gather around. Here's what I have in mind..."

# CHAPTER 18

Wallace watched as Krebb's men ran to take their positions around the installation. "You have too much faith in those men," he whispered. "Sometimes a scalpel is better than a sledgehammer."

Krebb chuckled. "You think you're the scalpel?"

"Of course."

"A scalpel is a precision instrument. I may have thought that of you once, but no longer. You're too reckless. Unpredictable. These men do as they're told."

"So do I. With incredible efficiency. That's why you've kept me around all these years."

"Yes, but you've also insisted on your insane side projects. Isn't your work for me enough to satisfy those murderous appetites of yours?"

"'Insane side projects'? People know my work all over the world."

"Your work?"

Wallace smiled. "Or, if you prefer, my art. You're the

one who wanted me to come back here after all these years."

"It was an emergency situation. All hands on deck. If Setzer hadn't talked to those sisters, none of this would have happened."

"You should have let me kill him fifteen years ago, the minute he left our group."

"That's funny, I thought about having him kill *you*."

Wallace chuckled. "I would have sent him back to you in pieces."

"You're not one to throw blame around. If you'd just killed Kendra Michaels instead of trying to toy with her in the garage of her building, we probably wouldn't even be here now."

"You're right. Instead, she was able to lead us right to the Morgan sisters. You're welcome. By the way, your man Banyon literally had Kendra Michaels in his grasp and lost a front tooth for his trouble."

Krebb checked his watch. "Banyon and Ohlmeyer should be on the hillside by now."

"They're dead already. Or they will be soon."

"What?"

"You should have sent me here alone. I've handled much tougher jobs for you."

"These are some of the best men who have ever worked for me."

Wallace snorted. "Have you read Adam Lynch's file? You should have, you gave it to me. They'll be lucky to leave this island alive."

"I like how you leave yourself out of that group."

"I know what I'm dealing with." He flipped up his jacket hood. "You can handle yourself out here by yourself, can't you, Krebb?"

"What do you mean?"

"I'll take care of this."

"Wallace, no!"

Wallace smiled and ran into the darkness.

---

Lynch crouched behind a bush on the hillside, waiting for Krebb's two men to reach their assigned positions. He unsnapped his shoulder holster, but he hoped not to use the gun. Even with a silencer, the shots would be loud enough to give away his position to anyone nearby. There were quieter options.

There was rustling on the hillside above him. He tilted his head. The sounds came from two positions: one directly above, another about fifteen yards to his right. Lynch slowly turned. The guys were good; he couldn't see either one. Fine. They'd show themselves soon enough. He crouched lower to hide in the shadows.

More rustling, more footsteps directly above. Had he been spotted?

With the shoot-on-sight order still ringing in his ears, Lynch imagined a red laser targeting dot playing across the back of his head.

The guy finally emerged from a clump of bushes. He held his automatic rifle in front of him.

In one motion, Lynch pulled a long-bladed knife from its scabbard and let it fly.

The knife buried itself in the man's chest, and he fell onto the ground. The only sounds were the crunching of brush as he rolled a few feet downhill.

His partner called out in a whisper: "Banyon...Banyon!"

Lynch pulled another knife and tried to zero in on the second man's location. *Come on, call out again. Once more...*

"Banyon!"

Lynch threw the knife, and it found its target on the second man's throat. He gurgled and wheezed for a good thirty seconds before falling dead to the ground.

Lynch scrambled up the hillside and took the automatic weapons from the dead men's hands.

---

It was a dangerous game he was playing, Wallace thought. If Lynch or the women didn't kill him, one of Krebb's trigger-happy goons might.

But it was intoxicating. He hadn't felt this alive in years. Well, maybe except for when he'd cornered Kendra Michaels in her garage the other day. He'd never gone after case investigators before; he usually preferred to keep them dangling on a string as they pathetically tried to bring him down. But to actually see Kendra Michaels cowering before him... He'd thought of little else, as invigorating as it had been to reacquaint San Diego with the Bayside Strangler. But those two young women didn't present near the achievement that Kendra Michaels would for him.

He couldn't let Krebb's men get to her before he did.

---

Kendra ejected and reinserted the cartridge of her automatic handgun. She, Chloe, and Sloane were crouched in the crawl space below an observation platform where a telescope had once been mounted. They'd been listening for any sign of Krebb's men or Lynch's return, but the only sounds were of the pounding surf and barking seals in the distance.

"I know where Harley is," Kendra whispered. "He can't get enough of those seals."

"Those seals have been keeping us awake since we've been here," Chloe said. "I think it's their mating season."

Sloane anxiously peered between the crawl space's wooden slats. "How long are we going to wait here?"

Kendra looked back at the dark hillside. "I know Lynch wants us to wait for a signal from him, but if we see an opening, I say we move closer to the boat."

Sloane shifted restlessly. "We prepared for this. I say we go now and—"

"Shh!" Kendra raised a hand to silence her. "Listen!"

It was a whirring sound in the distance. Kendra pushed aside another of the weather-beaten planks for a better view. An electric-powered boat slid onto the shore, crewed by four more men with assault rifles. A group of harbor seals approached the boat, possibly searching for food. As the gunmen disembarked, one of them produced a shock baton and turned toward the seals.

"No!" Kendra whispered.

The gunman powered up the baton and jabbed it at the seals. But before he could make contact, Harley jumped from the surf and sank his teeth into the man's arm.

The gunman screamed, and the shock baton went flying. Harley barked and ran back and forth, sending the seals scurrying into the water. The other men swung their assault rifles in Harley's direction and fired.

Too late. The dog leaped into the dark water and swam away.

"Wow," Chloe said. "I don't know how much he's protecting the rest of us, but he definitely has those seals' backs."

The gunmen now stood before Krebb, who was obviously giving them instructions. With military precision, the four men turned and ran for the installation.

"Shit," Kendra whispered. "We have problems. Four more guys."

"What now?" Chloe said.

"Get down!"

The three women dropped to their stomachs in the crawl space, hiding in the tall grass. Moments later, the four new arrivals swarmed around the sheds, forming a four-corners perimeter over the installation.

"Shit," Sloane whispered. "We're sealed in."

Kendra raised her head and peered through the wood slats. "The other two guys are going through the shacks one at a time from each end. It's only a matter of time before they make it over here."

Sloane bit her lip. "We need to get as many of them to the radio shack as possible."

"Why?" Kendra said.

"Because I did something before we left there." She smiled.

Was there a hint of devilish enjoyment in that smile? Kendra frowned. "Sloane…?"

"Why are you surprised?" she asked innocently as she

moved out of the crawl space. "I told you we prepared for this..."

---

Lynch was heading back to Kendra and the Morgan sisters with the seized assault rifles when Krebb's second boat arrived. He ducked low and watched the attack squad double from four to eight. Of course, he'd already subtracted two from its numbers, and he was confident he could take out the rest. But he'd have to plan carefully, especially since he had Kendra, Chloe, and Sloane's safety to factor in.

Lynch raised his binoculars and surveyed the scene.

Interesting. The new arrivals had adopted a four-corners strategy to secure the installation while the others continued to search the structures.

He could do this.

Lynch reached into his backpack and pulled out a thin-wired garrote. He flexed it between his hands, and it was virtually invisible in the darkness.

Perfect.

Lynch approached the first sentry, who was standing next to a shack that had once been a latrine. The man turned and tried to yell, but it was too late. Lynch snapped the garrote over his throat and squeezed. Blood oozed over the wire as it sliced through his throat. It was over in seconds.

Lynch backed away with the garrote and watched from the shadows. No one seemed to have seen or heard. He moved toward the next sentry, but something else caught his eye. Was that...Sloane?

It definitely was.

Lynch ran over and pulled her to the ground next to the radio shack. She fought him for a moment before realizing who it was.

"What in the hell are you doing?" he whispered.

"I'm trying to finish this."

"How?"

She smiled and then sniffed. "Smell."

"What?"

"Smell."

Lynch took a deep whiff. Natural gas. He looked back at Sloane. "Did you...?"

She nodded. "I turned on the spare gas tank that Detective Williams left with us. The back room should be a powder keg by now."

"What do you plan to do with that?"

She pointed to one of the assault rifles he was holding. "Mind if I borrow one?"

"Do you know how to use it?"

"I've fired one before."

"Where?" he asked doubtfully.

"Beverly Hills Gun Club. A bachelorette party."

He handed her the assault weapon. "Sounds fun."

"You have no idea."

She turned on a pocket flashlight and pushed it through a narrow opening between the structure's tin panels. "We'd better get back to the trees."

Sloane and Lynch ran for a nearby cluster of trees and crouched in the shadows. Sloane's flashlight cast just enough illumination that a faint glow was visible in the shack. "One of those guys is going to see it," she said. "But they won't go inside alone."

Lynch nodded in agreement. "I believe you're right."

Moments later, one of Krebb's gunmen came into view. He stopped short when he saw the light leaking between the tin panels. He raised a walkie-talkie to his mouth and spoke. A moment later, Krebb's other gunman approached from the other side.

"Now, if only the other three sentries will join them, we'll be—" He saw something. "Wait. I see two more coming from the rear."

"I saw them," Sloane said cheerfully. "And one of them was nodding to someone on the other side. We may have a full house."

"You're good at this," Lynch said. "I know some people who might want to see your résumé."

She smiled. "I already have a job."

"If this works the way I think it will, we need to run like hell to the boat."

She nodded. "Kendra and Chloe will meet us there. I told them what to expect."

"Good. The second those guys go inside, we should start firing through every opening in those panels."

"Got it."

The gunmen held up their fingers and silently counted down using a series of nonverbal hand signals, then burst into the shack with impressive synchronicity. Lynch and Sloane raised their guns and fired into the shack.

No more than four shots had been fired when BOOM! a bullet had sparked and ignited the gas-filled structure. A terrific explosion rocked the installation, and the fireball leaped over fifty feet into the air. Lynch shielded Sloane from the falling debris.

When they finally looked up, they saw that one of the men had somehow survived the blast. He staggered in front of the flaming building with his hair and clothes on fire, then fell facedown onto the ground. Unlike the others, he wore a shock baton on his belt, which now sparked and sizzled as his body was consumed by flames.

"Let's hit it," Lynch said.

"Right."

He and Sloane ran toward the boats.

---

"Move!" Kendra pulled Chloe to her feet and held her gun in front of her. Behind them, several patches of dry brush were burning. They ran toward the water as embers continued to fall from the sky. But a figure suddenly appeared in front of them.

"That's far enough, ladies."

Kendra and Chloe froze. Krebb was standing there holding his assault rifle. "Drop your weapon, Dr. Michaels."

Kendra held on to her handgun a moment longer.

Krebb brandished his AR-15. "Trust me. I can squeeze off thirty shots in the time it would take you to fire one. Throw your gun to the ground."

Kendra tossed her gun down. "Everyone knows what you've done," she said. "Killing us won't help you."

"What I've done?" Krebb smiled. "Everything I've done was for God and country. I'm no different than your Mr. Lynch. I suspect he's racked up quite a body count over the years. Or tonight alone."

Kendra shook her head. "You turned a monster loose on

our city. And when you found out what he'd done, you let him get away with it."

"You let him kill my mother," Chloe said.

Krebb seemed genuinely regretful. "Trust me, I would have given anything not to have that happen. Collateral damage is a fact of life in my world."

"Collateral damage?" Chloe asked incredulously. "Is that what Detective Chase was? And Detective Williams? Collateral damage?"

"Is that what you think we are?" Kendra said softly.

"I've been forced to make tough choices over the years," he said. "Not all of them have been easy to live with." Krebb suddenly wore a strange expression. His eyes fluttered, and blood ran from the corner of his mouth. He fell to the ground.

From the darkness behind him, Rod Wallace stepped forward, still holding his bloody knife. With his free hand, he picked up Krebb's assault rifle. "I almost went to one of those boats and took off." He smiled. "Aren't you glad I didn't?"

"It's you..." Chloe said.

"Yes. I understand you've been looking for me, Chloe. What do you want to know? Your mother's last words? What her final moments on Earth were like?"

"No. I'm far more interested in your final moments on Earth."

He nodded. "Appropriate."

Wallace spoke with unbridled confidence, and every movement could be called a swagger, Kendra thought. Like most other serial killers she'd known. She was surprised by his youthful appearance, and again by his close match to Bill's alternative sketch.

"You killed your champion," Kendra said, motioning toward Krebb's body.

"I was already living on borrowed time with him. He probably thought he'd have one of his thugs kill me, maybe even later tonight. Purely self-preservation on my part. But now...I'll take my leave. I'll come for you later, Kendra. But the time and place will be my choosing. It may be weeks, months, or years from now. Until then, just keep looking over your shoulder. And Chloe...I haven't decided what to do with you and your sister. But if I do decide to come for you, my offer is still open. I'll give you the opportunity to ask me anything you want about your dear mother. I remember her well."

With lightning-fast speed, Chloe pulled Williams' gun from her rear waistband and fired three shots into his chest.

The knife and gun fell from his hands, and he stumbled backward. He fell to the ground and looked up at Kendra and Chloe as the blood spread across his torso. His entire body trembled, and he tried desperately to catch his breath. "No," he gasped. "This isn't right. It can't...happen to me."

"Sure it can." She plowed two more shots into his chest. "See? Die, you bastard." Chloe held up the handgun as tears streamed down her face. "This was Detective Williams' gun. That was for him and Detective Chase." She aimed it at him at point-blank range. "And this one's for my mom."

She shot him in the head.

Kendra didn't have time to tell Chloe not to fire, and part of her hadn't wanted to. She was happy to see this evil asshole die, especially after he'd just promised to keep her looking over her shoulder for the rest of her life.

"I'm not sorry," Chloe said. "If you want to turn me in, go ahead."

Lynch's voice suddenly came from beside her. "There's no reason to do that. I'm sure there will be blame enough for all before this is over. We'll just have to sort it out."

Kendra turned. Lynch and Sloane had just run up with the assault rifles they'd obviously taken from Krebb's men. They stared at the two dead bodies on the ground in front of them.

Sloane turned toward her sister and Kendra. "You guys have been busy."

Kendra motioned toward the still-burning hillside. "You too."

"We can't take credit for Krebb," Chloe said. "Wallace took care of that one himself."

Lynch nodded. "Good. Some things are best left to the experts."

Chloe laughed even as she wiped the tears from her face.

Lynch stepped toward her. "Chloe, they followed us here to hurt us. We were within our rights to defend ourselves."

"I know. It's just...different than I thought it would be..."

A helicopter's engines roared from the north. Lynch listened for a moment. "It's a navy patrol. We made far too much noise here not to be noticed. For some reason, the US military takes issue with explosions going off on their installations." He turned to Kendra and pulled her closer. "Are you all right?"

Kendra nodded. She couldn't take her eyes off Chloe and Sloane, who were both still staring at Wallace's corpse. It was a moment they'd been working toward most of their lives, but she was sure it came with a mixture of emotions. She wanted to talk to them about it, but this wasn't the time. Not yet.

The navy helicopter's rotors kicked up a strong wind as it drew nearer.

---

There were hours of explanations and statements made as a steady stream of helicopters flew in from the Naval Air Station North Island in Coronado. Navy investigators swarmed over the scene as Kendra, Lynch, Chloe, and Sloane were separated and questioned. There was talk of detainment until a single call from Washington resulted in an immediate release and an official apology from the on-site naval officers.

As dawn broke over San Clemente Island, Kendra met Lynch next to the boat they'd rented. "Something made those navy guys very nervous," Kendra said. "One of them even offered to get me some breakfast."

Lynch smiled. "Lucky you. They just wanted me out of there."

She tilted her head. "Now, I wonder why? I assume we have your government contacts to thank?"

"I'm sure that had something to do with it. And I'm sure no one is anxious to have the activities of the Dayton Group come to light, especially since they clearly enabled a serial killer."

Another helicopter roared overhead and swung in a large arc over the area. Only when it landed did they see the FBI logo on the airframe. Michael Griffin climbed out and walked toward them, the still-spinning rotor blowing his hair in such a way that made Kendra admire the skillful styling that usually hid his massive bald spot.

Lynch shook his hand and smiled. “This isn’t your usual jurisdiction.”

“The navy permitted my visit as a professional courtesy. Officially, this is related to an active FBI investigation.” He lowered his voice. “Unofficially, the US attorney general wanted me to make sure you’re okay and to urge you to file a report on this incident posthaste to him and him alone. Our nation appreciates your service.” He nodded toward Kendra. “Both of you.”

“Wow,” Kendra said. “And me just a poor, weak woman trying to do her job. However can I thank you?”

“I know.” Griffin made a face. “That almost made me throw up in my mouth a little bit. But I promised to pass it along.”

Kendra turned toward Chloe and Sloane, who had stepped out of one of the tents the navy officers had erected and were using for their investigation. “You should be thanking them.”

“I will,” Griffin said. “They never gave up, did they?” He added pensively, “Even when the rest of us did.”

Griffin walked over, shook their hands, and introduced himself. He motioned toward his helicopter. “Can I give you a lift back to town? I have room for all of you.”

Lynch shook his head and pointed to the charter boat he rented. “This needs to go back to its owner in Catalina, but if the ladies would like to ride back in your copter, I don’t mind taking the boat back myself.”

“No, a short boat trip sounds good right now,” Kendra said.

Chloe and Sloane looked at each other for a moment, then Chloe responded to Kendra and Lynch with a grin. "Permission to come aboard?"

"Sure," Kenda said. "I think we could all use the time to decompress."

Griffin shrugged. "Okay. I need to find the base commander. I understand he's confused and more than a little upset by what went on here last night."

As Griffin walked away, Kendra heard the excited barking of seals in the distance. A moment later, there was a different bark.

It was Harley, she realized. She turned just in time to see him running along the shoreline in a playful gallop, followed by half a dozen seals.

Kendra shook her head. "He actually thinks he's one of them."

They stood there for a long moment, watching Harley and his new friends as the early-morning sun bathed the island in a pink glow.

# EPILOGUE

TWO HARBORS
CATALINA ISLAND

"What on earth is happening here?"

Kendra turned to see Olivia standing behind her on the beach, reacting in horror at Harley, who was howling like a coyote near the seals. "What have you done to my dog, Kendra?"

"Not guilty," Kendra said firmly as she gave Olivia a warm hug. "It's all his own fault. I've tried to talk him out of it, but he's not having it. We're sure he thinks he's a seal, or maybe he's just appointed himself as chief seal protector of the beach. He got very upset when Krebb's men were disturbing the seals on that island when they were attacking."

"He's always been extremely protective," Olivia said.

"I know, but this takes it to a whole new level. We're not sure what triggered it, but we're hoping he'll get over it quickly."

"It'll be okay," Olivia said. "It's actually kind of sweet."

Harley gave another howl as he saw and recognized Olivia on the beach with them. "I'm sure it's going to be okay."

Kendra nodded. "I am, too. Lynch is at the hotel teleconferencing with a security panel about what happened on the island last week. He promised me he'd be back to take care of Harley as soon as he could possibly arrange it. Though I don't know how he intends to—" She stopped short, staring at Olivia. "Lynch asked you to come and help me," she said. "Of course he did. You're the only one besides him that Harley pays any attention to. He realizes that you have the magic touch." She shook her head. "Lord, I'm sorry he dragged you out here. It's not as if I can't take care of Harley. We all love him, and I wrote and told you how he went after those slimy crooks and saved the day. He was magnificent."

"I'm glad you appreciate him." Olivia grinned. "It reinforces my judgment in bringing him to watch over you when Lynch wasn't doing what I wanted about your protection. But from what you told me, he wasn't too impossible once he arrived on the island."

"You might say that."

"I know you've had your issues with Griffin in the past, but you said he was very impressed with Lynch and how he dealt with things."

"Just your usual Lynch heroics." She made a face. "You know he can't resist."

"Then I suppose I'll have to forgive him for bringing me here to this fantastically beautiful place and trying to save my dog from your mismanagement."

"If you're inclined to do that, feel free." Kendra went back into Olivia's arms and whispered, "I'm so glad to see my best friend that I'll forgive anything. Thank you for every minute you've spent trying to help us during this nightmare, and I'll go back to the drawing board and make sure that I understand all the intricacies of Harley's delicate bonding with those seals. Then we'll go introduce you to the Morgan sisters before we arrange your transport back to the condo."

"You're setting up a complete day for me." Olivia's tone was teasing. "Did it occur to you I might be busy? I meant only to pick up Harley from the island and then go back home."

"I'm sorry." Kendra frowned. "I know how busy you are. Am I being pushy?"

"No, I guess not. Tomorrow is another day." Her smile faded. "But I wanted to tell you that you might have custody of Harley for a couple weeks beginning next month, if that's okay with you."

"Sure. Why? What are you going to do?"

"I have a few medical eye tests in Switzerland to take." Her tone was ultra-casual. "There's a report that there's been a breakthrough at the clinic in Geneva that might be of interest to me."

"Wonderful," Kendra said. "Promising?"

"I have no idea. I hope so. You know that I've been tested before and it's come to nothing. But I'm always hopeful. Miracles do happen." She smiled. "I have a friend who told me that a long time ago."

"Because she wants it so badly for you." She reached out and tightly grasped Olivia's hand. "Is there anything else I can do?"

"Not right now. I know you'll be there for me whenever I need you." She turned back toward Harley. "But right now it's that howling hound who needs me. Let's go get him and take him back to the camp to distract him."

Kendra sighed. "I tried that."

"You have to keep on trying." Olivia was putting the leash on Harley and Kendra noticed with frustration the blasted dog was sitting still, ignoring the seals, and rubbing against her. "Repetition is the key," Olivia said. "Every day. Every way. If it's worth it to you and him, don't stop." She patted Harley as he jumped up and followed her down the beach. She looked back at Kendra. "By the way, that applies to other skills and desires as well."

"I figured it did. You'd never leave me in the lurch like that."

"Absolutely not. Did I tell you how grateful I was that Lynch arranged this little vacation for me in this wonderful place?"

"I believe it was mentioned."

"Just checking...Come, Harley." She stopped again. "When are you going to talk to Lynch again?"

"I have no idea," Kendra said. "We've been talking ever since we left home. We seem to have no problem with conversation. Why?"

"Just wondering. Perhaps you need a more in-depth discussion with him." She was breaking into a run with Harley at her heels. "After all, he's very interesting. I've always liked him, you know. I'll see you back at the camp."

Kendra shook her head as she watched her run toward the campfire in the distance. Olivia's visit had been as complicated as usual, but not nearly as complicated as Kendra's feelings toward Lynch. Which, of course, Olivia had perceived even before Kendra herself.

Lynch. She had been trying to avoid thinking about him, but it was suddenly there before her. No time to think or plan or even have a little time to consider what she wanted to do or say to Lynch. Olivia might have even wanted that confusion to be present until she could have time to talk to her and influence her in the way she wanted her to go.

A magician, indeed…

All Kendra had left to do was to avoid Lynch for the evening, but that shouldn't be difficult. Just stay out of his way. Because of his background, everyone always wanted to talk to him or ask him questions. He was the golden boy of every organization or meeting connected with this attack. He'd already had trouble getting away from Griffin and those White House special advisors.

Yes, all Kendra had to do was avoid the golden boy until it was time to slip away and go to bed. After that she could arrange for a ride back to Avalon with one of the FBI agents on duty…She'd seen Metcalf earlier today before she'd been assigned seal duty. He was always helpful when she needed something. Plenty of time to think and plan when she was back at Avalon…

---

"No problem at all," Metcalf told her with a broad grin. "But I don't know why you'd want to go back to Avalon when you could spend the night in the encampment. It's fantastic here." His gaze went to where Griffin was having coffee by the fire with several of his agents. "Not only that but it's where the action is. It's not often that lowly agents get to hobnob with officers like Griffin."

"I didn't think of that." She shook her head. "Naturally

you'd prefer to stay here and make smart career moves up the ladder. Forget I asked. I'll find another way to get there."

"No, you won't. We wouldn't even be here if you hadn't called us and brought us to the island. I'll be glad to take you. We can have a drink or two and then I'll come back."

"Thank Lynch. It was his idea." She shook her head. "And no drinks. The reason I have to get back is that I've been away from my students too long as it is. You're not the only one who has to worry about climbing that career ladder." She patted his cheek affectionately. "But thanks for the offer. It was very kind of you."

"There you are, Metcalf." Lynch was suddenly beside them. He clapped Metcalf on the shoulder. "I've been looking all over the camp for you. Griffin has been bragging about you and your team to some of his buddies, and they want to meet you. It shouldn't take too long. But you don't want to offend him."

"No, of course not." He gazed anxiously at Kendra.

"Go!"

He waved and started to trot toward the fire. She turned back to Lynch. "You're suddenly being very caring about Griffin's feelings," she said caustically. "Particularly since you've been practically running his department and squeezing him dry of information lately."

"You're exaggerating." He dropped down outside her tent and crossed his legs. "But Griffin does owe me and so he'll welcome Metcalf with open arms because I let him use me." He leaned back against the post and gazed at her. "Though I do admit I've been floating around the camp and might have heard you talking to Metcalf."

"Might?"

"Well. I made a point of it when I saw how you were trying to avoid me. I figured it would save both of us time if I knew what was going on."

"You didn't talk to Olivia?" she asked suspiciously.

He shook his head. "Not after I threw myself on her mercy to get her to come here. My pride will only permit so much."

She made a rude sound.

He threw back his head and laughed. "It's true. You're the only one with whom I don't give a damn about pride. By the way, that kiss you gave Metcalf was very anemic. It made me feel terrific."

"It wasn't meant to have any effect on you at all."

"Then why were you going to run away with him and leave me in the lurch? That could have been very hurtful, if I didn't know you. But I realize you have problems and you have to work things out for yourself."

"Hurtful? With an ego like yours?"

"There you go again. Ego is necessary in certain situations. But I'm tired of this conversation." He got to his feet and pulled her up beside him. "Let's go for a walk and tip our hats to the seals and then you can tell me what barriers you're trying to put in the way of how we feel about each other. I could see it coming since we wrapped this search up and got the sisters back. You've been thinking too much and I haven't had time to concentrate on showing you how good we are together. Not that you should have to be reminded. You're very bright and you were amazing."

"Am I supposed to say thank you?"

"No, you're supposed to relax and let me have my way with you." He tilted his head. "Though a sentence like that should be said by a man with a mustache and a leer and I don't have either."

She suddenly found she was laughing. "You're ridiculous. Say what you mean. We shouldn't really be talking at all at the moment. That's what I intended when I asked Metcalf to take me back to Avalon to think things over. We're not children and we should act like adults."

"Bullshit," Lynch said. "We need to have a good time and care about each other and worry about tomorrow, tomorrow."

"Tomorrow," she repeated. "What will you be doing tomorrow, Lynch?" she asked soberly. "You're the golden boy and they're not going to leave you alone. Where will you go next?"

"Not to Spain, unfortunately. I have to finish up this job for the Justice Department that I left when I needed to come to you." He shrugged. "After that, we'll talk about it."

"No, you'll make a decision yourself that I have nothing to do with. That's the sensible way to handle it."

"As I said before, bullshit." He kissed her long and hard. "Golden boy? Screw it. Now let's go back to your tent and make love while we still don't have to deal with Harley. Okay?"

She shouldn't be this impractical. "It's probably the wrong plan but it seems right at the moment." She reached up, brought his head down, and kissed him back. "But we'll have to talk about it soon."

"Soon. That's a very good plan." He stepped behind her and kissed the nape of her neck. Then he took her hand and was leading her back toward the camp. That's right, he'd said it would be better if they could avoid Harley tonight...

Harley!

He felt her resistance and gazed down at her. "Kendra?"

"I can't go right now. I promised Olivia. I have to work some way that we can be sure Harley will be happy while we're taking care of him. I promised I'd do everything I could."

"But right now?"

"Of course." She smiled as she ran down the steps. "And I just had a thought. It's the seals that really make Harley happy. But they have to be safe and enjoy themselves, too. Right?"

"Yes," he said cautiously.

She nodded eagerly. "Olivia has done everything to help us, and it just occurred to me that we have the perfect way to repay her. You have the most gorgeous pool I've ever seen. It's bigger than most aquariums. Wouldn't it be wonderful for them?"

Lynch had a moment of imagining his extremely expensive pool being used as a home for a family of seals to make their own.

"Lynch?" She was looking at him eagerly and smiling. "Is it okay?"

"Oh, what the hell. Why wouldn't it be?" He took her hand again and they ran toward the tent.

# ABOUT THE AUTHORS

**Iris Johansen** is the #1 New York Times bestselling author of more than fifty consecutive bestsellers. Her series featuring forensic sculptor Eve Duncan has sold over twenty million copies and counting and was the subject of the celebrated Lifetime movie *The Killing Game.* Johansen lives in Georgia and Florida.

**Roy Johansen** is an Edgar Award–winning author and the son of Iris Johansen. His acclaimed mysteries include *Killer View, Deadly Visions, Beyond Belief,* and *The Answer Man.* He has written screenplays for Warner Bros., Universal Pictures, Disney, and MGM.

Iris and Roy have written eleven novels together, including the *New York Times* bestselling Kendra Michaels series.